She knew it was a mist...
his door.

But she had to settle the ~~...~~
orders.

He caught her watching th~~...~~ on his TV.
"Tell me you're a hockey fan and I'll get down on
one knee right now. That is, if I knew your name."

"It's Sierra."

He dropped to one knee.

"I didn't tell you because I want a proposal," she
said. "Only because we seem destined to run into
each other."

"So you believe in destiny?"

"No. It's just an excuse for people to avoid
responsibility for their actions."

"You don't think this is destiny?" He nodded at the
pizza boxes they held.

"Haven has only one pizza place. And right now,
I'm going to have dinner."

"Sure you don't want to stay and watch the game?"

"I'm sure," she said.

But it was a lie. The truth was, she wanted to stay.
Because she'd spent every night of the past three
weeks alone.

But Deacon wasn't simply another person. He was
a man. A man who made her all too aware she was
a woman. And in her situation, that could only be
dangerous.

Dear Reader,

It's the worst possible time for Sierra Hart to meet the man of her dreams, so it's a good thing that local attorney Deacon Parrish *isn't* the man of her dreams. To the contrary, he's arrogant and exasperating, incessantly flirtatious, annoyingly charming, and his smiles make her knees weak.

Okay, so maybe he could be the man of her dreams if she'd met him at a different place and time. But here and now, he's simply a complication she doesn't need—no matter how much she might want him.

Deacon Parrish isn't looking for happily-ever-after. Marriage and kids? No, thank you. No way. But flirting with the sexy new ADA? That's a plan he can get on board with. And the fact that she's going to be in town for only a limited time guarantees neither of them will get too attached.

So why, when he learns that Sierra is pregnant, doesn't he run far and fast in the opposite direction? Why does he, instead, suddenly find himself imagining a future with this woman?

As a former attorney, I occasionally find myself itching to get back into the courtroom—if only in my stories— which is one of the reasons I had so much fun writing Sierra and Deacon's story. I hope you have just as much fun reading it.

All the best,

Brenda

PS: Please check out my website, brendaharlen.com, for a complete list of Match Made in Haven titles and upcoming releases.

Her Not-So-Little Secret

BRENDA HARLEN

HARLEQUIN

SPECIAL
EDITION

PLEASE RECYCLE
THIS PRODUCT IS RECYCLABLE

Recycling programs
for this product may
not exist in your area.

ISBN-13: 978-1-335-72475-5

Her Not-So-Little Secret

Copyright © 2023 by Brenda Harlen

Harlequin Enterprises ULC
22 Adelaide St. West, 41st Floor
Toronto, Ontario M5H 4E3, Canada
www.Harlequin.com

Printed in U.S.A.

Brenda Harlen is a former attorney who once had the privilege of appearing before the Supreme Court of Canada. The practice of law taught her a lot about the world and reinforced her determination to become a writer—because in fiction, she could promise a happy ending! Now she is an award-winning, RITA® Award–nominated, nationally bestselling author of more than fifty titles for Harlequin. You can keep up-to-date with Brenda on Facebook and Twitter, or through her website, brendaharlen.com.

Books by Brenda Harlen

Harlequin Special Edition

Match Made in Haven

Captivated by the Cowgirl
Countdown to Christmas

Montana Mavericks: Brothers & Broncos

The Maverick's Christmas Secret

Montana Mavericks:
The Real Cowboys of Bronco Heights

Dreaming of a Christmas Cowboy

Montana Mavericks: What Happened to Beatrix?

A Cowboy's Christmas Carol

Montana Mavericks: Six Brides for Six Brothers

Maverick Christmas Surprise

Montana Mavericks: The Lonelyhearts Ranch

Bring Me a Maverick for Christmas!

Visit the Author Profile page
at Harlequin.com for more titles.

For Lauren,
who has always marched to the beat of her own drum
and has always made me proud.

Chapter One

There was one box of Frosted Flakes on the shelf.

Which shouldn't have mattered in the least to Sierra Hart, because she already had cereal in her cart.

The spoon-size shredded wheat (tucked between the loaf of twelve-grain bread and a package of low-fat, low-sodium crackers) was undoubtedly a healthier choice, and she was trying to make healthier choices. Over the past few weeks, she'd willingly reduced her intake of sodium and fat (*goodbye* convenient microwavable meals) and completely cut out alcohol (*au revoir* cabernet sauvignon), but her sweet tooth continued to protest the lack of brownies and cookies and ice cream.

And now, apparently sugary cereals that reminded her of her childhood, too.

Frosted Flakes had been her breakfast of choice while she was growing up in Summerlin South, a suburb of Las Vegas—or at least after her fourteenth birthday.

Prior to that, her favorite morning meal had been home-made breakfast burritos: scrambled eggs and crumbled bacon wrapped up with shredded cheese and tangy salsa inside a warm tortilla. Whenever Sierra had a test at school or a basketball game after, her mom insisted that she start her day with a home-cooked breakfast to fuel her brain and her body.

She shrugged off the memories. It wasn't so easy to shrug off the ache in her heart that, sixteen years later, had faded but not disappeared.

It was when her brother had come home that she'd started eating cold cereal in the mornings before rushing out of the house to catch the bus for school. Weekends usually meant toaster waffles, and sometimes Nick sat at the table with her, always with a textbook of some kind at his elbow despite having taken a hiatus from college.

He'd grumbled only a little about buying the sugary cereal for her when she was a teen, but she imagined he'd have a lot more to say if he knew she still craved it now.

But why should she feel guilty about the occasional indulgence when the other items in her cart were healthy?

When she'd lived in Las Vegas—and been on a partnership track at Bane & Associates—she hadn't had the time to cook. And with countless takeout options available, there had been little incentive to bother. But her new job in the Haven District Attorney's Office had, so far, afforded her a more regular schedule, and so she'd started to prepare her own meals.

At first, she'd been more resigned than enthused about tackling that particular chore, but she didn't really have much of a choice as dining options in town were severely limited. There was the Sunnyside Diner, famous for its all-day breakfast and not much else; Jo's Pizza, which offered wings and some simple pasta dishes alongside its namesake specialty; Diggers' Bar & Grill, a popular choice for those wanting standard roadhouse fare; and The Home Station, whose menu boasted creative and upscale cuisine.

Of course, even in Vegas there had been times when she wasn't in the mood for takeout and opted to pour herself a bowl of cereal instead. And quite often it was Frosted Flakes.

She started to reach for the box—

"Never go shopping on an empty stomach."

She drew her hand back and turned to the shopper who'd drawn her cart up alongside Sierra's. The other woman had long dark hair tied in a ponytail, pretty blue-gray eyes and a warm smile.

"That's what my sister tells me, anyway," the stranger confided. "But since I got pregnant, I'm constantly hungry, which makes it impossible to follow her advice."

"Um…congratulations?" Sierra finally ventured.

The expectant mother laughed. "And now you're wondering why you ever decided to move to this town where people overshare personal information in the breakfast foods aisle at the local grocery store," she guessed.

"I don't think it's just the breakfast foods aisle," Sierra said. "The guy working behind the deli counter told me all about his upcoming knee replacement surgery while he was slicing my oven-roasted turkey."

"That would've been Dustin Hobbs," the other woman said, reaching for a container of steel-cut oats and dropping it into her cart. "He's been grumbling about his bad knee for years."

"Since 2010—the year he carried three passes over the goal line for the state champion football team?" Sierra guessed.

"Sounds about right." A box of Corn Pops joined the oats. "You're Sierra Hart, aren't you?"

"Have we met?" Sierra was certain they hadn't, though the other woman did look vaguely familiar to her.

"Not formally, but our paths sort of crossed at April's House last weekend. I'm Sky Gilmore—Sky *Kelly*," she quickly amended, offering a smile along with her hand.

Though Sierra had only been in town two weeks, that was long enough to have heard about the Gilmores. In addition to being one of the founding families of Haven, they were owners and operators of the Circle G, one of the most successful cattle ranches in all of Nevada.

She'd also heard about the historic feud between the Gilmores and the Blakes, the gist of which was that both families had come to Nevada to settle the same parcel of land more than a hundred and fifty years earlier. Rather than admit that they'd been duped, they agreed to split the property. Everett Gilmore, having arrived first, took the prime grazing land for his cattle, leaving Samuel Blake with the less hospitable terrain. As a result, Crooked Creek Ranch—and the Blakes—struggled for a lot of years before gold and silver were discovered in their hills.

Although both families had ended up ridiculously wealthy, the animosity between them had remained for a long time. It was only in recent years—and as a result of a handful of reunions and romances—that the Gilmores and Blakes had finally managed to bury the hatchet.

"Do you work at April's House?" Sierra asked, shaking the woman's proffered hand.

"I'm a volunteer counselor," Sky responded.

"Tough job," she noted. And because Sierra had some experience of her own working with abused women and their children, she felt an immediate kinship with—and a lot of respect for—the other woman.

"I'm sure being an ADA isn't a walk in the park."

"It's just a temporary gig," Sierra told her.

"And your stay in Haven?"

"Also temporary."

Sky's smile was knowing. "That's what my husband said, too, when he came to Haven. Three years ago."

"What did I say?" a masculine voice asked from behind her.

Sky's smile was quick and warm as she turned her head. "That your stay in Haven was only temporary."

Obviously this was the aforementioned husband, and Sierra couldn't help but think that the counselor had lucked out when she fell in love with the six-foot-tall, dark-haired, hazel-eyed man standing beside her now.

"How was I to know that I would fall in love—with Haven almost as much as you?" he said.

Spoken by another guy, the response might have made Sierra want to gag, but not only did Sky's husband sound absolutely sincere, the way he looked at his wife when he said the words made her heart sigh.

"Well, I have no intention of falling in love with the town—or with you," Sierra said lightly.

Sky laughed. "Jake, this is Sierra Hart—the new ADA. Sierra, my husband—Jake Kelly."

"*Temporary* ADA," Sierra clarified.

Now Jake grinned. "And what do you think of Haven so far?"

"It has its charms," she noted.

"But being able to make a quick stop at the grocery store isn't one of them," he warned.

"So I've discovered."

"For the first few months that Jake was in town, he went to Battle Mountain to buy his groceries so that he wouldn't have to make small talk with the locals," Sky told her.

"Something to consider," Sierra said, only half joking.

"Which completely backfired on him," the other woman continued. "Because that's how he happened upon me, stranded on the side of the road one day."

"And while I don't mind strolling down memory lane now and again, I'm sure the ADA is more interested in finishing her grocery shopping," Jake said.

"You're right," his wife acknowledged. Then to Sierra she said, "I'll bore you with the story over coffee sometime."

"I'll look forward to it," Sierra said, a little surprised to realize that she meant it.

"It was nice to meet you," Jake said, nudging his wife along.

"And both of you."

Sierra watched them make their way down the aisle, walking side by side, so close that their shoulders were almost touching. They seemed completely in sync with one another, like her brother and sister-in-law, and Sierra's heart sighed again, more than a little wistfully, as they disappeared from sight.

Maybe one day she'd be lucky enough to meet someone who looked at her the way Jake looked at Sky and Nick looked at Whitney, but that was a dream she'd put on the back burner for at least the next seven and a half months. The move, the job and swearing off romantic entanglements had all been her choices, and while she didn't have any regrets, she couldn't deny that she yearned for something more.

"Excuse me," a deep voice said, at the same time an arm reached past Sierra to pluck a box of cereal from the shelf.

Not just *any* box but the *last* box of Frosted Flakes. The very same one that she'd been eyeing.

"Hey," she protested.

The cereal-stealer turned his head. His dark blue gaze locked with hers, and Sierra felt a frisson of awareness shiver down her spine.

Well, *damn*. She certainly hadn't expected *that*.

"Is there a problem?" he asked, sounding completely unconcerned about the possibility there might be.

She swallowed and tightened her grip on the handle of her cart. "Yes, there's a problem," she told him. "You took my Frosted Flakes."

Of course, the bigger problem was that Sierra seemed to be attracted to men who inevitably ended up trampling her heart, and she already knew that this was one she should walk away from—as far and as fast as her legs could carry her.

Unfortunately, her feet seemed glued to the floor and her brain stubbornly determined to battle over a box of breakfast cereal, even as her eyes enjoyed a leisurely perusal of the hottest guy she'd crossed paths with in the fourteen days she'd been in Haven. He had slightly tousled dark blond hair and a squarish jaw covered with golden stubble that, on another man, might have looked scruffy, but definitely worked for this one. He wore a dark brown bomber-style leather jacket, unzipped, over a blue sweatshirt, faded Levi's and brown cowboy boots. His shoulders were broad, his hips narrow, his legs long.

"*Your* Frosted Flakes?" he echoed, clearly amused by her declaration.

She yanked her errant gaze back to his mouthwateringly handsome face. "I was just about to reach for that box of cereal."

"Were you really?" he challenged. "Because you stood in front of it for at least three minutes without making a move to pick it up."

"I doubt it was three minutes," she said indignantly.

"*At least* three minutes," he said again.

"Which still doesn't give you the right to elbow your way past me to take it."

"I said *excuse me*," he reminded her.

As if being polite justified his actions.

"A gentleman would give up the box of cereal," she said, her tone both piqued and prim.

He grinned, and her knees turned to jelly. *Dammit.*

"You're definitely new in town," he decided. "No one from around here would mistake me for a gentleman."

She could see it now, in the devilish glint in those blue eyes. He was a bad boy. The kind a mother warned her daughters about. Not just dangerous but dangerously tempting.

Sierra knew that she should walk away—it was just a box of cereal!—but she decided to give it one last shot.

"You're really not going to give me the cereal?"

"I can't," he said, sounding almost regretful as he shook his head. "But I can give you some advice—add a couple tablespoons of sugar to a bowl of cornflakes."

"Why can't *you* add sugar to a bowl of cornflakes?" she challenged.

"I don't have to." He grinned and held up the box in his hand. "I've got Frosted Flakes."

She scowled, annoyed that his smug arrogance some-how added to his appeal. "I hope your milk is sour."

"That's harsh," he chided. "But the truth is, the ce-real isn't for me. I've got company coming tonight and they have very specific breakfast demands."

"They?"

She didn't realize she'd spoken aloud until she saw his lips twitch, as if he was fighting against a smile.

"Twins," he said, with a wink.

She shouldn't have been surprised. Men like this one always had women clamoring for their attention, and he was obviously willing to give it—and to more than one at a time.

Rather than continue this pointless conversation, she decided to relinquish her claim to the cereal and move on.

He deliberately stepped into her path as she started to push her cart past him.

"I'd be happy to share the cereal, if you wanted to come over for breakfast. Better yet," he said, with an-other wink, "you could *stay* for breakfast."

Her gaze narrowed in response to the blatant innu-endo even as her hormones stirred with interest. "Aren't you going to be busy with the twins?"

"Tonight and tomorrow, yes," he agreed. "But my schedule's wide open next weekend."

A not-at-all tempting offer, because as much as she had a weakness for bad boys, she had more important things to focus on while she was in Haven. "In your dreams, cowboy."

"I'm not a cowboy," he said, refusing to take the hint. "I'm a lawyer."

"Let me guess—" she zeroed in on the logo embla-zoned on the front of his sweatshirt "—Columbia Law?"

"That's right." He pulled a business card out of his pocket and offered it to her.

Deacon Parrish
Attorney at Law
Katelyn Davidson & Associates
355 Page Street
Haven, NV

"In case you ever need a lawyer—" he flashed that devastating smile again "—or breakfast."

"That's not going to happen," she said, ignoring the card in his outstretched hand and steering around him.

"Legal troubles or breakfast?"

He called out the question as she walked away.

Sierra forced herself not to look back.

"Neither."

Chapter Two

Deacon Parrish was a man on a mission—and a very tight schedule. He didn't have time to waste flirting with an attractive stranger in The Trading Post, but there had been something about the stunning brunette in the cereal aisle that had piqued his immediate interest and encouraged him to linger.

Haven wasn't such a small town that everyone knew everyone else, but it was a safe bet that he'd crossed paths with all the other residents at one point or another in his almost twenty-eight years. Which meant that this woman was either a visitor or newcomer, because he'd never seen her before. Maybe it was cliché, but he was certain he would have remembered.

He guessed that she was average height for a woman—but that was the only ordinary thing about her. In deference to the frigid January weather, she'd been wearing a long coat—black wool—and black knee-high boots with a modest heel. Beneath the coat, she wore a slim-fitting skirt the color of ripe cranberries and a matching jacket buttoned over a snowy-white blouse with a deep V neckline.

She was overdressed for grocery shopping, which suggested to Deacon that she'd come from work and led him to speculate as to what profession would require her to work on a Saturday. Real estate was the first thing that came to mind, and he'd heard that The Ruby Realty Team had recently hired a new agent. Perhaps she'd had an open house earlier that afternoon and was now picking up a few essentials on her way home. Or maybe she had a list of ingredients to cook a meal for someone special.

His gaze had automatically gone to the fingers curled around the handle of her shopping cart then. She wore what looked like a college ring on her right hand, but her left hand was bare. There was no sparkling diamond to herald an engagement and no wedding band to indicate a more permanent commitment.

He'd exhaled a grateful sigh of relief. Because Deacon didn't have any particular type when it came to the women he dated—blondes, brunettes, redheads, short, tall, skinny, curvy—but he did have two hard and fast rules when it came to dating. The first was to never make a move on another man's woman.

Once that concern had been alleviated, he'd shifted his attention back to her face, admiring the flawless skin, dark eyes fringed by darker lashes, high cheekbones and glossy pink lips. She was focused on the shelves as if choosing a breakfast cereal was a matter of great internal debate.

Deacon experienced no such indecision. He'd gone into The Trading Post knowing exactly what he was after, but when he reached past her for the familiar blue box with the tiger mascot on the front, he'd somehow started an unexpectedly provocative conversation that seemed to be about a lot more than Frosted Flakes.

Until she'd abruptly shut him down.

Perhaps she would have been more amenable to his flirtation if he'd relinquished the cereal, but that wasn't an option.

Not if he wanted peace in the morning.

And while he knew why *he* needed the cereal, as he made his way toward home, he found himself wondering why *she'd* been after the perennial kids' favorite and acknowledging that the absence of a ring didn't mean the absence of a family. Maybe she had kids at home who would kick and scream when she returned home empty-handed.

And if she had kids, she was off-limits to him. Because that was his second dating rule: no women with children.

It wasn't that he didn't like kids. In fact, he was crazy about his brother's two little girls. But aside from the fact that kids were an inevitable complication in any relationship—and potential collateral damage when a romance didn't work out—he simply wasn't dad material.

Maybe he sometimes wished it wasn't true, but there was simply too much of his own father in him to ever let himself believe otherwise. And yeah, it sucked that he still carried some emotional scars from the man who'd walked out on his family two decades earlier, but he couldn't deny that he did. And he knew that the only way to ensure that his kid never hated him the way he'd hated Dwayne Parrish was to never have a kid—or pretend to be a dad to someone else's.

Because Deacon wasn't the only one who'd been scarred by his dad's "parenting." His half brother Connor had suffered even more, being the preferred target of Dwayne's drunken fury—and deliberately putting himself in front of Deacon on the rare occasions that the man lashed out at his own son.

It was a testament to his brother's character that Connor had managed to turn his life around and not only let go of the past but embrace his future. Or maybe it was a testament to his feelings for the woman he'd married. Whatever the reason, Connor had been able to fall in love and have a family, and perhaps that example should have given Deacon hope that he might someday do the same. But while the brothers had both suffered at the hands of Dwayne Parrish, there was one crucial difference between them—only Deacon carried the man's blood in his veins.

It was a fact he tried not to think about too often, and he pushed it out of his mind now as he turned onto Sherwood Park Drive. As he drew closer to home, he saw the deputy sheriff's personal vehicle parked in his driveway.

Damn, he was late.

He'd no sooner pulled up alongside the curb and shifted his Jeep into Park when the back door of his brother's truck flew open and two little girls spilled out.

"Unca Dunca! Unca Dunca!" They raced toward him, blue eyes sparkling and wide smiles on their faces.

He set the bag from the grocery store on the hood of his SUV and crouched to catch the twins in his arms.

"Can we build a snowman?" Piper asked.

"Can we have hot choc'ate?" Poppy wanted to know.

"Can we watch a movie?"

"Can we have p'za?"

"Can we—"

"Can you give Uncle Deacon a minute to catch his breath?" the girls' dad interjected to suggest dryly.

"I'm good," Deacon said, rising to his feet with a smile on his face and a child propped on each hip—a more cumbersome task than usual as both girls were bundled up in snowsuits and winter boots.

"You're late," his brother admonished.

"Three minutes," he guesstimated.

The same amount of time he'd stood watching the stranger contemplate her cereal options.

Piper and Poppy lavished him with hugs and kisses then wriggled to be set down again. Deacon obliged, and they immediately threw themselves onto the snow-covered ground and began making snow angels.

"Two more minutes and I might not have had time to come in for a cup of the hot chocolate that you're going to make for the girls," Connor remarked.

"I don't know that Regan would approve of them having hot chocolate before dinner," Deacon said, picking up the grocery bag again and fishing his keys out of his jacket pocket.

"Which is why they love coming to Uncle Deacon's house—because he doesn't follow Mommy's rules."

"I follow some of them," he protested. "But not so many that I risk losing my 'Fun Uncle' title."

"It's not as if you've got a lot of competition," Connor noted. "Both of Regan's brothers have kids of their own, so they understand the importance of rules."

Deacon unlocked the door and called for Piper and Poppy to come inside as he exchanged keys with his brother. He helped out with the girls often enough that he and Connor had long ago discovered it was easier to swap vehicles than transfer car seats.

"But we're makin' snow angels, Unca Dunca," Piper said.

"Well, I'm going to be making hot chocolate," he said.

Apparently those were the magic words, because both girls jumped to their feet and hurried—as much as they could hurry in their heavy boots and bulky outerwear—toward the door.

"With whipped cweam?"

"An' spwin-kohs?"

"Snowsuits and boots off right here," Connor reminded his daughters as they pushed into the foyer.

They dutifully started yanking on zippers and tugging at Velcro fastenings to reveal fuzzy sweaters and printed leggings.

"Then can we watch *Fwozen*?" Piper asked, kicking off her boots.

"I wanna watch *'canto*," Poppy said.

"How about *Frozen* today and *Encanto* tomorrow?" Deacon suggested as a compromise.

"Okay," Piper said.

"'Kay," Poppy agreed.

"That's a lot of screen time," Connor noted, as the girls scampered off to the living room.

"Don't worry," Deacon said. "I've also got sharp knives and matches to keep them busy."

His brother slid him a look.

"Okay, we'll stick with coloring pages, building blocks and modeling clay."

"They've got some toys and books in their backpacks, too," Connor said, as he followed Deacon to the kitchen. "Which reminds me—Regan asked me to remind you to make sure they brush their teeth *before* story time, in case they fall asleep while you're reading."

"I know the drill," he assured his brother.

"And bedtime is eight o'clock. Actually, it's seven o'clock at home, but eight o'clock is okay for a sleepover.

But no later than eight," Connor cautioned, "or they'll be cranky all day tomorrow."

Deacon set a pot on the stove, filled it with milk. "This isn't my first sleepover—or theirs."

"I know, but Regan likes to remind me to remind you."

"And what are your plans for tonight?" he asked.

"I've got a table booked at The Home Station for dinner and dessert at home from Sweet Caroline's for after."

"What's the occasion?" Deacon asked curiously.

"Does there need to be an occasion for me to take my wife out for a romantic meal?" his brother challenged.

"Maybe not," he allowed. "But I'm getting the feeling there's something you're not telling me."

"Regan and I are thinking about having another baby," Connor finally confided.

"Because Piper and Poppy don't keep you busy enough?"

"Because we love our life with the girls and we've got a lot more love to go around."

"Do you really work in law enforcement?" Deacon wondered aloud. "Because it should be illegal for someone who carries a gun in his job to say something so sappy."

Connor shrugged, clearly unoffended by his remark. "Talk to me after you've had a child with the woman you love."

"That will be...never," Deacon said, reaching into the cupboard above the stove for the hot chocolate mix.

"Never say never," his brother warned.

Then Connor's gaze zeroed in on the old-fashioned glass canister, with the hand-printed label that identified it as *Hot Chocolate* in a decidedly feminine script, as if it was evidence at a crime scene.

"What kind of hot chocolate is that?"

Deacon measured out the mix in accordance with the (also hand-printed) directions on the back of the container and whisked it into the milk. "The same kind you get at Sweet Caroline's."

His brother's jaw dropped. "Who gave you the recipe?"

"No one gave me the recipe. According to Annalise, it's a proprietary mixture. But I did sweet-talk her into letting me buy some of it."

"You mean you slept with the Sweet Caroline's barista?" Connor guessed.

Deacon couldn't prevent the smile that curved his lips. "Not for the hot chocolate."

"How long has this been going on?"

"It's not going on," he said. "We went out for a few weeks and then things fizzled out."

"Have you ever gone out with a woman longer than a few weeks?" his brother wondered.

"Sure." He poured cold milk into two plastic mugs, filling them halfway, then topped them off with the hot chocolate.

"Have you ever thought that any of those women was the one?"

"Every one of them was the one—at least in the moment," he said easily.

"Are you trying to be an ass or does it come naturally?" Connor wondered aloud.

"It comes naturally," Deacon said, with a grin. "But if you're asking if I ever thought one of them might be someone with whom I want to spend the rest of my life, I'd have to say *no*, because I don't see my future following the same path as yours."

"You don't want to get married and have a family?"

"I don't see it happening," Deacon said again.

"Which isn't actually what I asked," his brother noted.

Deacon popped his head into the living room. "Who wants whipped cream on their hot cocoa?"

"I do!"

"I do!"

Two pairs of feet pounded as his excited nieces dashed into the kitchen, clamoring for their treat.

"I'm glad you're going to be dealing with the sugar rush and not me," Connor muttered.

"Is that your way of saying you don't want whipped cream?"

"Of course I want whipped cream."

He grinned and filled two ceramic mugs with the steaming liquid, then topped all four drinks with a generous heap of whipped cream and a sprinkle of chocolate shavings.

"You make the best hot choc'ate, Unca Dunca."

His heart melted like the cream on top of his hot drink.

Still, he felt compelled to remind her, "It's Deacon, Pop. Uncle *Deacon*."

She wrinkled her nose. "But that does'n rhyme."

Connor chuckled.

Deacon sighed. "I'm going to be Unca Dunca forever, aren't I?"

"Probably not forever," his brother said. "But at least another few years."

Chapter Three

Living in northern Nevada was taking some getting used to, Sierra acknowledged, as she tugged the fleece-lined hat over her ears and stuffed her hands into matching gloves. Then she opened the door to step outside and sucked in a shocked breath.

When she'd told her brother that she was taking a job in Haven for six months—starting in January—he'd warned her that it would be cold. Sierra hadn't been concerned. No one had ever accused her of being a shrinking violet.

But right now, she felt like a frozen violet—and she'd only been outside for fifteen seconds.

A quiet whimper escaped her as she thought longingly of the twenty-four-hour gym in the basement of her apartment building in Las Vegas.

Former apartment building, she reminded herself.

She'd vacated the premises at the same time she'd walked away from her eighteen-month relationship with

Eric Stikeman. She still missed the spacious two bedroom with the floor-to-ceiling windows and mountain view. Eric...not so much.

In any event, when she'd agreed to take the job in the Haven DA's office, she'd been hopeful that she might find similar accommodations here. Those hopes had quickly been dashed.

The good news was that she'd found a fully furnished townhouse in a newer development. Unfortunately, the furnishings hadn't included a treadmill.

The real estate agent had told her that there was a gym at the community center, but Sierra was reluctant to commit to a membership, not knowing how often she'd use it when her only goal was "moderate" daily physical activity. But the gym also offered yoga classes, and her friend Aubrey had frequently remarked that Sierra should take up yoga to help her relax.

Former friend, she amended.

And a reason for some of her current tension, as well as more evidence that she was a lousy judge of character—at least when it came to her personal interactions.

So for now, Sierra had decided that morning walks would provide not only exercise but also the opportunity to explore the area and maybe even meet some of her neighbors.

Apparently the locals were a hearty breed, as she crossed paths with more than a few residents out walking their dogs, spotted a couple others up on ladders taking down holiday decorations and observed several children playing in the snow.

But if she was going to continue walking in frigid weather, she was going to need a warmer pair of boots. And a thicker coat. And probably some thermal underwear, too.

On second thought, a gym membership might be cheaper.

She exchanged greetings with a man holding a leash attached to an Old English sheepdog and considered the benefits of a canine companion. It would be nice to have company, she mused, not only on her daily walks but at home.

But as appealing as the idea was for now, she was only going to be in Haven for six months. After her contract with the DA's office was finished, she'd be going back to Las Vegas, where she no longer had an apartment. Which meant that she'd be staying with her brother and sister-in-law until she could find a place of her own—which she wouldn't be able to do until she found a new job—and Whitney was allergic to dogs.

She paused on the sidewalk near where two little girls were building a snowman—or trying to with the limited amount of snow on the ground. Because the air might be frigid, but it was still desert, and snow was as scarce in the winter as rain was in the summer. Still, they'd managed to put one modest-sized ball of snow on top of a slightly bigger ball of snow.

Sierra didn't have a lot of experience with kids, but one of the partners at Bane had a four-year-old grandson who sometimes came into the office and these girls looked to be a similar age. One was dressed in a pink snowsuit with blue boots, the other wore a purple snowsuit and orange boots.

Twins, she guessed, and shuddered at the possibility of heightened nausea and vomiting, which she'd read could be experienced by women carrying multiple babies.

The girl in pink took the knitted hat off her own head to set it on the snowman.

"Now your scarf," she said to her sister.

The girl in purple dutifully began to tug at the knot by her throat.

"That's a nice snowman you've got there," Sierra said.

Both girls beamed with pleasure.

"He needs a scarf," Pink said.

"Can you help me wif it?" Purple asked, still tugging on her scarf.

"I don't know that your mom would want you dressing up your snowman in your accessories," Sierra said.

"It's okay," Pink told her. "Mommy's not here."

Sierra wasn't sure how to respond to that and was relieved when the front door opened and a man walked out.

Relieved, that was, until she recognized him as the thief of her Frosted Flakes.

"Here we are," Deacon said, his attention on the two girls. "Mini Oreos for the eyes and mouth and a baby carrot for the nose."

Then he spotted Sierra on the sidewalk. Their gazes locked.

"Oh," he said, obviously as surprised to see her as she was to see him. "Hi."

"Hi," she said back.

"She wikes our snowman," Pink chimed in.

"Well, of course she likes your snowman," Deacon agreed. "He's very handsome. Or he will be when you give him a face."

The girls took the proffered items and returned to their snowman-in-progress.

"Did you change your mind about needing a lawyer?" he asked Sierra.

She shook her head. "I was just out for a walk."

"You live around here?" he asked.

"A couple blocks over."

"I guess that makes us neighbors, sort of."

"Sort of," she agreed, before shifting her attention back to the little girls who were now stuffing mini Oreos in their mouths. "Your daughters are adorable."

"They're not mine," he said, shaking his head to emphasize the point. "They're my brother's kids."

"So...your nieces?"

Now he nodded.

She looked from one child to the other, noting their similar heights and features.

"Twins?" she guessed.

He nodded again. "Double Trouble, I call them."

The girls giggled at the obviously familiar nickname.

"We need mo' cookies," Purple said.

He glanced over, sighed. "You were supposed to use them to make the snowman's mouth, not put them in *your* mouths."

That remark earned another round of giggles.

"You know where the cookies are," Deacon told them. "You can go get one more package, but that's all."

They raced toward the door.

"I get the carrot," she said. "But why mini Oreos?"

"Because I'm all out of lumps of coal."

"None left in your Christmas stocking?"

His lips twitched at the corners. "Is it so hard to believe that I might have been on Santa's 'nice' list?"

"Were you?"

"I can be naughty or nice, depending on the situation," he told her.

And suddenly their conversation was inching toward potentially dangerous territory again, the air between them charged with electricity.

Deciding that a change of topic was in order, she

asked, "Did your nieces enjoy their Frosted Flakes for breakfast?"

"They always do," he said.

She should have left it at that, but she felt the teensiest bit uneasy thinking that she might have judged him not only too quickly but also unfairly.

"So why did you let me think that you would be spending the night with two women?" she asked him.

"Is that what you were thinking?"

She narrowed her gaze. "You know it was. You *winked*."

"And somehow you interpreted that as code for a threesome?"

She huffed out a breath. "I don't even know why we're having this conversation. It doesn't matter."

"Maybe it does," he countered. "Maybe I want to know why you'd assume a casual mention of breakfast with twins meant a night with two women."

"It was the wink," she said again.

"Or was it the fact that you looked at me and wanted me and guessed that most other women do, too?"

"What I guessed is that you'd be as obnoxious as you are arrogant—and I was right."

"Here's an idea," he said, seemingly unfazed by her retort. "Why don't we talk about my character flaws over dinner?"

"Because I don't date players."

"And, after two very brief conversations, you think you've got me all figured out, don't you?" he challenged.

She shrugged. "Some people aren't very complicated."

"Are you always so quick to rush to judgment?"

No, she wasn't. But she was apparently quick to

judge *him*, and that was something she'd have to give some consideration to on her own time.

For now, she simply said, "Goodbye, Mr. Columbia Law."

"It's Deacon," he reminded her. "And you haven't given me your number. Or even your name."

"Not an oversight," she told him.

She was right.

He'd acted like a dick, and she'd called him on it.

Well, she'd accused him of being arrogant and obnoxious, which was essentially the same thing. And not a completely inaccurate characterization of his behavior, Deacon acknowledged, if only to himself.

He was usually much smoother in his interactions with the opposite sex. But there was something about the cool reserve of the woman—who still hadn't even told him her name—that made him want to elicit a reaction.

He'd at least succeeded in that, even if the reaction wasn't quite what he'd hoped for. But as his high school baseball coach used to say, if you're going to go down, go down swinging.

"We got the cookies," Piper announced, running toward him, her sister close on her heels.

He imagined the snow they'd tracked inside melting on his hardwood floors but decided that he'd wipe it up later. Now he helped the girls put the finishing touches on their creation, took some pictures of them posing beside it and sent the photos to his brother and sister-in-law.

They both immediately responded to his text with heart emojis, then Regan sent another message:

We'll be there to pick them up in about an hour.

Make it 2 hours, he suggested. We haven't watched Encanto yet.

2 hours, she confirmed. And thank you again. xo.

"Okay, girls—take your hat and scarf off the snowman now so we don't forget them out here," he instructed.

"But he'll get cold," Poppy protested.

"He's a snowman," Deacon said. "If he wasn't cold, he'd melt."

"Like Fwosty," Piper said, nodding sagely.

"I don't want him to melt," Poppy said worriedly.

"I don't think you have to worry about him melting anytime soon," Deacon said.

It was far more likely that the snowman would meet his end courtesy of the seven-year-old bully who lived three doors down and already had a reputation for kicking over and stomping on the neighborhood snow people. Not that he was going to tell his nieces that.

"And even when he does eventually melt, it just means that you can look forward to building him again when the snow comes back," he said instead.

"Can we watch 'canto now?" Poppy asked.

"First, we need to pack up your stuff, so you're ready to go when your mom and dad come to get you, then we can watch *Encanto*."

"Can we have popco'n with the movie?" Piper wanted to know.

"An' Wed Vines?"

"You ate all my Red Vines last night," he reminded them. "But yes, we can have popcorn."

While the girls hung up their snowsuits, he wiped up the melted snow on the floor, then together they gathered up pj's, toothbrushes, books and toys before carrying their backpacks downstairs and settling in front of the television to watch the movie.

He adored the two little girls and was always happy to spend time with him. Of course, he would have been even happier if his brother hadn't confided that his babysitting services were being utilized so that the twins' parents could focus on making another baby.

Not that Deacon objected to his brother having an intimate relationship with his wife—because wasn't that supposed to be one of the benefits of marriage?— he just didn't want to hear about it. Especially when he was achingly aware that it had been far too long since he'd enjoyed any action between the sheets.

His own fault, Deacon knew. He'd had a good thing going with Mariah Traynor for almost six months— or they'd had some pretty good chemistry, anyway. But it turned out that they didn't have much in common beyond that. He was a Dodgers fan; she couldn't stand baseball. He cheered for the 49ers; she abhorred football. He enjoyed watching the Golden Knights; she didn't even know that Vegas had a hockey team.

Now, of course, he was kicking himself for ruining a good thing—or at least a sure thing. Because since then, he'd discovered that one really was the loneliest number.

And if Mariah wasn't the type of woman that he could envision spending the rest of his life with, maybe that was because he couldn't envision spending the rest of his life with any one woman.

Never say never.

The problem was, Haven wasn't exactly overflowing with single women.

Or maybe the real problem was that he'd already dated most of them—way back in high school when he'd been looking for love (or at least sex) in all the wrong places. And if he hadn't found love, he'd at least discovered the pleasures of physical intimacy. There had been plenty of girls willing to share those pleasures with him—and others who'd looked at him with obvious disdain, who'd snickered in the hallways when he walked by and whispered (not very quietly) about Faithless Faith Parrish's youngest son.

With his brother's words still echoing in his head, and Piper and Poppy singing about not talking about Bruno, Deacon went into the kitchen to make the kids' snack.

He tossed some mini marshmallows and M&M's in with the hot corn when it was popped, and Piper and Poppy immediately declared it was "the best popco'n ev-uh."

Of course, they weren't quite four, so he didn't put much stock in their use of the superlative. Case in point, they also claimed that he read "the best sto-wees," gave "the best hugs" and was, overall, "the best unca."

While he appreciated their enthusiastic endorsement, he was painfully aware of his own shortcomings. And he was definitely not looking forward to the day that they learned the truth about him.

Because he wasn't the best anything—he'd found that out long ago. But he was determined to be better than his beginnings.

Chapter Four

Sierra bought a pair of waterproof boots with a minus-forty-degree cold rating and a down-filled hooded coat so that she could continue to walk every morning, no matter the weather. She continued to explore the neighborhood in various directions, and if she avoided Sherwood Park Drive—where she now knew Deacon Parrish lived—that was simply because she wanted to discover new paths.

Unfortunately, not seeing him didn't stop her from thinking about him—and then she ended up annoyed with herself for thinking about him.

Damn hormones.

At least at work her mind was too busy to wander in his direction. And by the end of her third week on the job, Sierra felt more and more confident that the move to Haven—albeit temporary—had been the right move for her. Even if her brother and sister-in-law remained unconvinced.

Of course, they didn't know all the reasons that she'd chosen to leave Bane & Associates, and she had no intention of telling them. As a result, Nick worried that she was being impulsive, and while Whitney tried to be supportive, her sister-in-law wasn't happy that Sierra had decided to move so far away, especially now.

She understood why they wanted to keep her close, but she'd needed some distance from the mistakes she'd made. And while she knew she'd miss her family—and she did—Haven wasn't so far from Vegas that she couldn't go back to visit during the six months of her contract. She was also hopeful that Nick and Whitney would come to see her, when their schedules allowed, as her townhouse had plenty of room for guests.

For now though, she refocused her attention on proofreading the pretrial memo she'd drafted for her boss, then clicked the print icon on the screen and leaned back in her chair.

Her lips curved a little as she glanced around at the four walls that comprised her office. It was a small thing, the fact that she had an office—and it was a small office—but it was a big step up from the cubicle that she'd spent sixty hours a week in for the past three years. Not only four walls but also a door that closed, to afford her privacy for confidential phone calls or meetings with colleagues, and even a trio of windows with a view of the courthouse across the street.

A sharp rap of knuckles on the open door drew her attention back to the present as her boss stepped into the room carrying a file box.

She retrieved the pages she'd printed and stapled them together as Brett dropped the box on her desk. "What's that?"

"The Dornan file."

Sierra had taken careful notes when he'd briefed his staff on upcoming cases, so she immediately recognized the name. "The fraud case?"

He nodded.

"You want me to write up a sentencing memo?" she guessed, recalling that he'd mentioned he was working on a plea deal with Rhonda Dornan's defense attorney.

Now he shook his head. "She turned down the deal her counsel negotiated and got a new lawyer. She wants to go to trial."

"So what is it that you want me to do?" Sierra wondered aloud.

"Prep for the trial."

She felt a frisson of excitement shimmer through her. She'd been one of the most junior associates at Bane, hired right out of law school, so she wasn't surprised that she had to start out researching case law and drafting arguments for other lawyers to present in court. But almost three years later, she'd been inside a courtroom only a handful of times, and most often only to deliver documents to one of the partners.

"You want me to assist?" she asked cautiously, unwilling to get her hopes up.

"No," Brett said. "I want you to take the lead on this one."

She swallowed. "The lead?"

"Trial starts on Monday," he told her. "And I'm on vacation next week."

She remembered him mentioning that, too, but she hadn't expected the vacation to actually happen. At Bane, she'd known several colleagues who'd booked holidays only to cancel them when something came up at the office that required their attention. Because the work always came first, and any associate who wanted to move up the ranks had to demonstrate that nothing was more important than the job.

Sierra had never had to cancel a trip, because she hadn't been foolish enough to make plans to go away. But she'd bailed on outings with her friends more times than she liked to admit and had even stood up the occasional date when one of the partners dropped something on her desk at the eleventh hour.

"Disneyland," Brett said now, returning to the topic of his vacation with a shake of his head. "What was I thinking?"

Sierra smiled. "You were probably thinking that your kids will love it."

He had three sons, ages ten, seven and five, with his wife of almost fifteen years. A photo taken at their wedding was prominently displayed on his desk alongside another of Jenny and the boys, and he wore a chunky band on the third finger of his left hand. Brett Ryckell was a man devoted to his family and proud to let everyone know it.

"Have you been to Disneyland?" he asked her now.

"Once," she said. "A long time ago."

Before her parents had died and her life had been turned completely upside down.

"Any words of advice?" he asked.

"Take lots of pictures."

"I can do that," he said, as he started for the door.

She lifted the lid of the box, eager to dig into the files.

He turned and gave her a gently admonishing look. "It's almost six o'clock, Sierra."

"Yes, sir," she said, not sure what point her boss was trying to make in mentioning the time.

"Go home," he said.

"But…it's not even six o'clock."

"The contents of the box aren't going to change overnight," he pointed out. "You'll have plenty of time to familiarize yourself with the case before Monday."

"Yes, sir," she said again, reluctantly replacing the lid.

"Don't misunderstand me," Brett said. "I appreciate your enthusiasm, but I don't want you to burn yourself out before you've been on the job a month."

"I don't think there's any danger of that."

"Still, you should take some time for yourself, go out with friends."

"I haven't been here long enough to make friends," she said, even as she thought fleetingly of the woman she'd met in the grocery store the previous weekend. But despite Sky's suggestion that they should get together for coffee sometime, Sierra had yet to hear from her.

"Then you should go out and make some."

She managed a smile. "I'll work on it."

Truthfully, though, she didn't see the point in making friends when she was only going to be in town for six months. That was the length of the contract she'd been offered, temporarily filling in for ADA Jade Scott who was on maternity leave for the same period of time. And even if Jade decided that she wasn't ready to come back at the end of six months, Sierra wasn't in any position to stay in Haven beyond that.

She left the office with the file box and made her way to Jo's Pizza.

She'd heard nothing but good things about the place since her arrival in town, and she figured it was time to try the infamous pie for herself.

Jo's had a front entrance with a sign over the door that said Restaurant and a side entrance designated as

Takeout. Sierra opened the Takeout door and stepped inside, her stomach growling hungrily as she breathed in the scents of garlic, oregano and tomato sauce. If the pizza tasted half as good as the restaurant smelled, then Jo's would undoubtedly live up to its lofty reputation.

She turned toward the takeout counter and stopped mid-stride, because wasn't it just her luck that Deacon Parrish was there, flirting with a pretty blonde working on the other side of the counter?

Deacon needed to get a life.

Instead, it was six thirty on a Friday night and he was picking up pizza.

A single medium pizza that he would take home to eat by himself.

Even Lucy, daughter of the infamous Jo, had teased him about his lack of plans as she'd taken his order.

And she was right—he was an old man at twenty-eight.

Well, almost twenty-eight, but that clarification didn't make him feel much better about the fact that it was a Friday night and he had no plans.

Worse, he didn't want any plans.

He sincerely wanted nothing more than to go home, put his feet up on the coffee table—because it was his house and his coffee table, and there was no one to tell him to get his feet off the table—and eat his dinner while watching the hockey game on TV.

Well, there was maybe one thing that he wanted more—and wasn't it a happy coincidence that she'd walked through the door just as his pizza came out from the kitchen?

"Who's that?" Lucy asked curiously, having followed the direction of his gaze.

"I was hoping you could tell me."

She shook her head. "I can't say that I've ever seen her before."

"But you're about to get her name and number," he mused. "And if you happened to leave her order slip right here on the counter for your ninth-grade lab partner to take a peek at—"

"No," Lucy said bluntly. "You want someone to help you get a date? Join match-dot-com."

"Come on, Luce."

"No," she said again.

The phone rang just as his not-quite-neighbor approached the counter.

"I'll be right with you," Lucy told her, before snatching up the receiver.

"Hello, again," Deacon said, grinning.

"Hi," she replied, with a distinct lack of enthusiasm.

"Long day for you?" he asked.

She shrugged. "No longer than usual."

"I thought winter was generally slow season in the real estate market," he said, determined to engage her in conversation and at least learn her name.

"Sorry," she said, sounding more dismissive than regretful. "I don't know anything about the real estate market."

"You don't work at Ruby Realty?"

She seemed taken aback by the question. "What made you think that I did?"

He gestured to her attire. "The red jacket is part of their signature outfit."

"My jacket isn't red, it's cranberry."

Which was exactly what he'd thought the first time he saw her wearing it. "Isn't cranberry just a more specific shade of red?"

"I have a question for you," she said, declining to answer his. "If I was wearing a green jacket, would you assume I'd won it at the Masters?"

"Probably not, as women don't currently compete at the Masters."

"Touché."

"So you don't work in real estate, but you are new in town," he mused.

"Is that a statement or a question?"

"A statement."

"Because you know everyone in town?" she guessed.

"Maybe not by name," he acknowledged. "But I'm sure if I'd ever met you and known yours, I would have remembered."

She narrowed her gaze on him. "Are you capable of having a conversation with a woman without flirting with her?"

"I am," he assured her with a wink. "But flirting is so much more fun than regular conversation."

"Can I give you a word of advice?"

"I'm all ears."

"Save your flirtatious charm for someone who might be interested, because I'm not."

"Ouch," he said.

"You don't look particularly wounded," she noted.

"Because I know you're lying."

"I'm not lying," she said.

"You don't want to be interested," he said. "But the flush of color in your cheeks suggests that you are."

"Which can also be a physiological response to irritation."

"Can be," he agreed. "But in this case, I'd bet that it's indicative of attraction."

She rolled her eyes. "Apparently you're someone who likes throwing his money away."

"Okay, let's forget any kind of wager and instead grab a table so that we can share our pizzas and conversation," he suggested as an alternative.

"No, thanks."

"You've got that down to a fine art, don't you?"

"What?" she asked, with obvious reluctance.

"The affected disinterest and casual brush-off."

"I'm not trying to hurt your feelings," she said. "But I'm really not looking for any kind of romantic entanglement."

"What kind of entanglement are you looking for?"

"None," she told him.

But there had been a slight hesitation before her response—as if she regretted turning down the offer.

Interesting.

Lucy finally finished on the phone and returned to the counter. "Sorry about that," she said to his neighbor. "Are you here to order or pick up?"

Deacon effected a casual pose against the counter, as if he wasn't listening for her to give her name.

"Pick up," she said. "Medium pizza for—"

"Deacon Parrish!"

The excited squeal drowned out the rest of what she said, and he barely had a chance to turn his head to identify the source before a woman threw herself at him—so hard she nearly cracked his ribs. Soft breasts pressed against his chest and teased blond hair tickled his nose, but it was the cloud of Viva La Juicy perfume that took him back to tenth grade, which was, coincidentally, when he'd lost his virginity with Liberty Mosley.

"Oh. My. God." Liberty drew back a little to smile

at him. "I can't believe it's you." She pressed her red-painted lips to his. "I haven't seen you in…forever."

"It's been a few years," he acknowledged, sliding a cautious glance at his neighbor.

"Last time I saw you, you were just heading off to law school," Liberty recalled, oblivious to the fact—or maybe not caring—that she might have interrupted something. "And now you're a big-shot lawyer."

"Well, the lawyer part is right, anyway," he acknowledged.

"Where was it you went? Somewhere in New York, right? Harvard?"

"Harvard's in Massachusetts," he told her.

Her brows drew together. "I was sure your brother said you'd gone to New York City."

"I did," he confirmed. "Columbia."

"Wouldn't want to miss an opportunity to slip *that* into the conversation," he heard his neighbor mutter under her breath.

Before Deacon could respond, Liberty linked her arm through his and tipped her head against his shoulder. "Obviously we've got a lot to catch up on—why don't we order a pizza and take it up to Lookout Point?"

"For starters, because it's about ten degrees outside."

"I'm sure we can figure out a way to stay warm." The statement was accompanied by a smile that promised a lot more than conversation.

"Also, because your husband would likely object to that plan."

"I'm not married yet," she pointed out. "And anyway, Travis is out of town this weekend with his buddies—his last weekend of freedom, he called it, so I figure it should be my last weekend of freedom, too."

"And finally, because I've already got a pizza—"

Deacon continued, gesturing to the box on the counter "—and other plans for tonight."

And while Deacon had some very fond memories of Liberty, he wasn't interested in revisiting their history—and even less interested in hooking up with a woman who would be exchanging vows with another man in the near future.

She pouted prettily, but Deacon's attention was on the sexy brunette who was staring at the screen of her phone, pretending not to eavesdrop on his conversation.

Or maybe she really wasn't.

"How about tomorrow, then?" Liberty suggested hopefully, toying with the zipper of his jacket.

Out of the corner of his eye, Deacon saw Lucy return from the back with another pizza box. She set it on the counter and rang up the order. His neighbor paid for her food, picked up the box and headed for the door.

"No." His tone was firm and final. "It was nice to see you, Liberty. And congrats on your upcoming wedding, but I have to run."

"Deacon—wait!"

It was Lucy who called to him this time, and he turned with his hand on the door.

She gestured to the box on the counter. "Don't you want your pizza?"

Of course he wanted his pizza.

And by the time he raced back to the counter to grab the box and rush out the door again, his neighbor was already gone.

Chapter Five

Sierra's heart was beating a little too hard and a little too fast—though she didn't think it was an unusual physiological response for someone about to enter a lion's den.

Or at least knock on the door of the lion's den.

She paused to draw a deep breath (that stabbed at her lungs like icy needles!) before tapping her knuckles against the wood, then waited, the pizza box clutched in her hands.

"This is a surprise," Deacon said when he opened the door. "Did you change your mind about wanting to have dinner together?"

The smile that accompanied the question was warm and sincere and far too tempting.

"No," Sierra said quickly, refusing to let herself be tempted. "But I do want my dinner."

His brows lifted. "Isn't that what's in your hands?"

"No," she said again, lifting the lid of the box to show

him the pie. "I didn't order pepperoni, bacon and sausage."

In fact, just the smell of the bacon—usually one of her favorite foods—was churning her stomach, so she quickly closed the lid again.

"I haven't looked at mine yet. Why don't you come on in out of the cold and I'll see what I got?" he invited.

Enter the lion's den?

No, thank you.

Except that it was cold outside—*really* cold—and it seemed kind of rude to stand there, holding the door open and letting his heat escape, when he'd invited her in.

She stepped into the tiled foyer and closed the door at her back. She was both surprised and relieved there was no indication that the blonde from the restaurant had come home with him.

Or maybe she'd gone straight to the bedroom.

But Sierra didn't imagine that Deacon would have responded to her knock if he had a willing woman waiting for him.

So she pushed the idea aside and surveyed her surroundings. His house was a detached two story and obviously bigger than the townhouse she was renting, but the ground floor layout was a similar open-concept design, with the foyer leading into a family room that connected to a dining room. She suspected the kitchen was at the back of the house, facing the dining room, though she couldn't see past the stairs to the upper level to be sure.

Instead, she focused on the nearby living space. The walls were painted a warm cream color with a trio of abstract prints in neutral shades on the longest wall. The dark hardwood floors were covered with an oatmeal-colored rug, on top of which sat an oversize sectional of chocolate brown leather and mission-style tables in some kind of dark wood. Facing the sectional was an enormous flat-screen TV.

It was very much a masculine space—the proverbial bachelor pad—absent any decorative pillows or whimsical knickknacks.

But there was a photo of his nieces, mugging for the camera, in a frame on one of the end tables—a reminder to Sierra that, whatever his faults, Deacon obviously doted on the girls and, therefore, couldn't be all bad. And in the brief interaction that she'd witnessed between Deacon and the twins, it had been just as evident that they adored their uncle.

As her gaze shifted away from the photo, she spotted a lump of what looked like modeling clay beside it. No, not a lump, she realized, but a figure, with googly eyes and four strands of yellow yarn on the top of its head.

"Is that a self-portrait?" she asked, gesturing to the clay figure.

"I only wish I was that talented," he said. "The true artists in the family are Piper and Poppy."

And he was proud enough of their efforts to display them in his living space. Obviously there was a lot more to this man than she'd assumed, aspects of his character that she couldn't help but like, but none that affected her determination not to get involved.

"Who's winning?" she asked, hearing the play-by-play of a hockey game in the background.

"There's no score yet." He lifted the lid of the pizza box on the coffee table, made a face. "Tomatoes, green peppers and black olives?"

"That's mine," she confirmed.

"Are you a vegetarian?"

"Only when I'm selling real estate," she said dryly.

He chuckled at that—and *damn*, if the low, sensual sound didn't turn her knees to jelly.

The sound of a cheer emanating from the television thankfully diverted her attention, and she inched a little closer to peer at the screen.

"Are you a hockey fan?" Deacon asked, as they exchanged boxes.

"I enjoy watching the game, especially when the Golden Knights are playing."

"I'd get down on one knee and propose right now if I actually knew your name."

"It's Sierra," she said, because it seemed silly to continue to withhold such a basic piece of information.

He started to drop to one knee.

"I didn't tell you because I wanted a proposal," she was quick to assure him.

He straightened up again. "So why did you tell me?"

"Because we're neighbors, sort of," she said, borrowing his description. "And since we seem destined to run into one another around town, we should probably be able to exchange pleasantries on a first-name basis."

"Destined, huh?" He seemed to ponder that for a minute before he asked, "Do you believe in destiny?"

Though his tone was casual, there was something in his gaze that told her he was genuinely interested in her answer to the question.

"No," she said. "I think destiny is just an excuse for people to avoid responsibility for their actions."

"So you don't think it was destiny that there was only one box of Frosted Flakes on the shelf that day and we both wanted it?" he pressed.

"No," she said again. "I think it was a delay in the shipment from the supplier."

"And you stopping to talk to my nieces, not know-ing they were my nieces?"

"Geographical proximity."

"And crossing paths at Jo's?"

"A statistical probability," she decided. "In a small town with only one pizza place, it's almost inevitable that we'd run into each other."

"Haven isn't all *that* small," he protested.

"Compared to Vegas, it is."

"So that's where you're from," he mused.

"And where I'm going back to, when my contract here is finished. But right now, I'm taking this—" she held up her pizza box "—home to have my dinner."

"Are you sure you don't want to stay and watch the game?"

She hesitated, because the truth was, she did want to stay. Not because she was wildly attracted to him—although she was—but because she'd spent every night of the past three weeks alone and it might be nice to hang out with and talk to another person for a while.

Except that Deacon wasn't simply another person—he was a man who made her all too aware of the fact that she was a woman, and that made her wary.

It was the sound of cheers emanating from the tele-vision that tipped the balance.

"Actually, I think I will stay." She shrugged out of her coat. "Just for the first period."

Deacon grinned. "I've got beer and wine and soda. What can I get for you?"

"Water?" she suggested, unzipping her boots.

"You're a cheap date," he remarked, as he headed into the kitchen to get her drink.

"This isn't a date," she said firmly, because even

though she knew he was only teasing, she needed to be clear about that fact.

He returned with a glass of water and a couple of plates. "Okay, you're a cheap hockey-watching and pizza-eating companion."

"I can live with that," she decided, taking a seat on the opposite end of the sofa. Not only to reinforce the point that this wasn't a date, but also to ensure her stomach wouldn't rebel against the scent of the bacon on his pizza.

"Is it that you don't date or that you don't want to date *me*?" Deacon asked, transferring a slice from his box to his plate.

She plucked an olive off her own slice, popped it into her mouth. "I'm on a dating hiatus," she confided.

"Recent breakup?" he guessed.

"Not so recent."

"Broken heart?"

"Only bruised." She nibbled on a slice of green pepper.

"Are you going to eat that pizza or dissect it?"

She responded to his question by lifting the slice to her mouth and taking a bite, then moaned.

Deacon grinned. "Is this your first experience with Jo's Pizza?"

She nodded, still chewing. Savoring.

"It totally lives up to its reputation, doesn't it?"

She nodded again, swallowed. "I didn't think it was possible, but—" she couldn't wait to take another bite, continued with her mouth full "—ohmygod—this is…" She closed her eyes to better focus on the perfectly harmonized flavors and complimentary textures of crust and sauce and cheese and veggies as she searched for the right word. "Orgasmic."

"Should I leave you alone with your pizza?"

Her eyes popped open in response to his amused question.

She felt heat rise in her cheeks again.

"No," she said. "I'm good now."

"And I'm very intrigued," he told her. "How long do you plan for this dating hiatus to last?"

"Another seven months, at least. Maybe more."

His brows lifted. "That's a fair length of time. Is it random or specific?"

"I think it's my turn to ask the questions now," she told him.

"So ask me a question," Deacon said, happy that his sexy new neighbor was finally willing to get to know him—and let him know her.

Sierra reached for another slice of pizza. "Who was the woman you were talking to at Jo's?"

"Lucy Delgado—Jo's daughter. She and her husband mostly run the pizzeria now."

"I wasn't asking about the woman behind the counter but the one in your arms."

"That was Liberty Mosley," he told her, because after inviting her to ask questions, he could hardly balk at answering them.

"High school girlfriend?" she guessed.

"Off and on. Probably more off than on."

"And yet she seems to have some very fond memories of you."

He shrugged. "Aren't we all a little nostalgic when it comes to the past? Or at least select parts of it."

She acknowledged that with a nod before following up with another question. "What's Lookout Point?"

"A nearby golf course...and popular..." Now he did

balk, for a brief moment, as he scrambled for an appropriate description. "Uh, dating destination."

Sierra considered his response as she chewed another bite of pizza.

"You mean make-out spot," she finally said.

"Yeah," he admitted.

"So why did you turn down Liberty's invitation?"

"For all the reasons I told her—and one reason that I didn't."

"What's that?"

"I have a new neighbor who's piqued my interest."

Sierra's expression immediately shuttered. "Deacon—"

"I know," he interjected. "Dating hiatus, bruised heart, not-so-recent breakup. I heard everything you said—but I wanted to be as honest with you as you were with me."

Her gaze skittered away.

Because she was uncomfortable with his confession?

Or because she hadn't been as honest with him as he believed?

Before he could decide if he wanted to further pursue either of those possibilities, the buzzer sounded to end the first period.

Sierra leaned forward to close the lid of her pizza box, then she got up to carry her empty plate and glass to the kitchen.

Deacon wanted to invite her to stay to watch the rest of the game, but he didn't because it was evident what her answer would be. Truthfully, he was surprised that she'd stayed at all, but he was grateful that she had because he'd enjoyed her company.

He followed her to the door, waiting for her to put on her boots and coat before handing her the box of leftover pizza.

"Is that the right one this time?" she asked.

"You better hope so," he said. "Because I ate all of mine."

She smiled at that, and his heart bumped against his ribs before he remembered that she was on a lengthy dating hiatus.

But the reminder didn't discourage him so much as it motivated him to change her mind.

"You know, one of these days you're going to chase after me, and it's not going to be because you want my pizza," he told her.

"It was *my* pizza," she reminded him. "And don't hold your breath."

He didn't hold his breath, but he was smiling as he watched her make her way to the green Kia Soul parked in his driveway. Because he might have struck out, but he'd gone down swinging.

Even more important—he knew the game had only just begun.

When Sierra got home, she sat at the dining room table with the Dornan case file in front of her and the hockey game in the background. But after thirty minutes, she realized her mind was flitting around so much that she might as well have stayed and watched the last two periods with Deacon.

Still, she felt confident that she'd done the right thing in coming home, because she'd been trying to make it clear to him that she wasn't interested in any kind of relationship, and hanging out together for several hours on a Friday night would definitely send a mixed signal.

It wasn't just that she wasn't interested in a relationship, it was that the circumstances of her life right now made it impossible for her to get involved. At least for the next seven and a half months—and that's why the smart thing to do was to keep her distance from Mr. Columbia Law.

Which shouldn't be so difficult, she reasoned. After all, she was only going to be in town for six months.

Though it did seem an odd coincidence that their paths kept crossing. First at the grocery store on Saturday, the next day in front of his house and again at the local pizzeria only five days later.

But it wasn't destiny.

Maybe it wasn't even so odd but, as she'd pointed out to Deacon earlier, inevitable.

Though she didn't know what kind of law he practiced—she'd resisted the urge to google him—she knew that Katelyn Davidson ran a full-service law firm (and Sierra's new colleagues spoke highly of all the attorneys who worked there), so it seemed likely that she'd encounter him at the courthouse.

But likely wasn't destiny, either.

In any event, she was in Haven to do a job and, in the process, reassess her own career goals. Obviously her track to a partnership at Bane & Associates had been derailed by her abrupt resignation, but there was no way she could have stayed. Not after what happened in San Francisco.

Of course, there were plenty of other firms in Vegas, and she had a decent enough résumé that she felt confident she could get another job elsewhere in the city. But she didn't want another job where she'd be constantly on edge, wondering every day if she'd cross paths with Eric or Aubrey.

And so far, she was truly happy with the choice she'd made. She was enjoying the challenge of her work at the DA's office and excited about the opportunities her boss had given her.

But she did miss her brother and sister-in-law.

As if on cue, her phone chimed. She picked it up and smiled when she saw a message from Nick on the screen.

Just checking in to see how you're doing.

I'm good. Prepping for a trial next week.

Her phone rang. She swiped to connect the call.

"I hate texting," Nick said, in lieu of a more traditional greeting.

"I know," she agreed. "It's your chubby thumbs."

"I don't have chubby thumbs," he protested. "They're just big. Manly."

She chuckled.

"So are you still at the office?" her brother asked.

"No. My boss kicked me out before six."

"Wow. Your boss is a lot nicer than mine."

"Yours isn't so bad," she said, because Nick was his own boss now. After a decade of working at another firm, he'd decided to hang out his own shingle. Two years after that, he had three associates working with him.

"Well, I'm probably going to be stuck here for another couple of hours, anyway."

"Are you still tied up with the Chekhov trial?" she asked, referring to the insurance case that he'd been working on for the better part of six months.

"Yeah."

"Isn't this week three of what was supposed to be a two-week trial?"

"Yeah," he said again, and she could hear a world of frustration in that single syllable. "The insurance company has been delaying at every stage of the proceeding."

"Because they want to hold off having to make the big payout they know is coming," she guessed.

"Let's hope so," he said. "Anyway, closing arguments are on Monday, but we're heading to San Bernardino to see Whitney's parents this weekend, so I want to get this nailed down before we go."

"You'll knock it out of the park," she told him. "You always do."

"I appreciate your faith in me. And my wife would probably appreciate it if I made it home tonight, so I'm going to sign off now."

"Before you do," she interjected hastily, to prevent him from disconnecting the call, "I wanted to let you know that I got in to see the doctor in Battle Mountain that Dr. Shah referred me to."

"When was that?" Nick asked, and she knew she had his full attention now.

"Wednesday," she admitted, feeling just a little bit guilty that she'd waited more than forty-eight hours to tell him.

"I assume I would have heard about the appointment before now if there was any cause for concern."

"There's no cause for concern—I'm good," she assured him. Then she laid a hand on her still mostly-flat belly. "And the baby's good, too."

Deacon grunted in response to the elbow that slammed into his ribs.

"Who said this would be fun?" he grumbled.

"Early exercise helps you start the day with energy, focus and optimism," Claudio Delgado—Lucy's husband—told him.

"That might be true." He jumped up to intercept a pass. "If the form of exercise is sex."

"You getting too old for basketball?" Luke Ross—a childhood friend of the same age—taunted.

"No." And he proved it by sinking a basket. "But I'd rather be getting physical with a woman in the bedroom than sweating with you guys in a gym."

JJ Green—a local real estate agent—caught the ball and started toward the other end of the court.

"That was twenty-one," Claudio announced. "Game's over."

"Twenty-one to twenty," JJ called back. "The game has to be won by two."

Ben Powell—another childhood friend—swore as he started to chase the play.

JJ's toss kissed the backboard before dropping through the hoop.

"Now we're tied again," he said smugly.

"Since when do you have to win by two?" Luke demanded, as Ben snagged the ball and sent it through the air to Gerard Flaherty—the (very tall) husband of one of the lawyers who worked with Deacon.

"Since always," JJ said.

Gerard dribbled the ball around the defender, deliberately moving away from the net rather than toward it.

Deacon ran into the key, as if anticipating a pass. Claudio chased him.

Gerard set up outside the three-point line and took his shot.

Everyone stopped to watch the ball arc in the air before dropping through the net.

Swish.

"Twenty-three to twenty-one," Ben said smugly.

JJ muttered a string of curses beneath his breath as he made his way to the bench to grab his water bottle.

The other five men on the court followed suit.

"I thought Harvey was going to be here today," Gerard said, naming the courthouse security guard who was a usual Saturday morning pickup participant.

"He said he was," Deacon confirmed.

"But that was before I saw him getting cozy with Melanie Noble at Diggers' last night," Ben said.

"Which means he was likely enjoying Dekes's preferred form of physical exercise this morning," Claudio chimed in.

"Actually, I half-expected Dekes to bail on us today," Luke said.

"Why would I bail?" he wondered aloud.

"Because there was a bright green Kia parked in your driveway last night."

Ben's brows lifted. "Overnight?"

Luke shrugged. "How would I know? I just happened to notice the car as I was driving by."

Ben turned to Deacon. "Overnight?" he asked again.

"No."

"He said regretfully," JJ added with a smirk.

Deacon scowled at him as he lifted his water bottle to his lips.

"So...who is she?" Ben pressed.

"No one you know."

"How do you know?" his friend challenged.

"Because she's new in town."

"Sierra Hart?" Claudio guessed. "Lucy said you were flirting with her last night."

Sierra Hart. Deacon wondered why the name struck a chord with him now when he'd experienced no similar sense of recognition when Sierra introduced herself to him, using only her given name, the previous evening.

"Is it possible The Daily Grind rumor mill is failing?" Ben wondered aloud. "Because I stopped in to grab a coffee this morning and didn't detect a whisper of this."

"He was flirting with her at Jo's."

"Is she hot?" Luke wanted to know.

Claudio shrugged. "I wasn't there."

"Don't you have security cameras in the restaurant?"

"Sure," the restauranteur agreed. "But I don't review the footage looking for hot women."

"Because Lucy would kick your ass," Ben said.

"Because I'm lucky to be married to the hottest woman in town," Claudio said, managing to sound just a little smug.

"Lucy *is* hot," JJ acknowledged. "But Sierra is hot *and single*."

"How do you know?" Deacon wondered aloud.

"I listed the house she's renting."

"Hot and single," Ben echoed, sounding intrigued.

"I saw her first," Deacon reminded his friend, an unmistakable warning in his tone.

"Actually, it sounds like JJ saw her first," Gerard noted.

"I guess I did," the real estate agent mused. "But I also just booked a trip to take Veronica to Aruba for Valentine's Day."

"Are you finally going to pop the question?" Claudio asked.

JJ nodded.

"And another one bites the dust," Deacon remarked, shaking his head.

"Your time will come," Gerard said.

The words sounded to Deacon more like a warning than a promise.

He shook his head. "I don't think so."

"Dekes doesn't believe in happy-ever-after," Luke said, not without sympathy.

"Maybe Ms. Hart will be the woman to change his mind," JJ suggested.

Deacon was skeptical that anyone could do that—but, to his surprise, realized that he was more than willing to let Sierra try.

Chapter Six

Sierra was excited (and admittedly a little nervous) about her upcoming trial. Aside from one appearance in traffic court for the purpose of reducing a speeding ticket given to Harold Bane's seventeen-year-old grandson, she'd never had the opportunity to argue a case on her own.

But the Dornan case wasn't a complicated one, and a quick review of the file confirmed that all of the evidence required for a conviction was there. And by Sunday night, she'd pretty much memorized the police reports, drafted her opening arguments and made detailed notes for the examination and cross-examination of all the witnesses.

She set out Monday morning, confident that she was prepared to handle anything that might happen in court.

And she was—anything except discovering that the opposing counsel was Mr. Columbia Law himself.

Deacon was already seated at the defense table when

she walked in. And it was a good thing he was sitting down, because the realization that Sierra—his not-quite-neighbor, not-a-vegetarian, not-a-real-estate-agent—was the new assistant district attorney would have knocked him off his feet.

At least now he knew why Claudio's use of her full name had tripped something in his brain, because of course he'd heard mention of "Ms. Hart," the new ADA.

And apparently she'd been right about the fact that they were destined to run into one another around town—and who was he to fight against destiny? Instead, he pushed his chair back and rose to his feet to cross the divide, an easy smile on his face.

"You didn't tell me you were a lawyer," he said by way of greeting.

She shrugged. "I'm not one of those people who feels compelled to mention my job in every passing conversation."

"I mentioned it *once*," he said. "And only after you called me a cowboy."

"Being a lawyer doesn't mean you're not a cowboy," she noted.

Though a lot of people had romantic notions about cowboys, he knew that her remark hadn't been intended as a compliment. And maybe it should have bothered him that this woman had already formed an unfavorable opinion of him, but it didn't. Because the fact that she obviously had an opinion suggested that she'd been thinking about him—as he'd been thinking about her. And for now, he was going to count that as a win.

"There's a note in the file that Rhonda Dornan fired her previous attorney and hired Nolan Hollister to represent her," Sierra said, obviously eager to move on with business. "Where do you fit in to the picture?"

"At seven o'clock last night, Rhonda was informed by Nolan Hollister that he couldn't represent her at trial. At eight o'clock, she contacted Katelyn Davidson's office. Katelyn passed the case to me."

"I wonder if her retainer check to Nolan Hollister bounced," Sierra mused.

Deacon had wondered the same thing when he discovered the nature of the charges against his client. And perhaps it had, because Rhonda had promised to bring a certified check to court this morning for his representation.

Of course, it would be unprofessional to share any of that information with the ADA, so he remained silent.

"And I'm guessing, since you were assigned this case just about twelve hours ago, that you're not here to start the trial but to ask for a postponement."

"Just a short one," he said, adding a smile that more than a few women had described as irresistibly charming.

She glanced at her watch. "Thirty minutes?"

Apparently the new ADA wasn't easily charmed.

"A little longer than that."

Thirty minutes later, he walked out of the courtroom with his client's certified check in his briefcase and a forty-eight-hour postponement. It wasn't a lot of time, but he didn't think he needed a lot to get up to speed on the case.

"Do you have time for coffee?" Deacon asked Sierra. "And before you say *no*, remember that I know you were scheduled to be in court all day."

"And now that my schedule has been cleared, I can catch up on some of the other work that's waiting for me at the office," she said.

"What if I wanted to talk about the case?"

"I'd think you need some time to familiarize yourself with the details first," she pointed out.

"Or you could summarize those details for me," he suggested. "Over coffee."

"I don't drink coffee."

"You don't drink coffee?" he echoed incredulously.

"I don't drink coffee," she confirmed.

"I don't know anyone who doesn't drink coffee. Well, aside from Double Trouble," he clarified.

Before she had a chance to respond to that, Skylar Gilmore—now Skylar Kelly, he reminded himself—fell into step beside them.

"Well, if it isn't my sister's favorite junior associate and the new ADA," she said. "Were you guys battling in court this morning? And, more important, who won?"

Despite the fact that he'd grown up on the wrong side of the tracks that her ancestors had laid through town, Deacon had always liked Sky. Right now, though, he'd like her a lot more if she went away.

"The battle was adjourned," Sierra said.

"Does that mean you have time for coffee?" Sky asked.

"She doesn't drink coffee," Deacon interjected.

"You don't drink coffee?" Sky echoed, just as he'd done.

"But I do drink tea," Sierra said.

"I could do tea," Sky agreed, before turning to him to say, "Do you want to join us?"

"Thanks, but I'm going to head back to the office," he decided. Then he shifted his attention to Sierra, noting her obvious surprise—and relief—at his reply. "I'll touch base with you later, Ms. Hart, after I've familiarized myself with the case."

"I'll look forward to hearing from you," she said politely.

And though it was maybe no more than the expected response to his comment, he walked away with a smile on his face, pleased that this time he'd been the one to throw the curveball.

Oh yes, the game had definitely begun.

"The Daily Grind has the best coffee in town—and usually the hottest gossip," Sky said to Sierra, as they made their way down Main Street, away from the courthouse. "But if you're looking for something other than coffee—and/or you want a bit of indulgence—then Sweet Caroline's is where you want to go."

"I've walked by it," Sierra admitted. "But so far, I've managed to avoid the temptation."

"You won't be able to avoid it after today," Sky warned, opening the door to the bakery. "Because once you've tasted the deliciousness of Sweet Caroline's, resistance will be futile."

"I hope you're exaggerating," Sierra said. But as she followed the other woman inside and breathed in the mouth-wateringly decadent scent that permeated the bakery, she suspected she wasn't.

"Have you heard of Quinn Ellison?" Sky asked.

"The *New York Times* bestselling author?"

"That's the one," Sky confirmed. "She comes in here twice a week for the chocolate peanut butter banana croissant."

"Quinn Ellison lives in Haven?"

"Cooper's Corners actually, which is about fifteen miles from here."

"She drives fifteen miles to get a croissant?"

"No, she drives fifteen miles to get a *chocolate pea-*

nut butter banana croissant," Sky said. "And to stock her Bookmobile at the library."

"Apparently Quinn Ellison is every bit as interesting as the characters she writes," Sierra mused.

"She is, indeed."

"So…what days did you say she comes into town?"

Sky chuckled. "I didn't say. But it's Mondays and Wednesdays. Usually."

"It's Monday today," Sierra noted.

"And she's already been and gone," the woman behind the counter told them. "Took half a dozen croissants with her."

"This is Caroline," Sky said to Sierra. "The bakery's namesake."

"My mother started the bakery," Caroline explained. "I took over when she moved to Arizona a few years back."

"Caroline, this is Sierra Hart, the new ADA."

"Temporary ADA," Sierra clarified.

"You're filling in while Jade's on mat leave?" Caroline guessed.

Sierra nodded.

"Well, welcome to Haven. And to Sweet Caroline's."

"Thank you."

"What can I get for you ladies today?" Caroline asked.

"I'll have a hot chocolate and a chocolate peanut butter banana croissant," Sky said, as Sierra perused the herbal teas on display.

"Whipped cream on your hot chocolate?" Caroline asked.

"Of course."

"And do you want the croissant heated?"

"Yes, please."

"And for you?" Caroline asked, as her assistant got busy filling Sky's order.

"I'll try a cup of the raspberry bliss tea," Sierra decided. "Black."

"And?" Sky prompted.

She wanted to say "just the tea," but her mouth was watering as her gaze skimmed over the various offerings on display in the pastry case. "And a raspberry crumble bar."

Sky grinned.

"Good choice," Caroline said. "Do you want it heated with whipped cream?"

"Um." She looked to Sky for guidance.

"You have to go for the whipped cream if we're going to be friends."

"Yes, please."

Sky told Caroline to ring up their orders together and insisted on paying, promising to let Sierra pick up the tab next time.

"In case you were wondering, that's my way of saying that we're going to do this again."

"I'd like that," Sierra said, as they carried their mugs to a nearby table.

"Me, too. My best friend since high school moved to North Carolina in the fall, and I really miss having a female friend to talk to.

"I do have a sister—actually two sisters," she amended. "But Kate is busy with her career and her husband and kids—not necessarily in that order—and Ashley is only sixteen."

"Wow—that's quite an age gap," Sierra noted.

Sky shrugged. "Since everyone in this town knows everyone else's business and it's not exactly a secret, I'll tell you that Ashley is my half sister from a drunken encounter my dad had on the fifth anniversary of my mom's death."

She sniffled a little then and blinked away the moisture that covered her eyes. "I'm sorry. I'm not usually so emotional. But even though my mom's been gone a long time, I seem to miss her even more now that I'm going to be a mom."

"I know how you feel," Sierra said, fighting against her own tears. "About missing your mom, I mean," she hastened to clarify. Because despite having felt an immediate kinship with the other woman, she wasn't ready to share any more than that.

"You lost your mom, too?" Sky guessed.

"Both my parents, actually," she said. "They were killed in a car accident when I was fourteen."

"I'm so sorry," the other woman said. "And you definitely win the 'Most Tragic Childhood' round."

Sierra managed to smile, appreciating the attempt at humor. "Life does like to throw curveballs, it seems."

"Are you a baseball fan?"

"A Dodgers fan," she clarified.

"You can definitely be my new best friend," Sky decided. "And you're right about those curveballs." She touched a hand to the slight swell beneath her sweater. "Though sometimes they're exactly what we need, even if we don't realize it at the time."

Conversation paused for a moment while their desserts were delivered to the table.

"And now that we're best friends, do you want to tell me about the vibe between you and Deacon Parrish?"

Sierra's fork slipped from her fingers to clatter against the plate. "What? There was no vibe."

"There was definitely a vibe," Sky insisted. "And

why wouldn't you embrace having a vibe with a very sexy man?"

"There was no vibe," she said again.

"I know a little about denial," Sky said. "But since I want to be your friend and not your therapist, I'll defer to you on this."

Sierra wasn't quite sure how to respond to that, so instead she asked, "What were you doing at the courthouse today?"

"Offering emotional support to a woman swearing out a statement for a restraining order."

"Not a fun way to start the week," Sierra noted sympathetically.

"But a lot better than the way hers ended, with a visit to the emergency room."

"No doubt."

"Now, back to Deacon," Sky said.

"I thought you were deferring to me."

"And I did—in the moment. But now I want to know why you're trying so hard to deny your attraction to him. Is there someone special in Las Vegas?"

"No," she admitted. "But even if I was attracted to him—and I'm not saying that I am—I'm only in town for six months."

"Your contract at the DA's office is for six months," her friend acknowledged. "But there's no reason you couldn't decide to stay in Haven after that."

"Not having a job would be one reason."

"And another reason?"

Sierra looked at her blankly.

"The way you said *one reason* implied that there might be another," Sky said.

"Isn't a lack of gainful employment reason enough?"

"Which isn't a direct answer to my question."

"My family is in Vegas."

"And yet, you obviously had reasons for leaving Vegas."

"A romance gone bad," she said lightly.

Skylar considered this as she sipped her hot chocolate.

"You don't strike me as the type of woman to run away just because her heart was broken," she finally remarked.

"Okay, so it was a little bit more than that," Sierra acknowledged. "The breakup coincided with a…work incident…that made me realize I didn't want to stay at the firm where I'd been working."

"I'm sorry," her new friend said.

"It was a tough decision to make, but I have no doubt that it was the right one."

"Are you talking about your ex or the job?" Sky wondered.

"Both."

"So you're not still nursing a broken heart?"

She shook her head.

"In that case, let's circle back to our original topic of conversation—Deacon Parrish."

"You can circle as many times as you want," Sierra told her. "I have no interest in a romance with Deacon Parrish or anyone else."

"How about sex?" Sky asked with a grin. "Because I can assure you, there isn't any better way to combat the chill of a long, cold Nevada winter than hot sex."

"I don't know," Sierra said. "My new boots are apparently rated to minus forty degrees."

Sky laughed. "Spoken like somebody who has cold feet when it comes to relationships."

"Well, right now, these feet need to get me back to the office."

"I've got things to do, too. But we definitely need to do this again," Sky said, then she frowned. "Or maybe we shouldn't."

Sierra was a little surprised—and disappointed—by the other woman's abrupt reversal. "Why not?"

"Because I have no doubt that we'd be great friends, but I already said goodbye to one of those and it was really hard, so I don't want to get too attached if you're really planning to leave at the end of your six-month contract."

"I *am* leaving at the end of my contract," Sierra told her, needing to be very clear about that.

"Of course, Jake didn't plan on staying, either," Sky said with just a hint of smugness in her smile. "And I've still got more than five months to change your mind."

Chapter Seven

Rhonda Dornan was guilty.

She knew it, Deacon knew it, and he had no doubt that the ADA was going to prove it at trial. Which was why he'd spent the past three hours going over every piece of evidence with his client, to illustrate for her the strength of the prosecutor's case, though so far his efforts to convince her to change her plea had been futile.

"But there are mitigating circumstances," she kept insisting.

"And I will make sure those are taken into consideration at sentencing," Deacon assured the crying widow. "But they don't mean you're not guilty."

"I wasn't thinking clearly when I wrote those checks."

"But you did write the checks."

She didn't—couldn't—deny it. Not when anyone comparing her usual signature to the signatures on the checks could see that they were identical—even without the testimony of the handwriting expert on the district attorney's witness list.

"But I took the flowers to Twilight Valley, for the long-term care residents there to enjoy."

"Which was a thoughtful gesture," he acknowledged. "Or would have been if you'd actually paid for the flowers."

"But I made retribution."

"Restitution," he clarified. "And the fact that you paid back the people who were defrauded is another mitigating factor, but mitigating factors don't come into play until sentencing."

When he finally said goodbye to Rhonda, he had a much better understanding of the case that was going to trial—and absolutely no doubt that his client was going to be convicted.

Instead of immediately returning to his desk, he detoured to knock on the partially open door of his boss's office.

"Come in," Katelyn invited.

He pushed the door open wider and stepped inside.

She gestured to the chairs opposite her desk, inviting him to sit.

"How did it go with Mrs. Dornan?" she asked when he was settled.

"She's guilty."

"I had no doubt."

He frowned at that.

"Rhonda Dornan has been writing bad checks for longer than I've been practicing law," Katelyn told him. "It was her way of getting her husband's attention— and it usually worked, at least for a while. He'd repay whoever was wronged, adding a little extra to ensure they didn't grumble loudly enough to get the sheriff's attention, and take his wife out of town on a vacation.

"A year or so later, it would start all over again. The difference now is that Leopold isn't around to clean up her messes anymore."

"You're saying that her husband had money? That she wrote bad checks on purpose?"

"That's exactly what I'm saying," Katelyn said. "And now his money is hers, so don't feel guilty about billing her for every minute of your time."

"The trial—if she insists on going through with the trial—will likely take a few days, and I've got a couple of matters scheduled for small claims court Thursday afternoon."

"Are you okay letting Brenna handle them?" she asked, referring to another of the firm's junior associates. "Or should we ask the court to reschedule?"

"Brenna can handle them, if she doesn't mind."

"Why don't you get the files together for her before the end of the day?"

"I'll do that right now," Deacon said, rising to his feet. "But I have to admit, I hate going into court knowing that my client's guilty."

His boss smiled. "Welcome to the world of a defense attorney."

The rest of the week proceeded much as Deacon had anticipated.

Wednesday morning, the ADA gave opening arguments and called her first witness, then he went through the motions of cross-examination, though he made little progress in discrediting the testimony. Throughout the afternoon and all the next day, it was more of the same, with the ADA hammering more nails in his client's proverbial coffin through the precise and methodical presentation of her case.

Before court adjourned on Thursday, the judge informed both attorneys that the trial needed to be put over to Monday, as he had to go out of town to deal with a family emergency. He advised them to use the time to attempt to resolve the case, noting—with a pointed look at the defense attorney—that there didn't seem to be any doubt what the outcome would be.

Sierra didn't get many visitors.

In fact, aside from Ayesha Dhawan, who'd stopped by with a loaf of banana bread to welcome her to the neighborhood—and then stayed to chat for more than an hour—she hadn't had any visitors since she'd moved in. But if she was surprised by the knock on her door Saturday morning, she was even more surprised to find Deacon Parrish standing on her doorstep.

"Good morning, Sierra," he said politely.

"Good morning," she echoed, immediately following that up with the questions that sprang to the forefront of her mind. "But what are you doing here? And how did you know where I live?"

"Can't one neighbor visit another without there being ulterior motives?" he countered mildly. "Also, it was easy to figure out where you live because you drive a distinctive car."

And she loved every inch of the acid-green Kia Soul parked in her driveway, but she was still a little wary. "So you drove around the neighborhood looking for my car?"

"You said you lived a couple blocks over," he reminded her. "It wasn't a far drive. Which is a good thing, because I brought tea—and treats—from Sweet Caroline's."

"Magic words," she admitted.

He grinned.

"I suppose you expect me to invite you to come in now?"

"I brought tea and treats," he said again.

She stepped away from the door.

He followed her down the hall and into the kitchen. "Nice place."

"I can't take any credit," she said. "I rented it furnished."

And though it hadn't really mattered to her what the place looked like, Sierra had been pleased to discover that she liked her temporary home. The rooms were spacious and bright and mostly decorated in subtle earthy tones, but the kitchen was her favorite room in the house—with steel blue cabinets, white quartz countertops, stainless steel appliances and a set of French doors that opened onto the back deck. (She hoped to get some use out of the deck in the spring and summer, but right now, those doors remained tightly closed, keeping the frigid air out while letting in lots of natural light.)

"Do you have a dog?" he asked, eyeing the flap in the wall adjacent to the doors.

"No," she said. "But I'm guessing the previous tenant—or more likely the owner—did."

"That's too bad," he said, removing the cups from the paper tray. "I like dogs—and they like me. And if you had a dog who liked me, maybe you'd realize I'm not such a bad guy."

"I don't think you're a bad guy," she denied.

"Raspberry bliss tea, black," he said, setting one of the cups on the counter in front of her.

"Although now I'm wondering if you're a stalker," she said, only half joking.

He smiled. "Would it reassure you to know that Sky was at Sweet Caroline's and suggested it?"

"Maybe," she allowed. Except that now she had another reason to be concerned. "So Sky knows that you were coming over here?"

"Is that a problem?"

Yes.

"No," she denied.

He peeled the lid off his own cup, and she inhaled deeply, filling her lungs with the fragrant scent.

His brows lifted. "I thought you didn't like coffee."

"I didn't say I didn't like it. I said I didn't drink it."

"I'm not even going to pretend to understand that," he said. "So I'll tell you that Sky also mentioned that you were partial to Sweet Caroline's raspberry crumble bar."

"It's the only thing I've had from the bakery," Sierra said. "But it was pretty darn good."

"Well, I got you one of those and a couple other things to try."

"What other things?" she asked, her curiosity definitely piqued.

"An almond croissant, a lemon tart, a chocolate éclair, a mille-feuille and a salted caramel brownie."

"Now I *know* you want something from me," she decided.

He held her gaze for a long moment—a hint of amusement along with something deeper in his eyes. "Maybe. But why don't we take it one brownie at a time?"

She lifted her cup to her lips and nearly choked on the hot liquid.

"Are you okay?"

She nodded, not sure that her scorched vocal cords were operational.

Deacon sipped his coffee, did not choke.

"But for today," he said, continuing with their conversation as if she hadn't just been coughing and sputtering, "I was hoping we could maybe chat about Rhonda Dornan before the trial resumes on Monday."

"Is your client planning to change her plea?"

"Give her an incentive to do so," he suggested.

"The incentive is that she could start serving her sentence right away and be out by spring, pending good behavior."

"That's not much of an incentive," he protested, lifting the lid of the bakery box.

Of course Sierra couldn't resist peering inside, and then she couldn't hold back the sound of pleasure that hummed in her throat when she saw the exquisite offerings contained within.

Deacon grinned, obviously satisfied by her reaction.

"Are you trying to bribe an officer of the court?" she asked, making her way to the cupboard to retrieve two plates.

"Of course not," he immediately denied. "I'm just enjoying a chat with a professional colleague."

"A professional colleague who has all the evidence she needs to prove every element of the crime," she said, taking a knife from the utensil drawer.

He eyed the sharp instrument warily. "My client wrote a few bad checks—she didn't commit capital murder."

Sierra cut through the middle of the chocolate éclair, then put half on each plate and slid one of the plates toward him. "She willfully defrauded more than a dozen people."

"She was grieving the loss of her husband and not thinking straight."

"It isn't the first time she's written bad checks," Sierra told him.

He dropped his gaze to study the pastry in front of him.

"But I'm guessing you knew that, didn't you?"

"She's made full restitution to all of the victims," he said, ignoring her question.

"Is there any point in us even having this conversation?" she asked wearily. "Mrs. Dornan's first attorney worked out a plea deal with my boss, and then she decided to toss it aside."

"Her grief has interfered with her ability to make smart choices," Deacon acknowledged. "But she didn't protest too vehemently when I told her that I wanted to talk to you about a resolution of the charges."

Sierra sighed. "If your client agrees to plead guilty to the charges first thing Monday morning, I will agree to honor the terms of the original deal."

"Thank you."

"But if she hesitates at all, the deal is off the table."

"Got it," he said, swiveling on his stool so that he was facing her. "And now that we've taken care of business…"

"You can go, but you're not taking the pastries," she told him.

"The pastries are for you," he assured her.

"Well, you can take half," she relented. "I definitely don't need all that sugar."

Now he smiled. "Don't you know that the best things in life aren't what we need but what we desire?"

It was suddenly very warm in the kitchen, and Sierra knew it had nothing to do with the thermostat control on her furnace and everything to do with the heat emanating from the very hot body of the man sitting far too close.

"What do you want right now, Sierra?"

You.

She swallowed the answer that immediately sprang to her lips. There was no way she could admit that truth to him, because nothing could ever come of her foolish desire.

She didn't even know the man, really, so she definitely shouldn't be lusting for his body.

Darn pregnancy hormones.

"The lemon tart," she said instead.

His lips curved in a slow smile as he lifted the tart out of the box and set it on her plate. "You don't want to like me, do you?"

"Why would you think that?"

"Because every time you start to warm up to me, even just a little, you deliberately pull yourself back."

Apparently the man was much more observant than she'd given him credit for—or maybe she was more obvious than she wanted to believe.

"I work for the DA's office. You're a defense attorney. It's inevitable that our jobs are going to create conflict between us."

"My boss has represented plenty of defendants put in cuffs by her husband, but they don't let that interfere with their relationship," he told her.

"Your point?"

"I don't think your hesitation is professional. I think it's personal."

"You want me to be honest? Okay, you're right—I

don't want to like you. You're a little too good-looking, too effortlessly sexy, too annoyingly charming, and you remind me, a little too much, of my ex-boyfriend."

"Ouch. I mean, the good-looking, sexy and charming parts were okay," he said. "But being compared to an ex is rarely a good thing."

"You asked for honesty," she reminded him.

"I did," he agreed. "And now I'm going to be honest and tell you that, notwithstanding your attempted evisceration of my character, I like you."

"Why? You barely know me."

He shrugged. "Apparently I have a thing for contrary women."

"Or you just like a challenge."

"That might be part of it, too," he acknowledged. "But the truth is, from the first moment I saw you, I knew that you were someone who was going to matter to me."

"But I'm not," she protested. "I can't be."

He just smiled again. "I'll see you in court Monday morning."

Then he walked out, leaving Sierra alone with a whole lot of desire that she knew would never be satisfied by a box of pastries.

Chapter Eight

As a kid, Deacon loved Mondays. Especially during the school year. Because Mondays meant getting up early and getting out of the hellhole he'd called home. Then, for seven blissful hours, he could pretend that his life wasn't any different from that of Nathan Pineda or Chase Hampton or Travis Bell. And when he got home again, he could usually hide out in his room with the excuse that he had homework.

But dinner was a family affair, and he was expected to be at the table to eat with the family and then help with the cleanup afterward. He didn't mind the mealtime routine so much when his mom was home to cook and supervise the tidying. But his mom wasn't always home and his dad could be a mean sonofabitch, especially when he was drunk. And he was quite often drunk.

So after dinner, Deacon would go back to his homework, then he'd go to bed and get up and do it all over again the next day. And the day after that. And so on. It wasn't until the final bell went on a Friday afternoon that he'd get knots in his stomach. While his friends celebrated the end of the week and made plans for the weekend as the bus took them closer to home, the knots in Deacon's stomach tightened, because he knew that his dad was probably already drunk and angry and everything would only go downhill from there.

That had been his life until Dwayne Parrish went a little too far in disciplining his stepson one day. It was Deacon's fault—he'd knocked over his dad's beer, his dad had responded by knocking him over and Connor had immediately inserted himself between them. Because even at fifteen, his brother had the makings of a hero.

But he'd been no match for his stepfather, who was bigger and meaner and likely more than half drunk. Thankfully one of the neighbors heard the ruckus and called the sheriff.

It was Jed Traynor who'd worn the badge back then, and he'd shown up right about the same time that Faith arrived home from work. During all the commotion, Connor escaped out the back door, so the sheriff never saw how badly he'd been beaten, and Jed gave Dwayne a choice—leave the house voluntarily or be taken into custody to spend the night, or maybe a few years, in lockup.

Dwayne left voluntarily—and never came back.

Deacon's life settled down after that. And when he finally accepted that he no longer needed to tiptoe around the house, he started to enjoy weekends and the freedom they afforded from his Monday through Friday routines. The two-day break became even more important when he went away to school, not so much as a reprieve from classes as an opportunity to complete reading and assignments, to work hard and study harder. Because college wasn't just his escape from Haven—it was his chance to make something of his life, to prove that he was something more than the useless offspring of Faith Neal and Dwayne Parrish.

After two years as an associate in Katelyn Davidson's law office, he was finally starting to feel as if he'd done that. He'd also learned to fully appreciate weekends, especially when the time away from the office was spent with family or friends.

But as he drifted off to sleep Sunday night, he wasn't disappointed that the weekend was over, because he knew that he'd see Sierra in court the next morning, and he couldn't wait.

Late Friday afternoon, Sierra began to gather up the files on her desk to transfer them to her briefcase. After only a few weeks, she was starting to get used to packing up at five o'clock and suspected it would be a lot harder to readjust to the twelve-hour days that were the norm when she was living and working in Vegas.

As she zipped up the case, the blue box tucked in the outside pocket caught her eye, making her smile.

Rhonda Dornan had pleaded to the charges on Monday, per the terms of the original agreement, and the judge had signed off on her sentence of community service. The widow had seemed genuinely remorseful—and grateful—at sentencing, and she'd promised the judge that he wouldn't see her in court again. Sierra wasn't convinced, but that was a worry for another day.

After they'd finished in court, she'd surprised Deacon by offering to buy him coffee. Because he'd been right when he accused her of not wanting to like him, and she knew that wasn't fair. After all, it wasn't his fault that she was wildly attracted to him, and as long as she kept that fact to herself, she figured there was no reason they couldn't be friends—or at least friendly.

She'd suggested The Daily Grind rather than Sweet Caroline's, because the former was closer to the courthouse—and also, she told him, because she didn't want to be tempted by the offerings in Sweet Caroline's display case when she still had some in her fridge at home. But that wasn't actually true. After he'd gone Saturday morning, Sierra had taken the bakery box over to her neighbor, pawning the sweets off on Ayesha's family so that she wouldn't overindulge any more than she'd already done. (Of course, she'd almost immediately regretted doing so, and since then had been trying to alleviate her sweet tooth cravings with various "healthy cookie" recipes she'd googled. So far, none had quite hit the mark.)

Anyway, they'd had coffee together—or rather he'd had coffee and she'd had cranberry apple tea (not as flavorful as Sweet Caroline's raspberry bliss, but not bad)—and shared some conversation before going off in different directions. Though Sierra had been at the courthouse every day after that, she hadn't seen Deacon again until today, when he tracked her down to give her the box of cereal.

"Not a bribe but an apology," he'd told her.

"Apology accepted," she'd replied. "But contrary to what you apparently believe, I don't usually eat sugary cereal."

"And yet, you were ready to arm wrestle me for the last box of Frosted Flakes at The Trading Post the first day we met."

"A moment of weakness," she acknowledged.

"Do you have many of those?" he asked curiously.

"More than I'd like," she confessed.

He tipped his head toward her, a hint of a smile curving his lips. "Anything other than sugary cereal that makes you weak?"

Yes. You.

Even now, her heart was beating a little too fast and her knees were trembling, just because he was standing close to her.

She racked her brain for a more appropriate response. "Pastries from Sweet Caroline's."

"I probably could have guessed that one," he said.

"Then you know all my weaknesses."

"Not yet," he'd denied. "But I'm going to."

Then he'd given her a full, bone-melting smile before turning and walking away, and she'd stood there watching him go, a tiny part of her wishing that she might have met him at a different time, under different circumstances.

But she knew it was futile to wish for things that could never be, so she pushed the box deeper into the bag and pushed all thoughts of Deacon Parrish out of her mind.

"Four weeks down, only twenty more to go," Sierra said, as she slung the strap of her bag over her shoulder.

"Are you really hating the job so much that you're counting down the days?"

She felt heat rise into her cheeks as she glanced up to see investigative analyst Julie Keswick standing in her office doorway.

"I thought everyone else had gone," she admitted.

"Which doesn't answer my question," her colleague noted.

"I don't hate the job at all," Sierra said. "But I didn't anticipate that I'd miss my family so much."

"So why'd you take a job so far away from Las Vegas?" Julie wondered.

"Because I needed to get away from my family."

Her colleague chuckled at that. "What you need is a distraction," she decided. "I'm getting together with some friends tonight and heading to Sparkle—a new dance club in Elko. You should join us."

"I appreciate the invitation," Sierra said. "But I've actually got plans tonight."

"Hanging out with case files doesn't count as plans," her colleague protested.

"That's not what I was planning. Or not exclusively what I was planning," she amended, in response to the other woman's openly skeptical look.

Julie laughed. "Okay. But if you change your mind, you've got my number."

Sierra thought about the offer throughout the drive home. While she was pleased that the other woman had thought to include her, she was certain the invitation wouldn't have been issued if Julie had known of her condition.

Of course she was going to have to tell her colleagues about her pregnancy eventually—and probably sooner than she'd anticipated, considering that her pants and skirts were already starting to feel snug around her waist—but she wasn't in a hurry to make herself the hot topic of gossip at The Daily Grind. Not only because she was pregnant and unmarried—which shouldn't be at all scandalous in this day and age—but also because the circumstances of her pregnancy were a little unusual.

Then she pulled into her driveway, where a silver SUV was already parked, and the only thought on her mind was of her family, and her heart overflowed with joy that they were here.

Her brother stepped out of his vehicle at the same time she did hers, and she rushed into his arms.

"It's so good to see you," she said, somehow managing to push out the words around the lump in her throat. "But why didn't you tell me you were coming?" She turned her head then, looking for her sister-in-law, but the passenger-side door remained closed and the seat, she could see now, was empty. "And where's Whitney?"

"It's good to see you, too." His words were muffled in her hair as he held her tight. "And I didn't tell you I was coming because I was afraid that you'd tell me not to—especially as Whitney's stuck at home waiting for her jury to come back with a verdict."

"I would never tell you not to come," she assured him. "Though I might have pointed out that I've barely been gone a month."

"Can we continue this conversation inside?" he asked, shivering. "It's freezing out here!"

She chuckled. "Yeah, you were definitely right about the weather." She gave him one last squeeze before releasing him.

"I see you got a new coat."

"And new boots," she added.

She returned to her car to grab her briefcase while he retrieved his duffel bag from the backseat of his vehicle.

"How long has Whitney been waiting for her jury?" Sierra asked, as she unlocked the door and led her brother inside.

"Three days. She's trying to remain optimistic that they're deliberating the award rather than the verdict, but juries are unpredictable."

"Isn't that the truth?" Sierra agreed, hanging her

coat. "You're probably thirsty after that long drive—what can I get for you?"

He set his boots on the mat beside hers. "Any chance you've got coffee?"

"Decaf."

"So long as it's hot, it'll do."

She set her briefcase on one of the stools at the island, then found a pod for her single-serve coffee maker, dropping it into place and setting a mug under the spout. While Nick's coffee was brewing, Sierra filled a glass of water for herself from the dispenser in the fridge, then put some cookies on a plate and set it on the counter.

Nick selected a cookie, took a bite. "Did you make these?"

"Yes, and they're good."

"No," he said, setting the cookie aside. "They're not."

"Well, they're at least good for you," she said. "Made with all natural ingredients and carob chips instead of chocolate."

"Why?"

"Because I'm trying to eat healthy—for the baby."

"Trust me," he said. "The baby doesn't want those any more than I do."

She returned the other cookies to the container. Most likely, she'd toss them in the garbage later, but she wasn't going to give her brother the satisfaction of doing so now.

"And if you're on such a health kick, what's with the box of Frosted Flakes in your bag?"

"What?" She followed his gaze, felt her cheeks heat. "Oh. That was a gift from a colleague."

"A rather strange gift," he noted.

"Yeah," she agreed.

"But it's a good sign that you're making friends already."

"I said a colleague, not a friend."

"But you had a little smile on your face when you were thinking about…him?"

She sighed. "Stop."

"Stop what?"

"Prying into my life."

"I'm not prying," Nick denied. "I'm interested. And happy that your broken heart seems to finally be on the mend."

"Okay, it's true that I've rediscovered my love for Frosted Flakes," she acknowledged.

Now her brother sighed. "Are you ever going to tell me what went wrong with Eric?"

"No, because you and Eric were friends long before he and I started dating, and I don't want what happened between us to cause a rift between the two of you."

"You're my sister," Nick said gently. "And even without knowing the details, I know he hurt you, so the rift is already there."

"I'm sorry for that," she said.

"So if you were seeing someone new, I'd take it as a sign that you're moving on and be happy for you." He paused. "But I'd still be pissed at Eric."

"I appreciate the thought, but I can assure you that I don't have any plans to get involved with a new man—certainly not anytime in the next seven months."

Nick looked troubled by this assertion. "Because of the baby."

"Not only because of the baby, although I can't imagine any man wanting to get involved with a woman carrying someone else's baby—"

"Any man who truly cared about you wouldn't let a pregnancy get in the way," he interjected.

"—but also," she continued, "because I'm only going to be in town for another five months, so any relationship would automatically have an expiration date."

"That could be a bigger obstacle," her brother admitted. "And while some couples seem to make long-distance relationships work, the distance between here and Las Vegas is a little daunting."

"And yet, you drove all that way just to see me."

"I needed to see for myself that you were doing okay."

"I told you that I was."

"Are you suffering from any nausea?" he pressed.

"Occasionally," she admitted.

"It might be the cookies."

She balled up her napkin and threw it at him.

He caught it easily.

"And now," she said, pushing her stool away from the counter, "I'm going to cook dinner."

"Please, don't."

She narrowed her gaze.

"I just meant that I want to take you out for a meal," he said, eager to dig out of the hole he'd put himself into.

"You can take me out tomorrow," she said. "And you're going to pay—big-time—for disparaging my cookies, because I'm making a reservation at The Home Station, the fanciest place in town."

Chapter Nine

Deacon wasn't in the habit of getting tied up in knots over a woman, but there was no denying that he was all twisted up over the new ADA.

There were plenty of women in Haven, so why did he keep going back to the one who was always brushing him off?

And why did she keep brushing him off?

He'd considered the possibility that she had a boyfriend back in Vegas and discarded it for two reasons: one, he was certain that she would have told him if she did; and two, she'd mentioned that he reminded her of an ex-boyfriend. Which forced him to consider the possibility that she honestly wasn't interested, though he didn't want to believe that could be true. Because it didn't seem fair that he could be so tangled up while she was completely unaffected.

So when Ben had mentioned, at their morning pickup game, that a bunch of guys were getting together to enjoy some wings and watch the game at Diggers' that night, Deacon immediately agreed to join them.

A Saturday night with the guys was just what he needed to get his mind off a certain sexy brunette with dark eyes and kissable lips. And if the opportunity arose to flirt with other pretty girls, well, that would be even better.

Puck drop was scheduled for eight o'clock, but he pulled into the parking lot behind Diggers' at seven forty-five, giving him just enough time to stop by the reception desk at The Stagecoach Inn and chat with Mariah for a few minutes before heading over to the bar.

"Hey, stranger." Mariah greeted him with a warm smile. "What brings you around here on a Saturday night?"

He held up a silver hoop earring.

She laughed. "Ohmygod—I was starting to think it was lost forever."

"Me, too," he admitted.

The earrings had been a gift from her grandmother— their value more sentimental than monetary, but Deacon and Mariah had combed every inch of his bedroom when she realized she'd lost it, to no avail.

"Where did you find it?" she asked.

"Lodged under the corner of the cabinet in the bathroom."

She smiled again. "We had some good times in there, too, didn't we?"

"We did," he agreed.

"Well, I'm glad to have this back." She tucked the silver hoop into the pocket of her jacket. "Thank you."

"You're welcome."

It struck him suddenly that the whole interaction between them was civil and bland, proving that whatever chemistry had once drawn them together had fizzled out long ago.

"I'm seeing someone."

The way she blurted out the information made Deacon realize that she thought he was lingering, perhaps in the hope of picking up where they'd left off.

The truth was, he'd been about to say "see you around" and head over to the bar when Sierra walked into the lobby of the hotel.

With a man.

"It's been a few months now," Mariah elaborated, when he failed to respond.

"That's great," he said, his attention focused on the ADA and her companion.

Were they headed to the desk to check in?

Or did her companion already have a room key in his pocket?

They turned toward the hotel restaurant, and he exhaled a sigh of relief.

They were here for dinner, not a hookup.

But who knew what might happen after a romantic meal and a couple glasses of wine?

Deacon certainly didn't—and he didn't want to speculate.

The coat check was located outside of the dining room, and he watched as Sierra's date helped her remove her coat before handing it to the attendant. She wore a lot of suits in court—pants and matching jackets or sometimes skirts and jackets—but Deacon had never before seen her in a dress before and...*wow*!

The dress was a wrap style with long sleeves, a short skirt and a deep V neckline. The color was somewhere between gold and brown (maybe bronze?) and the fab-

ric hugged her curves in a way that he'd only dreamed
of doing.

There was a comfortable familiarity between her and
her date that suggested affection more than attraction. A
theory that was given further credence when she hugged
the man and he dropped a kiss on the top of her head
before they disappeared into the restaurant together.

Old friends, perhaps?

Or was that just wishful thinking on his part?

He vaguely registered the sound of Mariah's voice
and realized she was still talking about the new guy
she was seeing, about how great he was, how happy
they were together.

"Then I'm happy for you, too," he said.

The vibration of the phone in his pocket finally
dragged his attention away from the door through which
Sierra had disappeared. He pulled it out and glanced
at the screen.

Wings R on the table.

That was followed, almost immediately, by another
message:

FN Penguins just scored!

He quickly tapped out a reply:

Be there in 2 min.

"It was great to see you, Mariah, but I have to run,"
he said, lifting a hand in a wave as he headed toward
the exit.

He was no longer in a sociable mood, but he took solace in the fact that he could bang his fist on the table and his buddies would think he was reacting to the game.

Sierra said goodbye to her brother Sunday morning and stood at the front window to watch him drive away. His SUV had barely disappeared from sight when another vehicle pulled into the recently vacated spot on her driveway.

She immediately recognized Deacon's truck from his visit the previous weekend.

"This is getting to be a habit," she said, when she responded to his knock on the door.

"Can I come in?"

"You seem to be empty-handed."

"Should I go to Sweet Caroline's and come back?"

"No," she said, stepping away from the door so that he could enter. "I've got a cup of tea in the kitchen already."

"Any chance you've got coffee?" he asked.

"Decaf."

He made a face as he pulled his boots off and left them by the door.

"Is that a *no* on the coffee?"

"That's a no," he confirmed.

"Hot chocolate?"

That seemed to pique his interest. "What kind?"

"The kind that comes in a little pod labeled Hot Chocolate."

"Well, it can't be worse than decaf coffee," he decided.

She popped a pod into the machine and positioned a mug beneath the spout. When the hot chocolate was ready, she set the drink on the island in front of him.

"Now are you going to tell me why you're here?"

"I was at Diggers' last night with some friends—one of whom is the drummer for the Cowboy Poets."

"Who?"

He frowned. "You really haven't heard of them?"

She shook her head.

"Well, they're a pretty big deal around here, and tickets to their shows can be hard to come by, but Gavin hooked me up with a pair of tickets for their show Tuesday night.

"It's at The Vicar's Vice in Battle Mountain, and I thought you might want to go with me. I know having a first date on Valentine's Day puts a lot of pressure on the date, but I promise it will be a good show."

He was asking her to go out with him. On Valentine's Day.

Her fickle heart fluttered.

She ignored it.

"I appreciate the invitation, but I'm going to have to decline."

"You already have plans for Valentine's Day?"

"No," she admitted. "And I don't want any, to be honest."

"How about Friday night, then?" he suggested as an alternative. "Maybe dinner and a movie?"

Another flutter.

"No, thank you," she said, polite but firm.

He studied her over the rim as he lifted his mug to his lips. "Is your answer going to be the same if I suggest another activity on another day?"

"It is," she confirmed.

"Because of the guy you were with at The Home Station last night?"

She was startled by the question. "Because I'm not in a place right now to consider any kind of romantic involvement," she told him. "And, FYI, the guy I was with last night was my brother, who hasn't had any say about who I date since I went away to college."

"I didn't know you had a brother."

"Probably because we don't really know anything about the other."

He smiled. "A problem that could be easily remedied if you'd only agree to go out with me."

Damn, he really was sexy and charming—and far too tempting.

Which was why she needed to shut him down right now, before he proved to be a greater temptation than she could resist.

"Except that I don't see it as a problem," she said.

He finished his hot chocolate and carried the empty mug to the sink. "I'll get out of your way, then."

She had to bite her tongue to hold back the urge to apologize as she walked him to the door.

Because she was sorry that she'd had to say *no* when she really wanted to say *yes*.

Sierra had gotten in the habit of stopping at The Daily Grind on her way to the office in the mornings. Now that her stomach was no longer rebelling against the scent of coffee, she opted for the local café over the bakery because she was less tempted by the muffins and donuts in their display case than she was by the decadent offerings at Sweet Caroline's.

It was also closer to the courthouse, and that proximity meant it wasn't unusual for Sierra to see familiar faces there—another lawyer or a judge's secretary or an administrative assistant and, several times, Deacon. So she wasn't surprised to see that he was ahead of her in line when she entered the coffee shop Wednesday morning but, unlike the other times their paths had crossed, today he wasn't alone.

The woman he was with had blond hair cut in long layers that framed a heart-shaped face with porcelain skin, sharp cheekbones, a slightly pointed chin, green-gray eyes with dark lashes and a Cupid's bow mouth slicked with pink gloss. She was absolutely stunning, and though Sierra felt a stir of something in her gut that might have been envy, she couldn't deny that they made a gorgeous couple.

Deacon lowered his head to say something to his companion, and she tipped her head back against his shoulder and smiled up at him.

There was an easy affection between them that told Sierra they were close—two people who'd shared more than a single night together. And while she knew it shouldn't bother her—no doubt he had history with a lot of women in this town—it annoyed her to realize that after she'd turned down his invitation to go out on Valentine's Day, he'd immediately penciled another name into his calendar.

A completely irrational response, she acknowledged.

She'd told him she wasn't interested, and he'd taken her at her word. She should be relieved—even happy— that he'd found someone else to smile at, flirt with and deliver boxes of pastries to. Instead, she felt...annoyed. (She settled on that word again because she was unwilling to admit that her feelings might be a little deeper and a little more complicated than that.)

He ordered an extra-large coffee, black; the blonde asked for a decaffeinated, non-fat, sugar-free vanilla latte.

Deacon passed some money across the counter, then

dropped his change into the tip jar, and they moved down the line to wait for their drinks to be prepared.

The next customer—a brunette with a ponytail and a weary smile—ordered two extra-large coffees, one black, one with double cream and sugar.

"How's MG doing?" the woman behind the counter asked cautiously, as she punched in the order.

"He has good days and bad—though more bad than good, it seems these days."

"It's gotta be tough for him, to be laid up. And for you, too, Paige."

The brunette—Paige—nodded and offered her debit card for payment.

The other woman waved it away. "This one's on me."

"Thanks, Felicia." Paige managed a wobbly smile as she moved down the line.

The two women behind Sierra, obviously having heard the same exchange, started whispering to one another. And though she wasn't trying to eavesdrop, Sierra managed to put together enough pieces to figure out that there had been some kind of accident at the ranch (which ranch? she had no idea, except that it was apparently MG's ranch) and that he was lucky to be alive.

"Cranberry apple tea, black," Sierra said, when it was her turn to order.

She paid for her drink and followed Paige to the other end of the counter just as Deacon and his companion got their drinks.

The blonde picked up her to-go cup and kissed his cheek. "Thanks again for last night."

His smile was warm and sincere. "Anytime."

It was only when his companion had gone—and

Paige was getting her drinks—that he seemed to realize Sierra was standing there, waiting for her beverage.

"Good morning," he said.

She echoed his greeting coolly.

"Are you in court today?" Deacon asked.

"Not until this afternoon."

"Can we sit for a few minutes, then?"

Sierra murmured her thanks to the barista as she accepted her tea before turning her attention back to Deacon. "Was there something in particular you wanted to discuss?"

"No," he admitted. "I just thought it would be nice to have some company with my coffee instead of gulping it down on the run like I do most mornings. And a muffin," he decided. "Do you want a muffin?"

"No, thank you."

He went back to the counter, returning a minute later with a banana nut muffin on a plate.

"I didn't hear you offer to buy your…friend…a muffin," she noted.

"My friend?" he echoed, uncomprehending.

"The blonde whose lip gloss you're currently wearing."

"Oh." His lips curved as he rubbed a hand over his cheek. "Regan doesn't eat breakfast. And she's a lot more than a friend."

"Yeah, I got that impression," she acknowledged.

He eyed her speculatively. "Why are you mad at me?"

"I'm not," she denied.

"You sure sound mad," he noted. "And your tone is chillier than the weather this morning."

"I'm mad at myself."

"Because…" he prompted, tearing off a piece of muffin.

"Because I was actually starting to think that you were a decent guy."

"And now, because I didn't offer to buy Regan a muffin, you think I'm not?"

"And because, only three days ago, you invited *me* to go see the Poet Cowboys with you."

"Cowboy Poets," he corrected automatically. "And you turned me down."

"You're right," she acknowledged.

"And you think that I took Regan to the show," he realized.

"Or maybe you skipped the show," she allowed.

"But spent the night together."

"She thanked you for last night."

"You could have been the one thanking me for last night," he pointed out, a spark of what she was certain was amusement dancing in his eyes. "After all, I did ask you first."

"I told you that I wasn't looking for any romantic entanglements and I meant it."

He shrugged. "I'm not averse to skipping the romance and going straight to the sex, if that's your preference."

"Wouldn't I have to take a number—like at the deli counter in the grocery store?"

"Not necessary," he said. "We both seem to have a couple hours free right now."

"A not-at-all-tempting offer," she told him.

"I think you are tempted," he said. "And that's the real reason that you're annoyed."

He wasn't just arrogant—he was right.

She wasn't looking to get involved, and certainly not with another man who clearly had no understanding of loyalty or fidelity, and still there was something about Deacon that stirred her up.

Or maybe it was simply an overabundance of hormones running rampant through her system that was responsible for the inexplicable feelings churning in her blood.

"I'm on a dating hiatus," she reminded him.

"So you said," he acknowledged. "But seven months seems like an excessive amount of time to get over a not-so-recent breakup that supposedly only bruised your heart."

"It's closer to six months now."

His brows lifted. "The fact that you're counting suggests that you agree it's an excessive amount of time."

"Speaking of time," she said, desperate to change the topic before she gave anything else away, "I really do need to get to the office."

"Then I guess we'll have to finish this conversation another time," he said.

She nodded, grateful for the reprieve and eager to escape.

Because despite her growing attraction to Deacon Parrish, she knew that nothing could ever come of it. For the next six and a half months, her focus needed to be on taking care of the baby in her womb.

And the absolute last thing she needed was to give her heart to another man who was likely to break it.

Chapter Ten

Over the next week, Sierra saw Deacon only in passing. And though he'd lift a hand to wave or offer a smile from across the room, he didn't seek her out for conversation. He'd obviously moved on, and she knew it was for the best. There was no point in nurturing the seeds of romantic fantasies that could never come to fruition.

The strange thing was that she kind of missed him. Aside from her ill-advised attraction, she'd actually started to like him. He was smart and interesting; he listened to her and challenged her; he made her feel seen and heard and valued in a way she hadn't experienced in a very long time.

Unfortunately it seemed that her first instincts about him had been right—he was a player and she wasn't interested in being played. Not again.

Anyway, she was keeping herself busy enough, getting to know her colleagues at the DA's office and meet-

ing other people, not just at the courthouse but through
interactions at the grocery store and the library and even
the pizzeria. But Sky had claimed that they were going
to be best friends, and Sierra was happy that their bi-
weekly not-coffee dates seemed to be moving them in
that direction.

"I gave notice to Duke that I'm quitting my job at
Diggers'," Sky said, when she sat down across from Sierra at their usual table at Sweet Caroline's.

"Whatever will you do with all your free time now
that you'll only have two jobs?" Sierra wondered.

Her friend grinned. "Well, as Jake pointed out, in
about four more months we'll have a baby to fill some
of that time. And while I love hearing the personal con-
fessions that seem to be part and parcel of tending bar,
I don't love being on my feet until the wee hours of
morning."

"Duke's going to be sorry to lose you."

"He offered to give me a stool. Or a raise. Then a
stool and a raise." Sky rifled through her enormous
purse, obviously looking for something. She pulled out
a stainless steel water bottle decorated with numerous
and various stickers and set it on the table as she continued to examine the contents of her bag. "Here it is,"
she said, triumphantly holding up her phone. "I'm waiting to hear from the high school about a meeting with
a student, and I don't want to miss the call."

Sierra nodded, but her attention was on the water
bottle—more specifically, one of the stickers on it.

"Are you a fan of the Cowboy Poets?" she asked.

"A huge fan," Sky said. "Jake and I got to see their
show in Battle Mountain on Valentine's Day. But I'm
kind of surprised that you know their music—I didn't

think they had much of a following outside of this part of the state."

"I don't know their music," Sierra admitted. "But I was invited to that Valentine's Day show."

"Why am I only hearing about this now?" her friend demanded.

"Because I didn't think it was important, especially since I declined the invitation."

"Who... It was Deacon!" Sky said, answering her own question before she finished asking it. "Deacon invited you to the show, didn't he?"

"Yeah."

"And you turned him down...why?"

"Because I'm only going to be in town for another few months, and I have no interest in getting involved with anyone while I'm here."

"I'm going to ignore the first part of that statement," Sky said.

"Now who's in denial?" Sierra couldn't resist teasing.

"And focus on the second," her friend continued. "Because while I understand all the reasons that you might be reluctant to open up your heart again, I wouldn't be a very good friend if I didn't tell you that Deacon is a really great guy and you might be sorry if you let him slip through your fingers."

"Too late."

"What do you mean?"

"He asked me to go to the show, I said no and he took someone else."

Sky frowned. "I don't think he did. I mean, The Vicar's Vice was pretty packed but it's not very big, so I'm sure I would have seen him if he was there."

"Maybe he gave the tickets away," Sierra allowed. "But he definitely celebrated Valentine's Day with someone else because I ran into both of them at The Daily Grind the next day."

"Hmm."

"You don't believe me?"

"I believe he was there—and with a woman, but I suspect you might have misinterpreted what you saw."

"I also heard her say, 'Thanks again for last night.'"

"That sounds pretty damning," Sky acknowledged. "But I still think there might be another explanation."

"It doesn't matter," Sierra said. "Because he's moved on and, considering how often we find ourselves on opposite sides of a courtroom, that's a good thing."

"Keep telling yourself that—because I don't think you quite believe it just yet."

"Anyway…" She let her words trail off when her friend's phone chimed.

"That's the school," Sky said. "I'm sorry, but I have to run."

"No worries," Sierra said. "I've got an appointment to get to, too."

Deacon had a rare, unscheduled afternoon on Tuesday, so when his brother texted to ask a favor, he was able to agree. Fifteen minutes later, he was in the parking lot of Blake Mining.

"Thank you for this," Regan said, as she buckled her seatbelt.

Deacon waited for the click before shifting into Reverse to back out of the parking spot. "You know I'm always happy to help," he told his sister-in-law. "Mostly because I'm keeping a tally of all the favors that I do for you so that you can reciprocate someday."

"I'm pretty sure you're joking, but I don't even care

if you're not, because there's no way Connor and I could ever repay you for everything you do."

"Well, you did let me live with you all those holidays and summers when I came home from college."

"It was your home, too," Regan said.

"But it's lucky for all of us that I've got a place of my own now, because you're going to need that extra room for the new baby."

"Are we crazy?" she asked.

"That's probably a question you should have asked before you decided to have unprotected sex," Deacon told her.

She laughed. "I really hope Connor can get there in time for the ultrasound today—our first chance to see the baby."

"He'll be there," Deacon said confidently.

The deputy sheriff had been scheduled to testify in court that morning, but the lawyers had wasted so much time bickering over other matters that the judge had postponed his testimony until after lunch.

"How can you be so sure?"

Of course, he wasn't really sure, but he knew that what his sister-in-law needed right now was reassurance. "He didn't miss any of your appointments when you were pregnant with Piper and Poppy, did he?"

"No," she admitted, a smile curving her lips at the memory. "In fact, he was right there, holding my hand, when we found out I was carrying twins."

"And he'll be there this time when you get the same news."

"That's not funny," Regan told him.

"Actually, it is kind of funny," he said. "Could you imagine—*Double* Double Trouble?"

She shook her head. "I'd rather not."

* * *

Sierra had been hesitant to find a new doctor when she moved to Haven, albeit temporarily. She had a wonderful ob-gyn in Vegas, and she couldn't imagine sharing the same kind of rapport with a stranger. Or maybe she was worried that another doctor might not be as supportive of what she was doing as Dr. Shah had been from the beginning.

But the truth was, she hadn't really had a choice. Unless she wanted to make the long trip back to Vegas every four weeks for a checkup—which she definitely did not—she had to find a local doctor. Dr. Shah had recommended Dr. Camila Amaro.

At her first appointment, she'd spent almost an hour with the physician, going over not just her medical but familial history and talking about the unique circumstances of her pregnancy. And though the doctor's office in Battle Mountain was barely a twenty-minute drive from Haven, Sierra didn't worry about running into anyone she knew at the prenatal clinic, because the only other person she knew who was pregnant was Sky, and her friend's appointments were always on Fridays.

She certainly didn't anticipate that she might cross paths with Deacon Parrish there, but that's exactly what happened Tuesday afternoon. She was walking out of the clinic as he was walking in—with the same blonde woman he'd been with at the coffee shop.

Regan, he'd called her.

And she's a lot more than a friend.

Sierra halted in mid-stride, desperately looking around for an escape. But there was one door—and he was holding it open for her. Or maybe just holding it open, as his attention was on his companion and whatever she was saying.

So Sierra drew in a deep breath and walked right past him, murmuring a quick, "Thanks."

But she made the mistake of glancing up and their eyes met. His widened in surprise, but she hurried away before he could say anything.

She punched the button to summon the elevator, silently chastising herself for believing that going to an out-of-town clinic would allow her to be anonymous. Not that she planned to keep her pregnancy a secret forever—an impossibility in any event. But she had hoped to keep it to herself a while longer, and if she was going to confide in anyone about the baby she carried, her first choice certainly would not have been Mr. Columbia Law.

Connor rushed into the waiting room of the clinic just as his wife's name was called, allowing Deacon to breathe a sigh of relief that his brother would be there to hold Regan's hand while they got a first peek at their baby. Of course, it also meant that Deacon had to rush back to Haven to pick up the twins from day care, but that was a task for which he was much better suited.

Piper and Poppy chattered the whole way home, regaling him with the most minute details of their day. As he listened to them talk, he secretly marveled over the fact that, just about four and a half years ago, his brother and sister-in-law had been looking at their tiny images on a screen.

Actually, Regan hadn't been his sister-in-law then, but she and Connor had married a few weeks later. Though Deacon didn't believe that getting married was necessarily the right thing for every couple having a baby together, it had certainly been the right thing for his brother and sister-in-law.

Even if, at the time, Deacon had been certain that Connor had taken leave of his senses. Because the rarefied world of mansions and manicured lawns in which Regan grew up couldn't have been further away from the rundown neighborhood where Connor and Deacon had occasionally kicked a battered soccer ball around the patchy grass of their postage-stamp-sized backyard.

But there was no denying that Regan loved his brother and the family they'd made together, and Deacon was sincerely pleased that their family would be expanding.

When they got home, he sat Piper and Poppy at the table with a snack—veggie sticks and dip. Baxter, their faithful canine companion, took up position under the table, ready to snatch up any bits of food that might fall off the table.

While the girls were eating, he rummaged through the refrigerator to see what he could find for dinner and wondered what Sierra had been doing at the medical clinic in Battle Mountain. He wouldn't have given her presence there a second thought if not for the fact that she'd seemed determined to avoid eye contact with him.

Or maybe he was reading something into nothing.

He pulled out a tray marked Chicken Broccoli Casserole with neatly printed heating instructions on the label. Apparently the Channings' long-time housekeeper was still feeding her employers' kids—despite the fact they all now had kids of their own.

"Whatcha doin', Unca Dunca?" Piper asked, deliberately dropping a cucumber round onto the floor for the dog. Baxter snatched it up happily.

"I'm getting dinner started so your mom and dad don't have to worry about it when they get home—and so that they'll invite me to stay."

Poppy wrinkled her nose as she examined the contents of the tray. "I don' wike bwok-wee."

"I'll tell you a secret," Deacon said, programming the recommended oven temperature. "I'm not a big fan, either, but I do like Celeste's chicken broccoli casserole."

Poppy, having finished what she wanted of her snack—and fed the rest to the dog—hopped down from her seat. "Can we do T-shirts now?"

"I don't know what that means," he admitted.

The little girl giggled and lifted the hem of her sweater to show him what she was wearing underneath. "Dis is a T-shirt."

"I know what a T-shirt is," he said. "But I don't know how to make one."

"Wif paint an' spah-kohs."

"You want to decorate T-shirts?"

She nodded.

He glanced at Piper.

She shrugged.

"Mommy's got ev'rythin' set up," Poppy said, taking his hand and leading him to the dining room where, sure enough, the table was covered with newspaper and craft supplies, with two pink child-sized T-shirts laid out.

Baxter, who'd been watching over the twins since the first day Connor and Regan brought them home from the hospital, followed.

"I think I'd better check with Mommy," he said, and sent a quick text message to his sister-in-law.

Regan immediately replied:

Make sure they wear their smocks and keep an eye on them—that stuff can be messy.

"Mommy says okay, but you have to wear your smocks."

Poppy immediately handed him hers—designated as such by her name printed across the bottom of it—so that he could help her into it. When she was ready, he picked up Piper's smock.

She folded her arms over her chest.

"Don't you want to decorate a T-shirt?"

"I wanna dec'rate my shoes, but Mommy said *no*."

"I can't imagine anyone not wanting—" he looked more closely at the supplies on the table "—puffy paint and glittery glue on their shoes," he said. "But if Mommy said you should decorate a T-shirt, then you should decorate a T-shirt."

With a heavy sigh, she unfolded her arms and let him help her with the smock.

While they were occupied with their craft, he decided to check his email, in case he'd missed anything important while he was out of the office. He filtered out the junk, drafted a couple of quick replies and flagged other messages that required more detailed responses to be dealt with later, periodically poking his head into the dining room to see how the twins were making out.

The paint was messy, but they were giggling and obviously having a good time—even Piper—so he let them be.

Connor and Regan returned home a short while later.

"How did it go?" Deacon asked. "Was the doctor able to tell you what you're having?"

The expectant parents looked at one another, as if not quite sure how to answer the question.

"Twins," Connor finally responded. "We're having twins."

"Again," Regan added.

Deacon couldn't help but chuckle at the stunned expressions mirrored on their faces.

"This is your fault," Regan accused.

He held up his hands in a gesture of surrender. "I bear absolutely no responsibility for your condition."

"You *joked* about me having twins again on the way to the clinic."

"I'm pretty sure there were already two little zygotes when I made the remark," he felt compelled to point out in his defense.

"The babies are well past the zygote stage," his brother told him.

"Not the point," Regan told her husband.

"What are the odds of having a second set of twins?" Deacon wondered aloud.

"Apparently pretty good when a woman is a hyper-ovulator. Of course, Regan's always been an over-achiever," Connor said, with an affectionate glance toward his wife.

"So it's *your* fault," Deacon couldn't resist teasing his sister-in-law.

"Laugh all you want," she said, as the oven timer buzzed. "Because I promise you, I'll be the one laughing when it's your turn."

Deacon's name was on the docket as counsel for one of the defendants at First Appearance Court the following morning. Though Sierra trusted that he wouldn't comment on her doctor's appointment in the middle of the courtroom, she was nevertheless a little apprehensive. But when he approached the prosecutor's table, she found herself fighting to hold back the smile that wanted to curve her lips.

"Nice shoes," she remarked.

"Thanks," he said. "They're designer originals."

"Double Trouble?" she guessed.

He nodded. "And yet their mother wonders why I call them that."

"They look like they were new shoes."

"Cole Haan loafers that I wore for the first time yesterday."

"It could have been worse," she said, giving in to the smile now. "They could have decorated your cowboy boots."

"That would have been worse," he acknowledged.

Chapter Eleven

Sierra paused in the entranceway of Diggers', surprised by the crowd that was already gathered at six o'clock on a Friday. Though there weren't any signs indicating that the bar was closed for a private event, the brightly colored streamers and balloons decorating a trio of booths against the far wall suggested that a celebration of some kind was going on, giving her pause.

"Grab a table wherever you can find one," a server said, as she made her way past with a tray of drinks.

"Okay," Sierra agreed, though she'd already decided that she wasn't going to stay.

Her decision to stop at the local bar and grill had been an impulsive one, and though her stomach was seriously rumbling for some of Diggers' infamous wings, she didn't feel up to battling with a crowd tonight.

Or maybe what she didn't want was to be alone in the crowd.

She'd stop at The Trading Post and pick up some chicken wings to cook in her air fryer at home instead, she decided.

And turning to leave, she walked right into Deacon Parrish.

"Whoa," he said, catching her arms when she stumbled back, reeling from the accidental bump and, even more, the awareness that sparked as a result of the physical contact. "Where are you rushing off to in such a hurry?"

She ignored the heat pulsing through her veins and pulled herself together to respond to his question. "The grocery store."

He grinned. "Are you having another Frosted Flakes emergency?"

"It's chicken wings this time."

His brows lifted. "Did the kitchen run out?"

"No. I mean, I don't think so. I didn't get any farther than this because it looks like there's some kind of big party happening."

"It's not a party—it's the last Friday of the month, which is when a bunch of us get together for a few drinks and some of those wings you're in the mood for. Come and join us."

"The streamers and balloons indicate it's a party," she told him.

He glanced over her shoulder and winced when he spotted the decorations. "Well, it wasn't supposed to be a party."

Following his gaze, she realized now that she recognized several people—including Katelyn Davidson, Deacon's boss, Brenna Flaherty, another associate from Katelyn's office, and the deputy sheriff, who she'd recently learned was Deacon's brother.

"It's your party," Sierra said, feeling foolish that it had taken her so long to put the pieces together.

"It's not a party," he said again.

The slight pique in his tone made her realize that Mr. Columbia Law didn't like people making a fuss over him—or at least over his birthday.

Just then, the exterior door opened and a couple more people walked in, bringing a blast of wintry air with them.

"Helluva night for a party, Dekes," the taller man with curly dark hair said, stomping the snow off his boots.

Deacon just sighed.

"There better be cake," the shorter guy with reddish hair and an unshaven jaw grumbled.

"It's a birthday party. Of course there's going to be cake," Curly told him. "The question is—will a half-naked chick jump out of it?"

Deacon shook his head. "You're such a Neanderthal, Luke."

"I'll take that as a no," Curly—Luke—said, in a disappointed tone.

"Who's your special guest?" Red asked. Though the question was obviously directed at Deacon, he was looking at Sierra.

"Sierra Hart, the new ADA," he said, sending her an apologetic glance. "Sierra, meet Ben Powell and Luke Ross."

"A pleasure," Ben said, touching the brim of his cowboy hat.

"Why don't you go charm the bartender into pouring you a couple of beers?" Deacon suggested, literally nudging his friends along.

"I can do that," his friend agreed. "And what can I get for you, Sierra?"

"Lost," Deacon said firmly.

Ben finally took the hint and followed Luke into the bar.

"Sorry about that," Deacon said.

"I'm the one who should apologize—I didn't mean to crash your party."

"You haven't crashed anything," he assured her. "Come on in and have some wings."

"Is it a milestone birthday?" she wondered. "Or do you always celebrate like this?"

"Not always," he denied. "But…well, the last few years have been like this. My sister-in-law's doing."

"She's big on parties?" Sierra guessed.

"Something like that," he hedged.

"Which means there's more to the story."

"Not one you're likely to be interested in," he said.

"What if I am?"

"Then come on in and I'll tell you about it."

She was wavering.

Then another server walked by carrying a platter of wings covered in sweet, sticky sauce and Sierra's stomach rumbled.

"What kind of wings did you order?" she asked.

"Every kind," he promised.

"Honey garlic?"

"Of course," he said. "Because those are my favorite."

"Then I guess you're going to have a chance to tell me that story."

Of course, it was too loud and crowded in the bar to be able to have much of a conversation, especially when there was a steady stream of people coming up to the booth where they were sitting to wish Deacon a happy birthday.

But there were wings, as he'd promised. Platters heaping with wings of every flavor, served with celery and carrot sticks and blue cheese dip. There were also mozzarella sticks and onion rings and potato skins and garlic bread.

Sierra filled half her plate with the fresh veggies before she allowed herself to take a little bit of everything else. Unfortunately, by the time the platter of honey garlic wings made its way around to her, there was nothing left on it but smears of sticky sauce.

Deacon left the table for a minute to greet some more friends who came in, and Brenna Flaherty and her husband, Gerard, slid into the seat that he'd vacated. Sierra didn't mind—she'd gotten to know Brenna a little during the few weeks that she'd been in town, and she found out now that both Brenna and Gerard had known the birthday boy since elementary school.

When Deacon returned to the booth, taking the seat beside Sierra, he had another platter of wings in-hand.

"Honey garlic," he said, adding a wink as he set the platter between them.

She smiled her appreciation and transferred several of the wings to her plate as a trio of Deacon's friends made their way over, each carrying two shot glasses.

"Happy birthday." Ben set one of his shots on the table.

"Happy birthday." Luke set another shot next to the first.

"Happy birthday." A third man, whom Sierra had not yet been introduced to, added a third.

"Thanks, guys," Deacon said. "But you know I don't do shots."

"We know," Ben confirmed. "But we bought them for you, because it's your birthday. And now, being the good friends that we are, we're going to drink them for you."

And they proceeded to do exactly that.

Katelyn and her husband approached the booth as the three men tossed back the first round of shots, then the second.

"You guys better not be driving," Katelyn cautioned.

"It's okay," Luke said with an exaggerated wink. "We know a good defense attorney."

"They're not driving," Deacon hastened to assure his boss as his friends wandered off. "My brother's playing taxi tonight."

"Good thinking," the sheriff said. "You don't want to have to wake a judge up on a Saturday morning to attempt to get your idiot friends out of jail."

"Or maybe he does," Gerard said, winking at Deacon. "If he could guarantee that the new ADA got the call."

"Why would you say that?" Sierra asked curiously.

"Because he's been hot for her since day one."

"Shut up, Gerard." This was a whispered plea from his wife. "Shut up *now*."

"Why? Is it supposed to be some kind of secret?"

Brenna dropped her head to thunk it against the table.

Katelyn pressed her lips together, obviously trying to hold back a smile.

"Well, this isn't awkward at all," Deacon remarked dryly.

"What?" Gerard said.

His wife finally lifted her head, her cheeks as red as the single hot wing left on the platter in the middle of the table. "Sierra *is* the new ADA."

"Oh. Crap." He glanced first at Sierra, then Deacon. "Sorry, man."

"Anyway," Reid said, his hazel eyes dancing with amusement. "We just wanted to stop by to wish you a happy birthday again before we head out."

"You can't leave before we have cake," Deacon protested.

"We have to," Katelyn said. "We promised the babysitter that we'd be home by nine."

Sierra glanced at her watch as Deacon rose from his seat to hug his boss and shake hands with her husband. "I didn't realize that it was so late."

"When did nine o'clock become late?" Gerard wondered.

"When we started adulting," Brenna said, nudging him with her elbow. "We should be on our way, too."

"But we haven't had cake," her husband protested.

"Deacon and Sierra need to talk about the elephant you brought into the room."

"No," Sierra said. "We don't."

"Stay," Deacon chimed in, returning to his seat.

"Hey, there's another one of your…friends," Sierra said, grateful to be able to change the topic of conversation.

Brenna twisted her head to follow the direction of Sierra's gaze. "Looks like the newlyweds are back from their honeymoon."

"We should have gotten married in February," Gerard said. "A Caribbean vacation in February makes more sense than one in June."

"Maybe," his wife acknowledged. "But I didn't want to be trudging through snow in my wedding dress and then swapping my shoes for warm slippers at the reception, like Liberty did."

"You were there?" Deacon sounded surprised by this revelation. "I heard it was going to be a small wedding, mostly just family."

"Liberty probably told you that because Travis refused to let her invite anyone who'd seen her naked," Gerard said, then winced. "And I just did it again, didn't I?"

"That wasn't exactly a revelation," Sierra assured him. "Liberty was happy to walk down memory lane with Deacon when they crossed paths at Jo's a few weeks back."

"We all have a history," Gerard said. "Travis Bell, Luke Powell, Chase Hampton, Dekes and me have known one another since kindergarten."

"Wait a minute," Sierra said, holding up a hand. "Are you telling me that Liberty's husband's name is Travis *Bell*?"

Three heads nodded confirmation.

"So now her name is...*Liberty Bell*?"

More nods, smirks.

Sierra pressed her lips together, trying to hold back the laugh that bubbled up inside her.

"I suggested that she should keep her maiden name," Brenna told them. "She asked me why."

"It's probably not so bad, being Liberty Bell from Haven, Nevada," Deacon said.

"But she better hope they never move to Philadelphia," Gerard added.

They all lost the battle against laughter then.

A cheer went up from the crowd when the cake arrived, a huge slab brought in on a wheeled cart being pushed by the "a lot more than a friend" Regan.

"Hey—no outside food or drink," the bartender called out.

"A big corner piece of this cake has your name on it, Duke," Regan called back, with a smile and a wink.

"Carry on, then," he said, with a wave of his hand.

She wheeled the cart closer to Deacon and everyone—even the patrons on the other side of the bar—began singing "Happy Birthday."

Sierra had been having a good time with Deacon's friends. Now she wished she'd never accepted his invitation to join the party.

Did he know the other woman was going to be here?

He certainly didn't seem surprised to see her—or the least bit uncomfortable about her presence.

The deputy sheriff made his way to the front of the crowd. "Why aren't there any candles on the cake?"

"Because no one wants to eat cake that someone has spit all over," Regan told him.

"I would hope my brother would spit a lot less than the twins, and you let them have candles on their birthday."

"They each had one candle in their own cupcakes."

The deputy sheriff and the blonde continued to bicker good-naturedly as they cut and served the cake—moist lemon sponge, layered with white chocolate mousse and strawberry *pâté de fruit* jelly, with an Italian buttercream icing—and the pieces finally clicked together in Sierra's mind.

"So Regan's your sister-in-law," Sierra said to Deacon when Brenna and Gerard had gone, leaving them alone at the table.

"Uh-huh," he agreed.

"Why didn't you tell me that when I saw you with her at the coffee shop, the morning after Valentine's Day?"

He shrugged. "It seemed to me you'd already made up your mind about who she was—at least in relation to me."

"Because I heard her say, 'Thanks for last night.'"

"She was thanking me for giving them my Cowboy Poets tickets—and babysitting their kids—so that they could have a night out."

"Oh," she said, feeling foolish.

"Although now I kind of understand why you were annoyed that morning," he said. "You assumed I was flirting with you after spending the night with another woman."

"You could have just told me who she was."

"I could have," he acknowledged. "But green is a good color on you."

"You think I was jealous?"

"Weren't you?"

"No," she denied. *Lied.*

"So how long are you going to pretend there isn't something between us?" he challenged.

"I'm not pretending anything."

He shifted on the bench seat, moving a little closer so that his thigh was pressing against hers, his arm touching hers.

She swallowed.

"There's definitely something," he said.

"A basic physiological attraction, perhaps," she said dismissively.

He rephrased. "Chemistry."

"Equally irrelevant," she assured him.

He lifted a hand to tuck a strand of hair behind her ear, letting his fingertip trace the outer shell, making her shiver.

His lips curved. "Do you really think so?"

"I know so," she insisted.

"So if I kissed you now, you wouldn't kiss me back?"

Her breath hitched; her heart raced. "If you kissed me now, in front of all these people, I'd introduce you to my right hook."

His smile widened. "What I'm hearing you say is that it's the location rather than the kiss that you'd object to."

Her cheeks burned. "It's both."

He held her gaze. "Is it really?"

She bumped her hip against his, signaling that she wanted out of the booth. "Good night, Deacon."

He rose to his feet. "I'll walk you out."

"That really isn't necessary."

"Haven may be a friendly town, but it's late and it's dark," he said, helping her with her coat before donning his own and following her to the door.

"It's snowing," she said, smiling as she tipped her head back to watch the flakes falling from the sky.

"Doesn't it snow in Vegas?"

"Hardly ever. And while I'm not a huge fan of snow on the ground, especially when I have to shovel it, snow falling from the sky is different," she said. "Almost magical."

"Except in a blizzard—then it's dangerous," he told her.

"This isn't a blizzard. Is it?"

He chuckled. "No. Definitely not a blizzard."

A fat snowflake landed on her cheek, then melted against the warmth of her skin. He lifted a hand to brush the trace of moisture away with his thumb.

Her whole body went still.

Even her breath stalled in her lungs.

His hand fell away.

She exhaled slowly. Unsteadily.

"Do you miss Las Vegas?" he asked her now.

She was grateful for the question—the return to neutral ground. "Not as much as I thought I would."

"I didn't think I'd ever come back here after college," Deacon confided. "But there's a sense of community here that I've never felt anywhere else."

"I can see that." She started to walk again, away from the restaurant, and paused after taking about a dozen steps to stand beside the green Kia. "This is my car."

"Hard to miss," he noted with a smile.

"And now you know why I said it was unnecessary for you to walk me to my car."

"But it was necessary," he said. "Because you wouldn't let me kiss you in front of all those people."

"And I'm not going to let you kiss me now."

"Aren't you as curious as I am to know if the chemistry between us will flare or fizzle?"

"Curiosity aside, I don't think it's a good idea," she told him.

But she didn't move away.

Not even when he took a step closer.

Their gazes held for one heartbeat. Two.

"Yet one more thing about which we obviously disagree," he said, just before his mouth covered hers.

Chapter Twelve

Sierra would be lying if she said she hadn't thought about kissing Deacon, but she'd never thought it would actually happen. And while the rational part of her brain was shouting at her to end this madness—because it had to be madness—the desire rushing through her veins drowned out the shouting. And that was before his tongue dipped between her lips to tease and tangle with hers.

It was only a kiss, but it felt like so much more.

Made her want so much more.

She clutched at his jacket, holding on to him as she kissed him back.

It was a long time later, and only when they were both desperate for air, that he eased his mouth from hers.

"Tell me again that there's nothing between us," he said, whispering the words against her lips.

"Apparently there is some chemistry," she acknowledged breathlessly. "But I'm still not going to sleep with you."

She felt rather than saw his lips curve.

"I don't want to sleep with you," he said. "I want to strip you naked and spend hours exploring every inch of your body with my hands and my lips and—"

"I'm not going to have sex with you, either."

But her voice wavered, *dammit*.

Because she wanted all the same things he did, so much so that her body was practically quivering. And if circumstances had been different, she might have taken what he was offering and had no regrets afterward.

But circumstances weren't different, and she couldn't let herself succumb to the desire thrumming in her blood.

"I got a baseball glove for my tenth birthday," he said, surprising her with the abrupt change of topic. "Brand new. That in and of itself had been a big thing, as money was always tight in our house. Gifts were more often secondhand or homemade, and I can still remember the scent and suppleness of the leather."

She was surprised by this revelation—and even more so to realize that Mr. Columbia Law hadn't led the charmed life that she'd imagined.

"It was the very best birthday present I ever got," Deacon continued. "Until now."

"It was a pretty great kiss," she allowed. "But it's not going to lead to anything else. It can't."

"You keep saying that, but you haven't told me why."

"The why doesn't matter."

"It matters to—"

"Shh!"

His brows lifted. "Did you really just *shush* me? We were in the middle of—"

She touched a hand to his lips.

Deacon heard it then, a plaintive whimper in the distance. "Is it...a dog?"

Sierra squinted into the darkness as another whimper sounded. "It sounds like it might be, but I can't see anything."

Though streetlights illuminated the sidewalk and nearby storefronts, the narrow alley between the restaurant and adjacent office building was in shadow.

He turned on the torch app on his phone and directed the light at the ground before venturing into the alley, Sierra right behind him.

There was a trash can against the building, and a tiny creature cowering behind it.

"It *is* a dog," she said softly.

He caught her arm when she would have moved forward. "I'm pretty sure it's a rat."

She shook off his hold. "It's not a rat—it's a Chihuahua."

"It looks like a rat to me," he insisted, though he could see now that its legs were too long and its ears too big to be a rat. Not to mention that a rodent would likely have scampered away when they approached. Unless... "It could be a rabid rat."

Sierra dropped to her haunches, a respectful distance from the obviously wary creature. "Hey, little guy. What are you doing out here?"

The dog—if it was a dog—was shivering.

With fear?

Or cold?

Probably both, Deacon acknowledged. The animal was obviously lost or abandoned, and its short hair didn't look like it provided much—if any—protection against the elements.

Whatever the cause, the critter was trembling so much that its whole body shook, and Deacon knew there was no way they were walking away from it.

"Maybe he's waiting for a rendezvous with a female rat," he suggested.

Sierra glared at him over her shoulder, but when she turned back to the animal, her voice was soft and coaxing.

"I don't see a collar," she crooned softly. "But I can see your ribs. Are you hungry?"

The dog, mesmerized by her voice, took a couple of tentative steps forward.

"Be careful," Deacon felt compelled to warn her. "He might be vicious."

"Yeah, he looks really vicious," she said dryly.

She reached into her purse and pulled out...a pepperoni stick?

She peeled back the wrapper and broke off a piece of the sausage, then held it toward the dog.

His nose twitched and his tongue fell out of his mouth.

"Why do you carry pepperoni sticks in your purse?" Deacon asked.

"In case of a zombie apocalypse."

"I'm not sure if you're joking," he admitted.

She laughed softly. "I have them in case I'm stuck in court and get hungry—or find a lost dog in an alley."

"While you're coaxing him out, I'll give animal control a call—"

"Don't you dare."

Her outburst sent the dog scrambling back behind the trash can, earning him another glare.

"Shelters exist for situations just like this," he said, trying to reason with her even as he tucked his phone back in his pocket. "He'll be taken care of there. It's what they do."

"C'mon, sweetie," she said, talking to the dog again. "Don't let the big bad man's talk about shelters scare you."

"I would think he'd be happy to have shelter—it's got to be preferable to freezing."

The dog cautiously ventured forward again, his beady-eyed gaze darting from the sausage to Sierra to Deacon and back to the sausage again.

"I know it probably isn't what you should be eating," Sierra acknowledged, as the dog snatched the meat from her hand, "but beggars can't be choosers, right?"

Apparently the animal agreed, because he gobbled up the pepperoni and looked to her for more.

"One more little piece," she said, breaking off another bit. As he took the meat, she carefully lifted the dog off of the ground, tucking him into the crook of her arm.

"Oh, he is freezing," she said. "Poor little guy."

"Which is why he should go to a shelter," Deacon said again, feeling inexplicably envious of the dog as Sierra cuddled it close to her chest.

"But if he was abandoned here, and then he gets taken to a shelter and left there, he'll feel as if he's being abandoned all over again."

He unhooked the scarf draped around his neck and gently wrapped it around the shivering animal. "And then someone will come and adopt him, and he'll go to a new home and live happily ever after with a family that always wanted a pet rat."

"Stop calling him a rat," Sierra said, but the admonition was without heat this time.

Perhaps the sacrifice of his scarf had lessened her annoyance with him.

"And while you're painting a pretty picture, I don't think anyone—even a dog—would easily forget the trauma of being abandoned."

"Maybe he wasn't abandoned," Deacon suggested. "Maybe he ran away because his home life sucked and he wanted to find something better."

He felt the weight of Sierra's gaze on him and knew that she knew he was no longer talking about the dog. Or not exclusively, anyway.

The dog whimpered quietly.

"I'll take him to the shelter tomorrow," she decided.

"And what are you going to do with him tonight?" he asked, though he was certain he already knew the answer to that question.

"I'll take him home with me."

"You don't know anything about his history or his health," Deacon protested. "He could be sick or ill-tempered or covered in fleas."

"He doesn't look sick or ill-tempered," she pointed out.

The dog tipped his head back and looked at her adoringly, and Deacon knew he was in the middle of an argument that he couldn't win.

Still, he felt compelled to make one final point. "At least give him a bath before you let him onto your bed."

"That's a rule I enforce with all my overnight guests," she said, then ducked her head, no doubt to hide the color that filled her cheeks. "Please forget that completely inappropriate comment."

"Why would I want to do that?" he asked mildly.

"Because I've been trying really hard not to lead you on."

"Because you're adamant that nothing is going to happen between us?"

"Yes."

"Too late," he told her.

"Go back to your party, Deacon."

"I'm going," he said, because he could hardly abandon the friends who'd shown up to celebrate with him, even if he'd rather be with Sierra. Despite the fact that her attention was focused now on the scrawny dog in her arms. "But you've got my number, if you need anything."

"I've got your number," she confirmed, then surprised him by touching her lips to his cheek. "Happy birthday."

Sierra woke up Saturday morning with doggy breath in her face.

"We should have brushed your teeth after your bath."

A tiny pink tongue swiped at the end of her nose, making her laugh even as her heart squeezed inside her chest.

"Or maybe I should have let Deacon call animal control to have you taken to the shelter."

Her miniature canine companion let out a soft whine.

"Do you know that word?" she wondered aloud. "Have you been to the animal shelter before?"

Another whine and a reproachful look from big dark eyes.

She sighed. "What am I going to do with you, Dog?"

He wriggled closer.

"I can't keep you." She'd come to that realization the night before and had abandoned her efforts to find a suitable name for him, knowing it would only be much more difficult to say goodbye if she'd given him a name.

Dog just looked at her with his big dark eyes.

"I never even thought about getting a dog," she continued her explanation—well, her excuse, really—to the poor little pup. "Before I came to Haven, I didn't have time to care for a pet. I probably would have forgotten to even feed a goldfish."

This time his tongue swept over her chin.

She sighed. "Deacon was right. Not that I would admit it to him," she confided. "But I should have let you go to the s-h-e-l-t-e-r last night, because now I don't think that I can." She gently stroked the dog's head with a fingertip. "But what other choice do I have?

"I can't keep you," she said again, needing to convince herself as much as Dog. "You probably don't understand why, because it no doubt looks like a pretty good setup here. But it can't be your forever home because I'm only here temporarily—because I needed a short-term job to see me through most of my pregnancy. And I'm already near the end of the second month of a six-month contract with the DA's office. After that... I don't know.

"I mean, I'm going back to Vegas, obviously. But I don't have a place of my own there. Nick and Whitney said that I can stay with them for as long as I want, but they won't really want me underfoot when the baby comes. And I know you're really cute and don't take up much room, but Whitney's allergic to dogs, so I really don't think there's any other option."

But the thought of taking him to a shelter—of handing him off to a stranger and waving goodbye to him through a pane of glass...

She swallowed around the lump in her throat.

"On the other hand, I might be completely misreading your situation. Maybe you weren't abandoned but somehow got separated from your family and then got lost trying to find your way home.

"Maybe, right now, someone is posting flyers around town with your photo on them. Maybe you even have a microchip." She rubbed the dog's ears gently, feeling for evidence of such a device. "And maybe, instead of speculating, I should take you to the vet to find out for sure."

"I brought leftover birthday cake," Deacon said, when Sierra opened the door in response to his knock Saturday afternoon.

"You should keep the cake—it was your birthday."

"There was a lot of it left over," he told her.

"In that case." She accepted the plate with a smile.

Looking past her, he saw a tiny head peeking around the half wall that separated the entranceway from the living area.

"I brought some things for your pet rat, too."

"He's not a rat," she said indignantly. "And he's not mine."

"And yet, you obviously didn't take him to the shelter this morning." He reached down for the dog carrier that she hadn't noticed was on the porch beside him.

She stepped away from the door so that he could bring it inside.

"No," she admitted. "But I did take Dog to the vet, to see if he was microchipped."

"Dog?" he echoed.

As if responding to a summons, the Chihuahua took a few tentative steps closer.

Sierra shrugged as she carried the plate of cake into the kitchen. "He needed a name."

"Dog isn't a name, it's a classification," Deacon said, following behind with the crate.

"Anyway, Dr. Stafford said he's not microchipped," she said. "And no one had called the clinic—or the shelter—looking for a lost pet."

"How do you know no one called the shelter?"

"The receptionist checked while we were there."

"So you're keeping him?" he guessed.

She shook her head regretfully. "I can't."

"And yet, he's still here."

"Not for long."

He smiled at that as he unlatched the door of the crate to retrieve the bags he'd placed inside.

"Where did you get all that stuff?"

"Fur, Feathers and Fins," he said, naming the local pet store.

She watched as he unpacked a memory foam pillow bed, two stainless steel bowls decorated with paw prints, a bag of small dog kibble, a box of treats, an assortment of toys, a collar and a leash and waste bags to clean up after him on walks. There was even a puffy jacket with matching boots with Velcro fasteners.

"I think you went a little overboard," she said.

"Maybe," he acknowledged. "If there's anything you don't want or don't need, it can be taken back to the store."

"You should probably take it all back," she said. "Because I really can't keep him."

"Why not? It's not as if you don't have room for him. You've even got a doggy door."

A doggy door clearly intended for a much larger breed, Deacon acknowledged. Sierra's little dog probably couldn't even push it open—and was likely to hurt himself if he even tried.

"I've got room for him *here*," she agreed. "But it

wouldn't be fair to keep him for a few months and then leave him at a shelter when I go back to Vegas."

"That's true," he acknowledged, not wanting to think about her going back to Vegas. But as much as she seemed to enjoy her job in the DA's office—and was obviously good at it—she never missed an opportunity to remind him that it was only a temporary position. A six-month contract with a little more than four months left.

She sighed.

And then, as if another thought had just occurred to her, her expression brightened. "But *you* could keep him."

"Oh, no." Deacon shook his head.

"Why not? You like dogs."

"Yes, I like dogs." He picked the Chihuahua up with one hand, because it was that small, and tucked it into the crook of his arm. "But if I was going to get a dog, I'd get one that looked like a dog."

The Chihuahua snuggled into his elbow, yawned once, then closed his eyes and promptly fell asleep. As if he instinctively trusted that he was somewhere safe.

Deacon muttered a soft curse under his breath.

Sierra didn't even try to hold back the smug smile that curved her lips. "Admit it—you've fallen just as hard for Dog as I have."

"If you're going to keep him, he's going to need a better name than Dog," Deacon said.

"I'm not going to keep him—*you* are."

"Why don't you let him stay here for the next few months and I'll take him when you leave?"

"Or we could share custody," she said. "So that he gets to be comfortable at your place, too, and won't feel as if he's been completely uprooted when I leave."

"Shared custody of a Chihuahua," he mused. "Should we get Judge Wilkerson to sign off on our agreement?"

"I don't think that will be necessary."

"Well, even if we're not going to write up the paperwork, he still needs a name."

"Tiny?" she suggested.

He made a face.

"Bitsy?"

"You're not very good at this, are you?"

"I don't hear you offering up any suggestions."

"Remy," he said.

"Remy," she echoed, surprised that he hadn't suggested something like "Ratface" or "Mouse," and even more surprised to realize that she liked it.

Chapter Thirteen

"What do you say to taking Remy for a walk so that he can sniff out his new neighborhood?" Deacon suggested.

"I say *yes*," Sierra agreed.

All joking about shared custody aside, the dog was as high-maintenance as a child. Before they could go out, they had to size his collar and put it on him. Remy didn't object to that—it was almost as if he knew that the collar was a symbol that he belonged to someone, that he had a home. The coat he balked at initially, but once Sierra had wrestled it on to him, he seemed to tolerate it well enough. The boots were a different story. He did not appreciate their efforts in that regard—and yes, it was a two-person job, especially with the dog twisting and squirming and even nipping at them when they tried to put the boots over his paws.

"One thing I forgot to get was a muzzle," Deacon grumbled.

"I guess we'll have to take him without the boots," Sierra decided.

"Or we could take the ungrateful rat to the shelter."

"Stop that," she admonished.

"He bit me," Deacon reminded her.

"He didn't even break the skin."

"He still bit me."

And as if it wasn't enough that he had to shorten his stride to accommodate the tiny dog, Remy stopped every ten feet or so to lift his leg by a tree or a bush or a blade of grass sticking out of the snow.

"At this rate, it's going to take him six months to explore the neighborhood," Deacon remarked, when they finally made it to the end of the street and decided to turn back again.

Sierra didn't comment on that, and Deacon remembered that she wouldn't be around in six months. She only had a six-month contract and seven weeks were already gone.

"Did you want to come in?" she invited when they finally arrived back at her house.

"I should probably head home," he said. "It must be getting close to dinnertime."

"It is," she confirmed. "But you could stay and have dinner with me."

The lift of his brows indicated that he was surprised by the invitation.

"As a thank-you for the stuff you brought for Remy— and your help with him," she explained.

"In that case," he said, and followed her into the house.

"Do you like pasta?" Sierra asked, when they'd shed their outerwear and were headed to the kitchen.

"Moltissimo."

"Should I be impressed? Or is that the only word you know in Italian?"

"Posso dire qualche parola."

"Sono impressionato."

He grinned. *"Anchi'io."*

"You shouldn't be impressed," she told him, reaching into the drawer beneath the stove and pulling out a deep frying pan. "My knowledge of the Italian language dates back to Northwest High School. It's very limited and very rusty."

"You didn't sound rusty to me. Although I might be rusty, too."

She set the pan on the stove and dumped a package of ground beef in it. "Where did you learn Italian?"

"Francesca Moretti—an Italian exchange student."

"Pretty?" she guessed, retrieving a jar of spaghetti sauce from the cupboard.

"Very." He picked up the spatula she'd set on the counter and used it to break apart the lump of meat in the frying pan.

"I invited you to stay for dinner, not help make it."

"Am I doing something wrong?"

"I don't think there's a wrong way to brown ground beef."

"Then let me do it."

So she did.

And since he was taking care of the meat, she decided to put together a salad to serve with the pasta.

"You mentioned that you went to Northwest High School," he noted. "But I just realized that I don't know where you went to law school."

"Nowhere near as lofty as Columbia," she told him.

"I've never heard of that one," he deadpanned.

She rolled her eyes. "UNLV."

"A good school," he said. "I got my undergrad degree in poli sci there."

"Me, too," she admitted.

"It's interesting that we both did our undergrads in the same program at the same school but our paths never crossed on campus," he mused. "Almost as if destiny was waiting for the right time for us to meet."

"Or maybe it's because the student population at UNLV is approximately twice that of Haven," she countered. "Also, I was probably a couple years ahead of you."

"Why would you assume that?"

"Because it was your twenty-eighth birthday last night and I'm...older than that."

"How old are you?"

She chopped celery to add to the salad. "Didn't anyone ever tell you that it's rude to ask a woman her age?"

"You brought up the subject," he pointed out.

Because it was true, she relented and answered his question. "I celebrated the big three-oh on my last birthday."

"Wow, you are an old lady," he teased.

She reached past him to retrieve a pair of tongs from the utensil holder on the counter, not-quite-accidentally elbowing him in the ribs.

He chuckled.

They chatted some more about mostly inconsequential topics while they finished preparing the meal.

And it was nice to have company, Sierra admitted. Even if it was male company that made her achingly aware of specific female needs.

"I've got a couple of beers in the fridge from when my brother was here," Sierra said, as she scooped the pasta into bowls. "Do you want one?"

Deacon hesitated for a second. "Yeah, I guess I could have one."

While he plated the garlic bread she'd warmed in the oven, she retrieved a bottle from the fridge, twisted the cap and set it on the table.

"I expected that Remy would be ready for his dinner, too," she remarked, taking a seat across from Deacon at the table. "But apparently he's more tired than hungry right now."

"I guess half a block is a long walk when your legs are that short."

"Speaking of Remy," she said, selecting a piece of garlic bread. "We should draw up a schedule to establish who has him and when."

"Or we could not worry about a schedule," he said.

"You're not reneging on our agreement, are you?"

"No, I'm not reneging," he assured her. "I'm just suggesting that you should have primary custody and I'll exercise visitation."

"Does that include exercising him when you visit?" she asked.

"Whatever you want."

"I want him to become as familiar with you as I'm hoping he'll become with me, so that when I leave, he'll still feel that he has a home."

"I could come by to take him out after work on Mondays, Wednesdays and Fridays."

"That would be great," she agreed. "But I have...a class on Wednesdays at six, so I'll give you a key that you can use if I'm not here."

His brows lifted. "You won't go out for dinner with me but you'll give me a key to your house?"

"Because going out for dinner implies a date. Exchanging keys for access to the dog is a sign of friendship—

not that I'm asking for a key to your house," she hastened to assure him, rising from the table to carry their empty dishes to the sink.

Deacon followed with the salad bowl. "It would be strange for me to have a key to your place and you not have one to mine."

"But if Remy's going to be living here full-time, there's no reason that I'd need a key to your place."

"Unless you had a shower emergency."

"A shower emergency?" she echoed dubiously.

"Such as your water tank going on the fritz," he said. "If that happened, you could come over to my place, strip out of your clothes—music optional—"

"Let me assure you, that is *not* going to happen."

"Water tanks can be finicky," he warned.

"I was referring to the stripping part."

"It's much more efficient to take your clothes off before you shower."

She shook her head, a smile tugging at the corners of her mouth. "You're enjoying this, aren't you?"

"Picturing you naked in my shower?" He grinned. "Absolutely."

She swatted at him with a tea towel.

Remy finally woke up from his nap then and wandered into the kitchen. Sierra measured kibble into his bowl and gave him fresh water while Deacon finished loading the dishwasher.

"Did you want another beer?" she asked, removing the empty bottle from the table.

"No, thanks," he said. "One's my limit."

She'd noticed the night before that he wasn't a heavy drinker. Though he'd had a beer in his hand most of the night, it hadn't taken her long to realize it was always the same bottle—almost a prop more than a beverage.

"Alcoholic parent?" she guessed.

He seemed taken aback by her question, but after a brief moment's hesitation, he nodded. "My dad was a drunk and a bully."

"I'm sorry."

He shrugged. "We all have our demons."

No doubt there was a lot more to the story, but he obviously didn't want to talk about it, and she felt she should respect his secrets if she wanted to keep her own.

"It's getting late," Deacon said. "I should probably be going."

She glanced at the illuminated display on the stove. 6:42.

"I'm sorry—which one of us did you say was old?" she asked, unable to resist teasing him.

"Okay, it's not actually late," he acknowledged. "But I've taken up a lot of your time today."

"I'm not sure I should admit this, but I enjoyed your company."

"See? I'm not such a bad guy when you get to know me."

"I never thought you were a bad guy."

"Am I a bad kisser?"

She narrowed her gaze. "I think you know the answer to that question."

"Maybe I want to hear you say it."

"We are not going to talk about that kiss," she said firmly.

"Why not?" he challenged.

"Because it never should have happened."

And because she hadn't stopped thinking about it since it happened. And because, even now, her lips were tingling in anticipation of touching his again.

"Okay, let's talk about our second kiss," he suggested.

She shook her head, dismissing the temptation that urged her to press her body to his. "There's not going to be a second kiss."

"Why are you so opposed to giving us a chance?"

"You're not going to let this go, are you?"

"I wish I could," he said. "But I can't think of any reason for us not to explore the obvious attraction between us."

"There is a reason," she insisted.

"Did you do one of those ancestry DNA tests and discover that we're fourth cousins or something?" he asked, when she failed to expand on her response.

"Nothing quite that scandalous," she assured him.

"Then what is it?"

She took a deep breath and said, "I'm pregnant."

Chapter Fourteen

"Pregnant?" Deacon echoed, stunned.

"You really didn't know?" Sierra asked skeptically.

He shook his head slowly. "How could I have known?"

"Because you saw me at the prenatal clinic."

He remembered seeing her in Battle Mountain when he took his sister-in-law to her appointment, but... "I didn't realize it was a prenatal clinic."

"What did you think it was?"

"A woman's health clinic. For all I knew, you were having an annual exam or renewing a prescription for birth control."

"I was there for a four-month prenatal checkup," she said. "The baby's due in August."

Baby. She was going to have a baby.

This wasn't just another brush-off—this was real.

"And the baby's father?"

"I'm not sure what you're asking," she hedged.

"Where is he?" It was probably none of his business, but he wanted to know.

"Las Vegas."

"Is that why you left?"

She shook her head. "I left because I wanted to make a career change—and to put some distance between me and my ex."

"Does he know about the baby?"

"No. And there's no reason for him to know. He's not the baby's father."

His brows lifted at that. "Rebound relationship?"

"No."

"One-night stand?"

"No," she said again.

"I'm not sure what options are left," he admitted.

"Does it really matter how this baby came to be? The fact is, I'm pregnant. But I haven't told anyone else yet, so I'd appreciate if this stayed between us for now."

He nodded.

"I'll probably share the news with my boss and my coworkers in the next week or so."

The news being that she was going to have a baby.

And while she was talking matter-of-factly about her next steps, he was trying to stop his head from spinning.

"And Sky, of course," she said. "I don't want her to hear about it from anyone else."

"You and Sky seem to be pretty chummy," he noted, latching on to a topic that was completely unrelated to pregnancies and babies. "Did you know her before you came to Haven?"

"No." Sierra shook her head again. "In fact, I met her the same day I met you. And the same place—the cereal aisle of the grocery store." Now she smiled. "But she didn't steal my Frosted Flakes."

"You're never going to let me forget that, are you?"

"Probably not."

But thinking back to that day now... "I guess you wanted the cereal to satisfy a pregnancy craving?"

Now she nodded.

"And that's why you don't drink coffee," he realized.

She nodded again.

"And also why that kiss should never have happened," she told him.

"Maybe," he acknowledged regretfully. "But I'm not sorry that it did."

The hint of pink that colored her cheeks told him that she wasn't sorry, either. That in that moment, she'd wanted his kiss—maybe even wanted him.

But, of course, her pregnancy changed everything.

As her next question proved.

"Do you think... Can we be friends?"

The tentativeness of the request tugged at his heart.

"As long as being friends doesn't require me to abandon my shower emergency fantasy."

She laughed then, as he'd hoped she would.

"Trust me, in a few more weeks—maybe less—you won't want to picture me naked."

"I guess time will tell. And speaking of time, I really should be going."

She walked him to the door. "Thanks again, for all your help with Remy. And all the stuff you brought for him."

"It was my pleasure."

He donned his boots and coat, then paused at the door. "I guess I'll see you Monday. If not at court, when I come over to walk Remy."

"That reminds me—" She dashed off and came back half a minute later with a key.

He slid it onto his ring, then took off his own house key and gave it to her.

"Don't you need this to get into your house?"

"There's a spare in my garage."

She tucked the key into the front pocket of her jeans. Slim-fitting dark denim that hugged her feminine form.

On top of the jeans she wore a soft knit sweater the color of ripe plums.

She certainly didn't look like a woman who was going to have a baby in five months.

She looked hot. Sexy. Desirable.

But she was going to have a baby, and that changed everything for Deacon.

Everything except how much he wanted her.

Having a dog waiting for her at home was giving Sierra a taste of what it meant to be a working mom. True, she didn't have to worry about day care for her canine dependent, but she did worry about other things. Such as if he was hungry or thirsty (despite the fact that she fed him in the morning and made sure his water bowl was full before she left the house) or scared or lonely (even though she left the television on so that the house wouldn't be too quiet) or getting into mischief. (The vet had recommended crate training to avoid this potential problem, but Sierra hadn't seen any hints of destructive behavior that made her think confinement was necessary. She had, however, blocked off the stairs to the upper level so that he wouldn't hurt himself trying to climb them when he was alone.)

But by the end of the first week, she was starting to feel more comfortable with their routines and confident that when she said goodbye to Remy in the morning, he didn't spend the rest of the day stressing about whether she would come back again. But he was always at the door when she walked in, and he'd bark happily when he saw her, not just his tail but his whole back end wagging. And it was kind of nice to have someone make a fuss over her, so she made a fuss over him in return.

He was just as excited to see Deacon, too, when the other lawyer showed up to take him for his evening walks on Monday, Wednesday and Friday. And it was a relief to Sierra to know that Remy would be not just taken care of but happy when she went back to Las Vegas and left him with Deacon.

Sky texted while Deacon was out with the dog Friday night, and Sierra exchanged a few messages with her friend while she cooked chicken and vegetables for her dinner. She was fluffing the brown rice when they returned.

"I made stir-fry," Sierra told him. "And there's enough for two, if you wanted to stay for dinner."

"That sounds a lot more appealing than what I had planned," he admitted.

"A microwaveable meal?" she guessed.

"Yeah."

"I've eaten my share of those," she confided. "But yes, this should be better."

He washed his hands at the sink while she dished up the meal.

They chatted mostly about work while they ate. In general terms, of course, not discussing any details of any particular case that might breach confidentiality or disclosure rules.

"You're tiptoeing around something," Deacon remarked, as he set his fork and knife on top of his now empty plate.

She didn't deny it. "I want to ask a favor."

"Because it's not enough that I'm already walking your dog three days a week?" he teased.

"*Our* dog," she reminded him. "And I was hoping you might be able to dog-sit tomorrow."

"You do know it's okay to go out and leave the dog alone?"

"I know. But he's been alone every day this week when I've been at work, and I hate the idea of leaving him alone again tomorrow just so that I can go shopping with Sky."

"I'm surprised you don't want to take him with you."

"I guess I could," she said. "But a crowded mall might be too much stimulation for him."

"Or good socialization," he countered.

"If you don't want to look after him—"

"I didn't say I didn't want to look after him," Deacon interjected. "I said I didn't think he needed looking after. But I'm happy to have him over to my place for a few hours—or however long you're going to be gone."

"Thank you. I'll drop him off on my way out."

So that's what Sierra did, and then she drove to Battle Mountain to meet her new friend at a store called Baby Bump. Sky had recently been lamenting the fact that none of her clothes fit comfortably anymore. Of course, the other woman was nearing the end of her second trimester now and happy to show off her growing belly, while Sierra was doing everything in her power to hide hers.

She wasn't ashamed of her pregnancy, but she also wasn't ready to be the subject of any more local gossip. It had been a hot enough topic that the DA had hired an attorney from Las Vegas, and while she felt confident that she'd proven herself capable of doing the job, she was still an outsider and, therefore, a more likely target of scrutiny.

"So what's going on with you and Deacon?" Sky asked, as she rifled through a rack of tops.

"Nothing," Sierra said quickly.

Maybe too quickly, she realized, as her friend's gaze narrowed thoughtfully.

And then she compounded the error by asking, "Why? What did you hear?"

Sky smiled as she selected a dark blue peasant-style blouse. "What do you think I might have heard?"

"Nothing," Sierra said again, though she suspected that the heat filling her cheeks belied her words.

"So it's not true that you went to his birthday party last Friday night?"

"I didn't go to his party," she denied. "I went to Diggers' not knowing that there was a party."

"But then you stayed and hung out with him all night."

"I left before ten o'clock, so I'm not sure it's accurate to say *all night*," she hedged, handing a pretty paisley top to her friend to consider. "And how do you know any of this? You weren't there."

"No." Sky added the paisley top to the growing pile of clothes she intended to try on. "But my sister was."

Sierra had forgotten for a minute that everyone in Haven knew everyone else—and that Katelyn Davidson, formerly Katelyn Gilmore, was Sky's sister.

A salesperson took Sky's selections to a dressing room while she continued to browse.

"I also heard that you and Deacon are sharing custody of a dog," her friend continued.

"Did you hear that from Katelyn, too? Because I

know you didn't hear it from Deacon, who refuses to admit that Remy is a dog."

Sky made a face as she considered—and rejected—a pair of stirrup pants. "What does he think Remy is?"

"A rat," Sierra admitted.

Sky chuckled. "I'm guessing he named the dog?"

"He did," Sierra confirmed. "But how did you guess that?"

"Because it's the name of the main character in *Ratatouille*."

"What's *Ratatouille*?"

"An animated movie about a rat who dreams of being a chef."

"I'm going to kill him," Sierra muttered under her breath.

"Don't tell me," her friend cautioned. "I'm not a lawyer, so our conversation isn't protected by attorney-client privilege."

"A threat to do harm isn't protected, anyway," Sierra informed her.

"I'll keep that in mind," Sky promised, dragging her friend into the changing room with her so their conversation wouldn't be put on hold while she tried on clothes. "But tell me how you and Deacon found this dog—and was it before or after the kiss?"

Sierra felt her cheeks burn. "How did you know about *that*?"

Her friend grinned as she quickly shed her clothes, showing no hint of self-consciousness. "Jake and I stopped by to pick up food for my cousin MG and saw your lips locked together. And you cannot know how much I've been dying to ask you about it."

She wanted to ask about MG, curious to know if Sky's cousin was the same man she'd heard the whispers about in the coffee shop several weeks earlier, but she felt compelled to respond to her friend's comment about the lip lock first. Because she knew if Sky had seen them kissing, anyone could have. And that Haven rumor mill might be running out of control if she didn't do some damage control. Fast.

"It was just a kiss," she said, because she knew she couldn't let it be more than that.

"A kiss that practically steamed our windows." Sky wiggled into a pair of maternity jeans.

"I'm sure you're exaggerating."

"Only a little." She donned the paisley top, studied her reflection in the mirror and made a face.

"It's a cute top," Sierra said.

"More your style than mine," her friend said. "So I guess you were mistaken when you said that he'd lost interest in you." Sky somehow managed to sound smug even with a shirt over her head.

"I was mistaken then," Sierra acknowledged. "But I'm sure of it now."

"Why? What happened after the kiss?"

"I told him…that I'm pregnant."

Sky hesitated a beat, then offered the paisley shirt to Sierra. "You should try this one on."

Deacon had just slid the pan of pork chops, potatoes and carrots into the oven when Sierra texted to let him know that she was on her way back from Battle Mountain—which meant that she should arrive just about the same time that dinner would be ready.

"How was your shopping trip?" he asked, when she showed up at the door.

"You wouldn't need to ask if you saw the mountain of packages in the back of my car."

"A success, then," he guessed.

"It was." She crouched down to pet the dog who, upon hearing her voice, raced to the foyer to greet her.

"I bought a few things for you, too," she said, opening the bag she carried to show Remy a buffalo plaid hooded pullover, a soft gray cable-knit sweater, a fuzzy blue sweater and a dark green faux suede coat.

"That's quite the wardrobe for a tiny dog," he remarked.

"I'm glad to hear you say that he's a dog," she said. "Because you named him after a *rat*."

Busted.

Deacon tried to keep his expression neutral, his tone casual. "You said you liked the name Remy."

"Because I didn't know it was the name of a rat in a kids' movie," she retorted.

"*Ratatouille* is a family movie," he felt compelled to point out. "Have you honestly never seen it?"

"I've honestly never seen it."

"We should watch it. If you saw the movie, you'd understand that naming our dog Remy isn't the insult you apparently think it is."

"I have no interest in a movie about a rat."

The oven timer buzzed, drawing him back to the kitchen.

"We'll watch it after dinner," he decided, ignoring her protest.

"Dinner?" she echoed, her attention momentarily diverted from the indignity of Remy's name.

"It's nothing fancy—just sheet pan pork chops, potatoes and carrots."

She breathed in the scent of the meat and veggies when he took the pan out of the oven. "Fancy or not, it sure smells good."

He retrieved a couple of plates from the cupboard and began to dish up the meal.

She found the cutlery drawer and got forks and knives.

"This is a really nice surprise," she said. "Thanks."

"You've cooked for me twice—it seemed that I had some catching up to do."

After dinner was done and the kitchen cleaned, Sierra suggested that it was time to be taking Remy home.

"Not just yet," he protested. "We've got a movie to watch."

"You were serious about that?"

"Of course."

"How are we going to watch it? Do you have Disney+?"

"I have twin almost-four-year-old nieces," he reminded her. "Of course I have Disney+."

"Do you have popcorn?"

He grinned. "And I have popcorn."

Over the next few weeks, Sierra spent a lot of time with Deacon—and Remy. They had interesting conversations about all manner of topics, and though he never hesitated to challenge her opinions, he always listened to her. But the more time they spent together, the more she found her thoughts wandering down paths it had no distance wandering.

Such as when he warned her against letting Remy sleep in her bed, because there was no way he would share his with the dog when she went back to Vegas. It had been a casual comment that somehow got Sierra thinking about Deacon in his bed…wondering if he wore pajamas or boxers…or nothing at all.

But she knew it would be foolish to get romantically involved when she was only going to be in town a few more months. And while Deacon had once flippantly suggested that they could skip the romance and go straight to the sex, that had been before he knew about the baby.

The revelation of her condition might have effectively quashed his attraction to her, but the actual condition seemed to have the effect of amplifying her own desire. She'd read that pregnancy hormones could increase a woman's libido, but she'd been certain it wouldn't be a problem for her. After Eric's betrayal, she'd vowed to take a break from men and dating. She hadn't anticipated meeting Deacon Parrish—or that their interactions, no matter how brief, would stir her up inside.

And while her hormones were in favor of stripping him naked and having her way with him—if he was still amenable to the idea, and that was a big if—the rational side of her brain kept reminding her that her body wasn't currently her own.

In addition to the conflict between her hormones and her head, there was another battle happening inside her heart. Because being with Deacon, and seeing him interact with others—especially his adorable nieces—only served to escalate her attraction to him.

So she tried to focus her attention on other things—doing her job, exploring the town, meeting new people and making sure Remy knew he was loved. She walked the dog every morning and every night after work—except the days that Deacon came by to take him out, per their agreement.

They generally exchanged only quick hellos and goodbyes in the early part of the week, but he usually hung around a little longer on Fridays. Occasionally to share a meal and sometimes long enough to watch the hockey game together if the Golden Knights were playing.

After a few weeks, Sierra realized the extended Friday night visits were more regular than occasional—and often the highlight of her week. Especially when he sat close to her, so that she could tip her head against his shoulder when she started to feel sleepy.

"You don't have to come every Friday," she told him, as they tidied up the kitchen after dinner. "I know that was the original deal, but this must be putting a kink in your social life."

"You seem to have all kinds of ideas about my social life, most of which bear little resemblance to the reality," he told her.

"I'm just saying, if you wanted to make plans that didn't include walking the dog, we can manage without you."

"Since subtlety doesn't seem to work very well with you, I'm going to be blunt," Deacon decided. "I don't want to make plans with anyone else. I want to make plans with you.

"And yes, I know why you don't want to get involved. But respecting your decision doesn't miraculously stop me from wanting you."

She was stunned. "You still want me?"

"Every minute of every day," he said, with an intensity that made everything inside her quiver.

And yearn.

Oh, how she yearned for him.

Was it the pregnancy hormones?

Or was it Deacon?

She couldn't be sure. But she knew that after only one kiss, she craved more.

More kisses. More touches.

So much more.

Not that she could admit any of that to Deacon, so instead she said, "Perhaps this shared custody thing was a bad idea."

"You don't have to worry about me jumping your bones, Sierra. I can control my urges."

"Maybe I'm worried that I can't control mine."

Okay, apparently she *could* admit it to Deacon— though the flare of heat in his eyes warned her it might not have been wise to do so.

"I promise not to fight you off," he told her.

"I'm sorry. I shouldn't have said that."

"Because you don't want me?" he asked, almost challenging her to backtrack now. To lie.

"Because nothing can happen between us," she said, sincerely regretful. "Because… I've been advised to abstain from sex until after the baby is born."

His gaze immediately sharpened. "Is everything okay—with you and your pregnancy?"

"I'm fine. The baby's fine. It's just…complicated."

He considered her response for a moment before he nodded. "Then I guess we'll have to suffer together."

Chapter Fifteen

"Isn't that the new ADA at the table by the window?" Regan asked, when Deacon lowered himself into the empty seat across from her at The Daily Grind.

He glanced in the direction she'd indicated, as if he hadn't seen Sierra the minute he walked through the door. As if he hadn't noticed that she was wearing the cranberry jacket again—this time over a black turtleneck sweater with black pants, having adjusted her wardrobe to the northern winter. Or that she'd done something a little bit different with her hair today, so it had that sexy, slightly tousled look, as if she'd just rolled out of bed—inspiring a man to fantasize about taking her back there again.

"Deacon?"

His sister-in-law's prompt drew his attention back to her table. "Yeah, that's Sierra."

"I didn't get an introduction at your birthday party,

but I can see why you're smitten," Regan said. "She's gorgeous."

He frowned. "Who said I was smitten?"

"Your brother."

"I don't know why he'd say something like that."

"Because he saw the two of you facing off in court last week."

"When? I didn't see him."

Her smile was smug. "Exactly. So why did you bring your coffee over here to sit with me instead of taking it over there?"

"Because I didn't want to hurt your feelings."

"Nice try," she said. "Now try the truth."

"It's complicated," he hedged.

"Isn't it always?" Regan said, not unsympathetically.

He intended to leave it at that. But his brother's wife was also his friend—and one he'd found himself confiding in frequently over the years.

"Do you remember the day that I drove you to your doctor's appointment?" he asked her now.

"As if I could ever forget it." She sipped her latte. "It was the day we found out I was pregnant with twins— again."

"Well, as we were entering the clinic, another woman was exiting."

"I'd guess a fair number of women are in and out of that clinic on any given day," she remarked dryly.

"I'm sure you're right," he agreed. "But this particular woman was Sierra."

"Oh." Then, *"Oh."*

He nodded.

"I'm beginning to understand the complication," Regan said.

He nodded again.

"Where does the baby's father fit into the picture?"

Deacon wasn't entirely sure. It seemed to him that Sierra had been deliberately cryptic about the details of her pregnancy, but there had been one point about which she was clear. "She assured me that they don't have any kind of romantic relationship."

"Okay, then—what's the problem? Is it that you don't want to be a dad to another man's kid?"

"I don't want to be a dad—period."

The blunt assessment made his sister-in-law frown. "Why not?"

"Isn't it obvious?" he challenged.

"Not to me."

"Maybe because you never knew my dad."

"You're right. I didn't know him," she said. "But I know that he was an abusive alcoholic, and I'm sorry that you had to grow up with that.

"I also know that the absence of a positive role model can make parenting a challenge. But your brother was raised in the same house, and I can't imagine a better father to our daughters than him."

"He is an amazing dad. But Connor is only my half brother," he reminded her. "He doesn't carry the burden of Dwayne Parrish's DNA."

Regan seemed to consider this as she took another sip of her drink. "That's true," she finally acknowledged. "Instead, he carries the burden of never having known his father. Of not even knowing who his father is. Half of your brother's DNA is a question mark. His dad could be a schoolteacher or a serial killer—he doesn't know and he has to live with the not knowing."

"I never looked at it from that perspective," Deacon admitted, duly chastened by his sister-in-law's words.

"I'm not trying to make you feel bad," Regan said,

in a gentler tone. "I'm trying to make you see that biology is only a small part of the equation. What matters more—a lot more—is how you feel about both the mother and her child.

"If you really like Sierra, and it seems obvious that you do, then you shouldn't let the fact that she's going to have a baby scare you away."

"You don't think I should be concerned about the possibility that I might turn out like him?"

"Your past isn't nearly as important as your present," she insisted.

"Do you really believe that?"

"Absolutely."

"You never had any qualms about me babysitting your girls?"

"Never," she replied without hesitation. "Because you are the best—and their undisputed favorite—uncle."

"I'm not sure I deserve that kind of praise."

"You didn't even raise your voice when they painted your shoes."

"My new Cole Haan loafers," Deacon clarified. "And I think I was too stunned to speak."

"But when you did, you commented on their creative use of color."

He sighed. "They were so proud of their handiwork. I knew that if I got mad, they'd be crushed."

Regan smiled and touched a hand to his arm. "And that is why I have no doubt you'll be an amazing dad when the time comes."

It was Friday night, and though dinner wasn't long past, Sierra was rummaging through her cupboards.

"What are you looking for?" Deacon asked her.

"Salt and vinegar potato chips." She closed one door,

opened another. "I'm sure I bought some when I was shopping last weekend."

"I saw an empty bag in the trash can in the garage when I dropped Remy's evening deposit in there."

She sighed. "I guess I finished them."

"Do you want me to pop over to the convenience store to pick up another bag?" he offered.

She hesitated, just long enough to let him know that she wanted to say *yes*, before she shook her head *no*. "I've got some fruit in the fridge. I can have an apple or a pear.

"I've got grapes, too," she discovered, when she opened the refrigerator to examine the contents. "Do you want some grapes?"

"Grapes are an after-school snack for a ten-year-old, not a game-watching snack for grown-ups," he protested.

"I could make popcorn," she said.

"In an air popper with no added butter?" he guessed.

"It's healthy."

"I think I'd rather have the grapes."

"I'll make a fruit tray," she decided.

He glanced at the time displayed on the stove. "There's at least twenty minutes until puck drop—I'm going to go out to get some real snacks."

She should have objected—not to the snacks but to his plan to come back to watch the game. She felt a little guilty that he'd been spending so much of his time with her, but she didn't say anything, because that tiny bit of guilt was greatly outweighed by the pleasure of his company.

He returned from the store with the coveted salt and vinegar potato chips, a bag of white cheddar popcorn and a veggie tray.

"You dissed my suggestion of fruit, but you came back with veggies," she noted.

"The veggies aren't for me—they're for the baby," he told her.

"And the popcorn?" she prompted.

"You want some popcorn?"

"If you don't mind sharing."

He emptied the bag into a big bowl, and they sat close together on the sofa, watching the game and sharing the snack. But when there was a stoppage in play, she found herself asking, "Wouldn't you rather be watching the game at Diggers', where you could flirt with the pretty servers?"

"If I wanted to be at Diggers', I'd be at Diggers'," he told her, turning his attention back to the screen when the puck dropped again.

"You should want to be at Diggers'," she said. "It isn't normal for a young, single guy to spend his Friday nights hanging out with a pregnant friend."

Deacon slid her a look. "Are you going to talk through the whole game?"

"Maybe." She considered for a brief moment then revised her response. "Probably."

"Well, I guess that's proof we've come a long way from the early days when I could barely get you to say two words to me."

"I didn't like you at first," she admitted.

"Yeah, you did." He winked. "But you didn't want to like me."

She rolled her eyes. "And that's one of the reasons— because you're entirely too cocky for your own good."

"And yet here we are."

"Seriously, you're wasting your time with me," she told him, even as she leaned back against his shoulder.

Remy, not wanting to miss out on the cuddles, put his front paws up on the edge of the sofa cushion. Deacon scooped the little dog up with one hand and deposited him in Sierra's lap.

"That's not how I see it," he said, giving the Chihuahua a gentle scratch beneath his chin. "But even if I am, it's my time to waste."

A body check against the boards sent both players crashing to the ice.

Sierra turned her face into Deacon's shirt, her hormones stirring anew as she breathed in his familiar, masculine scent. She tamped down on her hormones and reminded herself that she was trying to be as good a friend to Deacon as he'd been to her.

"Do you know Madison Russell?" she asked, forcing herself to stop sniffing him and resume their conversation.

"Judge Wilkerson's clerk?" he guessed.

Sierra nodded as she stroked Remy's soft fur. "Who apparently has a major crush on you."

Deacon frowned. "She's barely twenty years old."

"Twenty-two," she told him.

"Still."

"I was in the judge's chambers to get an order signed and overheard Madison talking about going to Sparkle—that new dance club in Elko—with some friends tonight."

"And you're telling me this…why?" he asked, sounding genuinely baffled.

"Because I thought you might want to go."

"Are you saying that *you* want to go?"

She huffed out a breath. Obviously she was going to have to spell it out for him. "No, I thought you might want to go *because Madison is going to be there.*"

He shook his head. "I've outgrown the club scene."

"You're twenty-eight years old," she pointed out.

"My mother always said that I was an old soul."

It was an offhand remark that served the dual purposes of distracting her from the original topic and also providing an opportunity to learn a little about the family he was usually reluctant to discuss.

"You don't talk about your mom very much," she noted, her tone deliberately casual.

"No," he agreed.

She waited for him to expand on that single word, but he remained tight-lipped, focused on the game.

"Can you tell me about her?" she prompted, after another minute had passed, the silence broken only by the play-by-play on the television.

"My mom was a good person who made some bad choices, and the people in this town never let her forget it," he finally said.

"Does she still live in Haven?"

He shook his head. "She died ten days after my high school graduation. Brain tumor."

She touched a hand to his arm. "I'm sorry."

"Yeah, it sucked," he agreed. "But it was a long time ago."

Still, it was obvious the loss had left a mark, as she knew only too well the loss of a parent could do.

It was something else they had in common.

"You don't talk about your dad much, either," she remarked.

A muscle in his jaw flexed, the only hint of any kind of emotional reaction, before he deliberately relaxed it.

"He was one of my mom's particularly regrettable choices," Deacon said, his tone flat. "He took off when I was eight. I haven't seen or heard from him since, and I definitely don't miss him."

"I lost both of my parents, too," Sierra told him, shifting the focus of their conversation away from his family in an effort to ease some of his obvious tension.

He turned so that he was sitting almost sideways, facing her. "I didn't know that."

She shrugged. "It's not something I like to talk about—mostly because...it was my fault."

She felt the unexpected burn of tears behind her eyes.

After more than fifteen years, she should have been able to talk about her mom and dad without being flooded by the emotions that had overwhelmed her fourteen-year-old self, but apparently not. Or maybe it was that this was serious confession time. Because she'd never told anyone about the guilt that she'd carried in her heart since that day—not even Nick.

But she suspected that her brother knew. Because he knew the details of the tragic accident that had taken their parents' lives. And yet, he'd never blamed her— even though she knew that he should.

"Why would you think it was your fault?" Deacon asked.

"Because they were on their way to watch me play basketball." Remy, as if sensing her distress, nudged at the hands folded in her lap. She untwisted her fingers to stroke his soft fur. "My parents were both lawyers. Both very busy and very successful, and while I appreciated that their work gave us a comfortable lifestyle, I sometimes resented their preoccupation with their careers.

"Anyway, I was playing in a big tournament hosted by one of the local high schools—a showcase of future varsity talent. Our team was playing well, and I'd scored double-digit points in each of the three previous games. But my parents were working a big case and hadn't managed to make it to any of them, so I had a bit of a hissy fit, and they promised to be there for the championship.

"They never showed, but I was more angry than worried, certain they'd just decided my game wasn't as important as whatever work they were doing. It was only after, when we were getting onto the bus to go back to school, that one of the tournament officials tracked down my coach to tell her the news—that their car had been hit head-on by a stolen vehicle being chased by police. They were both killed."

According to the police report, her mom had died instantly. Her dad had been rushed to the hospital with life-threatening injuries that he'd succumbed to three days later.

"A horrible accident," Deacon murmured sympathetically. "But an accident. You're not responsible for what happened, Sierra."

"I'm the reason they were on that road at that time. If I hadn't asked them to come to my game, they would have been safe at the courthouse, miles away."

"Or maybe the police chase would have happened on a different route at a different time...but with the same result."

"You're suggesting destiny killed my parents?"

"I'm saying you can't know. And you need to stop blaming yourself."

"I miss them." Her confession was an anguished whisper.

He pulled her into his arms. She didn't resist.

"It's okay to miss them," he told her gently. "And it's important to hold on to all the good memories. But you've got to let go of all the other stuff so that you can live your own life."

"Is that what you've done?"

He hesitated before saying, "I'm working on it."

She snuggled into him then, wanting to give back some of the comfort he'd given to her, and drifted off to sleep listening to the beat of his heart.

Chapter Sixteen

Sierra had always been an avid reader, and though her chosen profession required almost constant reviewing of reports and briefs and case law, she still enjoyed disengaging from work and losing herself in a good story when she could get her hands on one. Boxes of books had gone into storage when she'd moved out of the apartment she'd shared with Eric, but she hadn't seen any point in carting them to Haven when she would only be here for a few months. And since she didn't want to add to the quantity already in storage, she decided to put her name on the waiting list at the local library to get her hands on a copy of the latest Quinn Ellison title.

Her pickup notification came on Friday, so after Remy's morning walk on Saturday, she decided to pop over to the library. She'd visited the community center a few weeks earlier to get a library card and sign up for her prenatal yoga class, and the parking lot had been mostly empty then. Of course, it had been the middle of the day in the middle of the week, and today was Saturday—apparently a popular day for residents to visit the community center, as the parking lot was nearly full.

A sign on the library door advertised a reading of *The Intergalactic Adventures of Cosmic Cat—Vol. 29* by renowned children's author Anderson Hawley. No doubt the reason the library was so busy today.

She picked up her book from the Holds shelf, then followed the chorus of giggles to the back of the room where a group of about twenty kids, ranging in age from two to ten, were sitting in a semicircle facing the author.

There seemed to be a pretty even split between girls and boys in the audience, though most of the adults were moms with only a couple of dads—and Deacon Parrish.

Well, wasn't that a surprise?

She ducked back into the stacks to peer out between the rows of books so she wouldn't be caught staring. He was cross-legged on the floor, with one little girl on his lap and a second beside him.

Apparently Uncle Deacon had been recruited to take his nieces to story time. And maybe the sexy lawyer, with his broad shoulders and seductive smile, should have looked out of place there, but he didn't. In fact, he appeared to be completely at ease surrounded by kids and every bit as absorbed by the story as they were.

She didn't know if it was Anderson Hawley's voice or the silly antics of the titular character, but she was quickly mesmerized—and remembered, with a touch of melancholy, attending story time at the local library with her mom during the happy years of her childhood.

A brief question and answer period followed the reading, and Sierra found herself lingering for that, too. It was only when the crowd began to disperse that she realized she'd missed her window to escape undetected, because suddenly Deacon was standing in front of her.

He glanced at the cover of the book she held against her chest.

"That's a good one," he told her.

"You've read it already?"

He nodded. "I preordered it for my Kindle, so it downloaded automatically at midnight the day of release."

"I have a Kindle," she admitted. "But I prefer to hold a book in my hands."

"I've heard that's common for people over thirty," he said.

She narrowed her gaze on him.

He grinned, unrepentant.

"I wike to read, too," the little girl in the pink sweater chimed in.

"Me, too," her purple-clad sister said, nodding her head with so much enthusiasm her pigtails bounced up and down.

"'Cept we can't get books today cuz we fo-got our libray cards."

"So we're gonna get ice cweam instead."

"I wanna donut!"

"Can we have ice cweam an' a donut?"

"No," Deacon said firmly.

His denial was met with identical twin pouts and pleading eyes.

"Piper," he told Sierra, gesturing to the twin in pink. "And Poppy," he said, identifying her sister.

They were cute names for cute kids who looked close to starting a mutiny.

"I should let you be on your way," Sierra said. "You've obviously got your hands full."

"And that's without the sugar high that will inevitably follow the ice cream I already promised them," he acknowledged.

"So how did you end up at story time today?"

"My brother had to work and my sister-in-law wasn't feeling well."

"Mommy was thwowin' up," Piper interjected.

"It was gwoss," Poppy said gleefully.

"She's not really sick," Deacon said. "Just pregnant."

"Ah, the joys of morning sickness."

"'Cept it wasn' mo'nin'," Poppy said.

Her sister's gaze narrowed on Sierra. "You're the wady who wiked our snowman."

"I am," she confirmed. "My name's Sierra."

"Are you Unca Dunca's goo-fwend?" Poppy asked.

"No," Sierra responded, refusing to look at the man in question. "Just his friend."

"But if you're a goo and his fwend, that means you're his goo-fwend."

Deacon smirked. "You can't argue with the logic of an almost-four-year-old."

"Unca Dunca's got a goo-fwend," Piper chanted in a singsong voice.

"Unca Dunca's got a goo-fwend," Poppy echoed.

"Unca Dunca?" Sierra said, her brows raised.

His smile faded. "They struggled to say Deacon when they first started to talk, and Unca Dunca seems to have stuck."

"It's cute," she decided.

"I'm sorry." He cupped a hand around his ear. "Did you just say that I'm cute?"

She rolled her eyes. "I said *the name* was cute."

"So you don't think *I'm* cute?" he pressed.

"That's not the first word that comes to mind when I think of you," she said.

"But you do think of me?"

Way more often than she should. Not that she would give him the satisfaction of acknowledging that truth.

"Annoying is probably the first," she said, ignoring his question. "Or maybe arrogant."

He just grinned. "I'm waiting to see where *charming* and *sexy* fall on the list."

"Did I mention *cocky*?"

"I think that falls under the same umbrella as *arrogant*," he told her.

"I think it warrants its own mention," she countered.

"How about generous?" he suggested. "Which I'll prove by buying you a cone if you want to come across the street for ice cream with us."

"One scoop or two?"

"As many as you want," he said.

"I want two," Piper said.

"Fwee," Poppy said, holding up three fingers.

"You guys get kiddie cones," Deacon told them.

Sierra had to fight the smile that tugged at her lips in response to their immediately crestfallen expressions.

"What do you say?" Deacon prompted.

"As much as I'd love a double scoop of rocky road, I need to get home to Remy."

"Never let it be said that I don't know how to take a hint," Deacon said, offering the pint-size container to Sierra when she opened the door for him a few hours later.

"It wasn't a hint," she protested, though her gaze seemed to be transfixed by the Scoops logo.

"Then you don't want this?" He started to draw the container back.

"Of course I want it," she said, practically snatching the ice cream out of his hand. "Thank you."

"Note to self—do not get between Sierra Hart and rocky road."

"It's my all-time favorite," she told him.

"I didn't forget you," he said, offering a treat to the dog, who was looking up at him expectantly.

Remy scampered off with his dog biscuit.

"You told me a long time ago that dogs like you," she noted. "You didn't tell me it was because you carried treats in your pocket."

"I only started carrying the treats for Remy."

"So you say," she retorted teasingly.

He followed her into the kitchen, where she put her ice cream in the freezer.

"You should know that Piper and Poppy ran into the house announcing to their mom that Uncle Deacon has a girlfriend," he told her.

"Don't you mean 'Unca Dunca has a goo-fwen'?"

"Either way, I just wanted you to be prepared for the rumors to start flying around town."

"I'm not worried that courthouse staff might overhear a couple of almost-four-year-olds chanting on the day care playground," she said. "As long as you understand that we're friends and why we can't be anything more than that."

"Actually, I'm not sure I do," he admitted.

"Have you forgotten that I'm pregnant?"

"Of course not," he assured her. "I also haven't forgotten your assurance that you don't have any lingering romantic feelings for the baby's father."

"Trust me—I *never* had any romantic feelings for him."

"And yet," he said, with a pointed glance at the very slight curve of her belly.

"A long story," Sierra said. "And not one I'm ready to share."

"How about popcorn?" he said. "Would you share some of that?"

"You always complain when I make popcorn because I don't put butter on it."

"I was thinking about real movie theater popcorn. At the movies. Have you been to Mann's Theater yet?"

She shook her head.

"*Thor: Love and Thunder* is showing in half an hour."

"I saw that in Las Vegas. Last summer."

"I've seen it, too," he told her. "Not in town, obviously, because Mann's is a second-run theater, but I enjoyed it enough to want to see it on the big screen again."

"It was a good movie." She felt her lips curve as she recalled one scene in particular where Thor was literally unrobed by Zeus.

"You're thinking about Chris Hemsworth's naked butt, aren't you?" Deacon's tone was accusing.

She felt heat climb into her cheeks. "I am not."

"You are, too."

"I was thinking about *Thor's* naked butt."

He shook his head despairingly. "Is that a *yes* or *no* on the movie?"

"It's a *yes*, as long as we're clear that this is just a movie and not a date."

"Just a movie," he confirmed.

Yet despite their mutual agreement that it wasn't a date, it felt an awful lot like a date. Especially when the lights went down in the theater and her fingers brushed against his when they both reached into the popcorn bucket at the same time. And when he drove her home afterward and walked her to the door, excited butterflies danced in her stomach in anticipation of the possibility that he might kiss her.

But he didn't.

Instead, she went inside alone, secretly wishing for something that she knew could never be.

The last time Deacon had overnight guests had been when Piper and Poppy stayed with him.

This weekend, instead of almost-four-year-old twins, he was hanging out with an almost-four-pound dog. All because Sierra had read some article about how moving was a traumatic experience for a dog, and she wanted Remy to get used to not only spending time with Deacon but also at his house.

Sierra had opted out of their usual Friday night dinner, ostensibly so that he could maximize his time with Remy. But when he picked up the dog, he couldn't help but notice that she looked a little pale, and she admitted that she'd been battling a headache all day.

So Deacon had picked up a pizza and watched TV with Remy beside him. And ignored Sierra's warning against giving the dog "people food"—to his own detriment. About thirty minutes after he'd peeled a couple of slices of sausage off the pizza for the dog, he suffered the consequences of the animal's shockingly pungent flatulence.

Saturday, having learned his lesson the hard way, he gave Remy only his own food and approved treats.

Sunday, Deacon was looking over the schedule for the upcoming week when there was a knock on the door.

"I brought my tools," Connor said, holding up the metal box he carried.

"Thank you?" Deacon said cautiously.

"You said you wanted a hand installing the new cabinet in your powder room."

"I didn't say I wanted to do it today."

"I know," his brother admitted. "But Regan was taking the twins to her parents' house for a visit this afternoon and staying for dinner—and I needed an excuse to beg off."

"You lied to your wife to get out of spending time with her family?"

"It's true that I promised to help you," Connor pointed out in his defense.

"And when Regan comes over to see the new cabinet?"

"Damn," his brother muttered. "She will, too, won't she?"

"Of course she will."

"So I'll tell her that you decided you didn't want to do it today."

"And that's why you were able to make it to Miners' Pass for dinner after all," Deacon said, naming the street where Haven's wealthiest families all lived.

"Alright," Connor agreed reluctantly. "I'll go for dinner because Celeste's cooking is almost good enough to make me forget that Regan's mother will never believe I am."

"Regan doesn't care what she thinks, so why should you?"

"You're right, I shouldn't."

But Deacon suspected that growing up the way they'd grown up meant they'd always be trying to prove themselves.

"Anyway." Connor glanced at his watch. "I've still got a few hours before dinner."

Deacon opened the door to let his brother in.

"Do you have coffee on?"

"No, but I can remedy that in about two minutes."

Connor followed him to the kitchen.

"When did you get a dog?" he asked, eyeing the tiny creature snoring on his pillow in the corner. "Assuming that is a dog."

"He is," Deacon said. "But he's not mine."

Connor looked pointedly from the dog to the personalized mat with the bowls for food and water and then the bin of toys, his brows raised.

"Okay, he's mine this weekend," Deacon admitted.

"You're dog-sitting?"

"Actually, it's more like a joint custody arrangement."

"Really?" Connor sounded amused.

"He'll go back to Sierra tomorrow."

"You're sharing custody of a dog with the new ADA?"

"Temporary ADA," Deacon felt compelled to remind his brother—as Sierra was always quick to remind him. "Which is the reason for this arrangement."

"I'm going to need you to fill in some more blanks," Connor said.

"I was with Sierra when she found the dog outside of Diggers' one night. I wanted to take him to the shelter, but she—against my advice—decided to take him home. Then she realized that she was getting attached to a dog that she couldn't take back to Vegas with her because she's going to be staying with her brother and sister-in-law, who's allergic to dogs, so she asked me if I'd take him when she left."

"And instead of reminding her that the shelter would find him a permanent home, you decided that she'd provided you with the perfect opportunity to spend more time hanging out with her."

It was an uncannily accurate assessment of his thought processes.

"Anyway, he's with Sierra most of the time, but she wants him to spend a few nights here every now and then, to ensure it's a familiar place to him when he comes to live here."

"You're not going to take him to the shelter when she goes back to Vegas?"

"Of course not," he immediately replied, insulted that his brother would even suggest such a thing.

"Because you've fallen as hard for this ridiculous little dog as you have for Sierra," Connor noted with a grin.

Deacon didn't respond, because he wasn't ready to acknowledge that his brother was absolutely right.

Chapter Seventeen

After Connor had gone, Deacon filled Remy's water bowl and measured out his dinner.

The dog was happily chowing down when Deacon's cell phone chimed with a text message.

He glanced at the screen.

Any chance you can keep Remy another day or two?

He immediately replied to Sierra's request:

Of course. What's up?

I think I've got a touch of the flu.

He knew it was making the rounds. In the past week alone, the trial coordinator, a court reporter and two judges had been out with it. While each had apparently bounced back from the bug within a couple of days, none of them was (as far as he knew) pregnant. And he couldn't help but worry that Sierra was on her own and obviously feeling unwell.

What do you need? Ginger ale? Chicken soup?

Just to stay in bed and not have to worry about the dog.

Then that's what you should do. Remy and I were planning a Marvel movie marathon tonight, anyway.

She responded to that with a smiley face.

Seriously, how long have you been sick?

It started in the middle of the night Friday.

Fever? Nausea? Vomiting?

Yes.

Have you eaten anything?

I'm not hungry.

While he didn't get sick often, Deacon had some experience with the flu, so he could understand that food wasn't appealing when battling nausea. Rest, which Sierra seemed to be getting, was crucial, and so was staying hydrated.

Was she drinking plenty of fluids?

Instead of sending another text message to ask that question, he called to the dog.

"Come on, Remy."

The Chihuahua lifted his head but, obviously tuckered out after chasing the ball Connor had kept tossing for him, made no move to get off his pillow.

"We're going to see Sierra."

Remy responded to her name with a happy yip and scrambled to his feet.

At any other time, Deacon would have walked over to her house. But he wanted to make a couple of stops first, so he put Remy's harness on him and buckled him into the passenger seat of his truck. Half an hour later, he texted from her driveway to let Sierra know he was using his key to let himself in.

She didn't reply to the message.

Once inside, he unclipped the dog's leash. Remy immediately went searching for Sierra—checking the living room, then the dining room and kitchen before making his way to the stairs. He sat there at the bottom and looked at Deacon expectantly, obviously waiting for him to carry him up to the bedroom, as Sierra always did.

Deacon hadn't considered that she might be in bed. Yeah, she'd said she wanted to sleep, but he'd assumed she'd be flaked out on the sofa in the living room with the TV on—as he tended to do when he wasn't feeling well.

Walking into her house with a key that she'd given him was one thing, venturing into her bedroom was another. But he set the bags he carried on the counter in the kitchen, then picked up the dog and made his way up the stairs.

"Sierra? Are you up here?"

She didn't respond, so he followed the sound of a television down the hall, pausing in the doorway of a room dimly lit by the screen. She was huddled under a mountain of blankets, and he tapped his knuckles on the open door before crossing the threshold.

"Sierra?" he said again.

"Mmm."

He approached cautiously, noting the half-full glass of water on her bedside table and bottle of Tylenol beside it.

The covers were tucked right up under her chin, and her hair was tangled around her face. He gently brushed the hair aside and touched the back of his hand to her forehead.

He wasn't really sure what he was checking for, but his mom had always done the same thing when he said he wasn't feeling well. If Sierra had been a little warm, he probably wouldn't have known it, but her skin was noticeably hot and clammy.

Her eyelashes fluttered, then parted.

"Deacon? What are you doing here?"

"I brought you soup," he said.

"Oh." She tried to smile, but the effort wasn't very successful. "That was sweet, but I'm really not hungry."

"You need to eat something."

Her eyes drifted shut again.

"When do you last take Tylenol?"

"Five o'clock."

The display on the clock on her bedside table read 6:10 p.m., so just over an hour ago.

He found a facecloth in the linen tower in the bathroom adjacent to her bedroom, moistened it with cold water and returned to the bedroom to lay it across her forehead.

"Mmm...that feels good."

"I've imagined you saying those exact words when I had you in bed, but not under these circumstances."

She managed a weak smile.

"Do you want to come downstairs to eat or do you want me to bring the soup up to you?"

"I'm really not hungry."

"Not eating wasn't one of the options."

She exhaled a weary sigh. "You can bring it up, please."

He couldn't find a serving tray, so he improvised, arranging the bowl of soup, napkin, spoon, a sleeve of saltine crackers and a glass of ginger ale on a baking sheet.

By the time he returned to her bedroom with the food, she'd managed to sit up in bed, the pillows propped up behind her back.

"I should have gone downstairs so you didn't have to come back into my germ-filled room," she protested weakly. "Now you're going to get sick."

"Doubtful. But if I do, you can return the favor and play nurse to me. Short skirt optional."

"Pretend I'm rolling my eyes at you," she said. "Because I'm too tired to actually exert the effort."

"Rolling eyes noted," he assured her.

She nibbled on a couple of crackers and managed half a dozen spoonfuls of soup before she decided that she was done.

He took the baking sheet/tray from her and set it on the dresser, leaving her with the glass of ginger ale.

"What are you doing?" she asked, when he began opening and closing drawers.

"Looking for some clothes for you."

"I don't need to get dressed—I'm not going anywhere."

"You're going to the hospital."

"It's the flu, Deacon. If everyone who got the flu ran to the hospital, it would be overflowing with sick people."

"If you don't think you need to see a doctor—"

"I don't," she interjected.

"—then think about the baby."

Her hand immediately went to the barely noticeable curve of her belly and her brow furrowed.

"Okay," she finally relented. "I'll go to the hospital."

He pulled out a sweater he was sure he'd seen her wear before and a pair of stretchy leggings, holding them up for her perusal. "Do these work?"

"Sure."

He deposited them on the foot of the bed.

"I'm going to need more than that," she told him. "I'm not in the habit of leaving the house commando."

Right. She needed underwear.

"Top drawer of the other dresser," she told him.

He pulled open the drawer and found himself staring at a colorful selection of bras and panties. He gritted his teeth and plunged a hand into the sea of lace and silk, grabbing the first items he touched and tossing them onto the bed with the other garments.

"Ordinarily I'd protest that those don't match, but right now I don't really care," she admitted.

"The doctor won't care, either," he told her, shoving the drawer closed.

And right now, he was trying really hard not to picture his (pregnant and sick) friend in sexy underwear—a not entirely successful effort.

"Do you need a hand getting dressed?"

He held his breath, torn between wanting her to say *yes* and hoping she'd say *no*.

"I think I can manage."

"How about undressed? I'm pretty good at that part."

"I have no doubt, but no, thank you."

He took it as a good sign that she'd been able to respond to his teasing and carried the remains of her meal downstairs so that she would have some privacy to dress.

When they got to the hospital, he pulled into a drop-off zone and left his hazards flashing while he ran inside to get a wheelchair, then he wheeled Sierra into the ER before going to park his vehicle. By the time he got back, she'd checked in at the desk and was in triage.

"What brings you in today?" the nurse asked in a bored voice.

"I think I have the flu."

"You and a lot of other people," the nurse responded.

"How many of those other people are pregnant?" Deacon asked.

That question seemed to generate at least a modicum of concern from the health-care worker. "How far along?"

"Eighteen weeks," the expectant mother said.

The nurse input that information. "Your doctor's name?"

"Camila Amaro."

"Lucky for you, she's on call tonight."

"I'd feel a lot luckier if I hadn't got the flu," Sierra joked weakly.

A few minutes later, they were ushered into an exam room by a nurse who checked the patient's vitals, drew some blood and sent her into the bathroom with a specimen cup. And a few more minutes after that, when she'd transferred from the wheelchair to the bed, the doctor came in.

"Couldn't wait until your next appointment to see me?" the white-coated specialist teased.

"I was willing to wait," Sierra told her. "Deacon didn't give me a choice."

The doctor shifted her gaze to him. "You're Deacon?"

He nodded.

"Friend or family?"

"Friend."

"I'm Camila Amaro," she said, introducing herself before turning her attention to the chart on which the nurse had recorded Sierra's vitals.

"We're going to get you hooked up to an IV, and then we'll take you down to perform a quick scan to check on the baby, okay?" Dr. Amaro said, speaking to Sierra now.

"Okay," she agreed.

"I don't think there's any reason to be concerned about the little guy, but an ultrasound will let us be sure."

The doctor had barely finished speaking when the nurse returned with the IV drip. Dr. Amaro went ahead to get set up for the ultrasound and told Sierra an orderly would be there in a few minutes to transport her to diagnostic imaging.

"They run an efficient operation here," Deacon noted.

"We do our best," the nurse told him. Then to Sierra she said, "Your friend can go with you to your ultrasound, if you want."

Sierra looked at Deacon. "What do you think?"

"Whatever you want."

"I want you to come…unless this is weird for you."

It definitely felt weird, but his discomfort was greatly outweighed by his desire to be there for her.

"Then I'll go with you," he said.

So he followed along as the orderly steered the bed through the halls and into an elevator, delivering her promptly to the diagnostic imaging department where Dr. Amaro was waiting.

Sierra didn't have to change into a gown. Instead, she was instructed to push her leggings down to her hips and lift her sweater. The doctor then squirted gel on her belly and used some kind of wand to spread it around. As she did, an image appeared on the computer screen.

Sierra smiled. "There he is."

"He?" Deacon echoed.

She nodded. "It's a boy."

He squinted at the screen. "How can you tell?"

She managed a soft chuckle. "I can't tell, but Dr. Amaro identified all the relevant parts during my last scan."

"It's a boy," the doctor confirmed.

Deacon remembered seeing an ultrasound picture of Piper and Poppy at about eight weeks, which had looked like nothing more to him than a couple of whitish blobs on a dark background. At eighteen weeks, Sierra's baby actually looked like a baby. And it was fascinating to him to not only see the baby moving but also hear the rhythmic beat of his heart.

"Heart rate is 144 beats per minute," Dr. Amaro said.

"That seems fast," Deacon said, and immediately wished he'd kept his mouth shut.

"For you or I it would be," the doctor agreed, obviously unconcerned. "For an eighteen-week fetus, it's right in the middle of the normal range."

"That's good then, right?" Sierra asked.

"Very good," Dr. Amaro said. "More good news—

your placenta is healthy and right where it should be, and your amniotic fluid level is good."

Sierra exhaled a quiet sigh of relief.

"All in all, the baby's doing just fine."

Sierra looked at Deacon. "I told you I didn't need to come to the hospital," she said, sounding tired and just a little bit smug.

"The baby's doing just fine," Dr. Amaro said again. "But your heart rate is a little high and your blood pressure is a little low, both signs of dehydration."

"Which is why I've got the IV, right?"

"Yes, but it's not an instant fix, so I'm going to keep you here overnight for observation."

"But—"

A pointed look from the doctor had Sierra cutting off her own protest.

"Instead of enumerating all the reasons you don't want to spend the night in the hospital—because none of those reasons is as important as your well-being and that of the baby—why don't you thank your friend for bringing you in?"

It wasn't really a request but a directive.

"Thank you, Deacon," Sierra dutifully intoned.

"You're welcome," he said, lest he be chastised by the doctor for not following her script.

"You can wait here while I finish the paperwork to get you admitted to a room," Dr. Amaro told her patient.

"Thank you," Sierra said again.

"Do you need me to bring anything back for you?" Deacon asked. "Pajamas? Toothbrush? An actual book because you don't like to read on a Kindle?"

"I'll be fine," she told him. Then to the doctor she said, "It's just one night, right?"

"At this point, I'm optimistic about your chances of

going home in the morning, but I'm not making any promises."

"If Sierra can go home tomorrow, what time should I be here to pick her up?" Deacon asked the doctor.

"You can't pick me up," Sierra protested. "You have a trial starting tomorrow."

"Jury selection is tomorrow," he said. "And I have complete faith in Brenna to handle that on her own."

"I start my rounds early," Dr. Amaro said. "If the IV does the trick, I should be signing Sierra's discharge papers by eight a.m."

"You don't need to come back tomorrow," Sierra said to him, continuing her protest when the doctor had gone. "I can get a cab or—"

"I'll be here at eight," he said, in a tone that brooked no argument.

"I appreciate everything you did today, but I'm not your responsibility, Deacon."

"Maybe not," he acknowledged, giving her hand a gentle squeeze. "But you are my friend."

She managed a wobbly smile. "Thank you for being my friend."

"Always," he said, and meant it.

Even if he suddenly found himself longing to be so much more.

Chapter Eighteen

The doctor did, indeed, start her rounds early. And by 8:00 a.m., Sierra was sitting in the passenger seat of Deacon's truck, on her way home.

She felt a little bit guilty that he'd driven all the way from Haven to Battle Mountain only to turn around and immediately drive her all the way back again, but he'd refused to even consider letting her make other arrangements. And when he pulled into her driveway, he didn't just walk her to the door but insisted on seeing her inside, settling her on the sofa where he'd already set up a pillow and blanket. Then he made her tea and toast, handed her the remote control for the television and kissed her on the top of the head before heading off to the courthouse with a pointed reminder that she was to call him if she needed anything.

She sat on the sofa, cradling the mug of tea in her hands, her heart overflowing with gratitude for everything he'd done.

Had anyone else ever taken care of her like this?

Her mom, obviously, when she'd been little. And maybe Nick. She remembered her brother blending frozen fruit into smoothies for her when she'd had her wisdom teeth removed—and having to spoon the thick liquid into her mouth, because the dentist had forbidden sucking through a straw, which he told her would put too much strain on the stitches.

But she couldn't recall anyone who wasn't related to her ever going to such lengths. Apparently Mr. Columbia Law was a lot more than a hotshot lawyer with a handsome face and sexy body, and she was immensely grateful that they'd found their way to being friends.

After she ate her toast (or at least half of it) and drank her tea, she decided to close her eyes and have a quick nap. When she woke up, three hours later, she was feeling much more rested and even strong enough to venture upstairs to change the sheets on her bed—only to discover that Deacon had taken care of that, too. He'd even put clean towels in the bathroom.

It was going to be a very lucky woman who managed to snag that man someday, she acknowledged. His willingness to take care of menial chores around the house was the least of it, and if she felt just a twinge of regret that she couldn't be that lucky woman, she was still grateful for his friendship.

She made her way back downstairs, ate the rest of her (now cold and hard) toast with another cup of tea, then fell asleep rewatching *Bridgerton* for the third time.

At the end of the day, Deacon stopped by to see how she was doing and to bring her some more soup. Minestrone. The day after that, he brought Remy to visit. And harvest vegetable soup. On the third day, she was standing at the stove when he arrived.

"What are you doing?" he asked.

"Making dinner."

"But… I brought you soup."

"Thank you," she said, not wanting to seem ungrateful. "But I'm sick of soup. I want real food."

"You should have told me that. I would have been happy to pick up whatever you wanted."

"I am capable of putting a meal together."

He came into the kitchen then and peered into the pan.

"Grilled cheese is real food?" he asked, sounding amused.

"Apparently I need to make a trip to the grocery store."

"Make a list," he said. "I'll pick up what you need."

"I need to take care of myself."

"You're just getting over the flu," he reminded her. "You need to be careful not to overdo it."

"I'm over the flu," she said. "In fact, I'm going back to the office tomorrow and would like to pick up my dog to bring him home after work, if that's okay."

"Our dog," he reminded her.

"Our dog," she agreed. "And I'm more grateful than I can express for everything you've done, but I'm really fine now."

"Okay," he agreed. Then, "Any chance one of those sandwiches is for me?"

"That's why there are two plates on the counter."

He got out two bowls to divvy up the chicken and rice soup he'd brought, and they ate it along with the sandwiches.

After they'd finished the meal—Sierra managed half a sandwich and most of her soup—they tidied up the kitchen together. Deacon wanted Sierra to sit and rest, but she reminded him that she'd been resting for nearly five days already.

When she straightened up after bending to close the dishwasher door, she sucked in a breath and pressed a hand to the side of her belly.

Deacon was immediately there. "Are you okay?"

"Yeah." She smiled to reassure him. "I think... I felt the baby move."

The worry on his face immediately eased.

"First time?" he guessed.

She nodded. "I've had these weird little flutters that I thought might be the baby, but this was different. This was a more distinct—oh." She smiled again. "A definite kick."

Then she took his hand and guided it to the same spot.

His eyes went wide, and she knew that he'd felt it, too.

"I guess you really do have a tiny human being in there."

"Seeing him on the ultrasound didn't convince you?"

"He looked like a baby, but that was still just an image on a screen. This is..."

She lifted her gaze when his words trailed off and suddenly realized that they were standing close, her hand on his hand on her belly.

Sierra knew that she should take a step back; put some distance between them. Instead, she stayed right where she was, her eyes locked with his.

"This is?" she prompted softly.

His response was barely more than a whisper, "Real."

It certainly felt real to Sierra.

Not just real but right.

She leaned in, breaching the scant distance that separated them, and tipped her head back to touch her lips to his.

* * *

She was kissing him.

Deacon's head was reeling over the fact even as her lips—so soft and sweet—moved against his. And while she might have taken him by surprise, he had no intention of letting this opportunity slip through his fingers. Though he knew there was at least one not-so-little reason that kissing Sierra was a bad idea—that being the slight (but growing) swell of her belly pressed against him—he didn't ever want to stop.

His tongue touched the seam of her lips, then slipped between when they parted for him. A soft hum of approval sounded low in her throat and she lifted her hands to his shoulders, holding on to him as the kiss went on and on.

As she'd been the one to start it, he let her be the one to end it. She did so far too soon for his liking, pulling her mouth away from his and dropping her head against his chest.

She exhaled a regretful sigh. "We can't do this."

"It seems to me that we can—and were."

She pulled out of his arms then and took a deliberate step back. "I'm sorry. I know I've been giving you mixed signals."

"You have," he agreed. "But I'm happy to forget all the earlier signals and get back to the kissing."

"Except that kissing is a slippery slope. And I'm not in any position to get involved in a personal relationship right now," she continued her explanation.

"It seems to me that we already have a personal relationship."

"And I'm grateful to you for your friendship."

"Friendship is always a good starting point," he agreed.

* * *

Sierra's boss wanted her to ease back into work, so he didn't assign her any court duty until a full week after she returned to the office following her bout with the flu. And her first assignment was First Appearance Court with Judge Graves. The overwhelming majority of cases were put over at First Appearance, which allowed the court to get through the docket quickly. Still, a two-page docket usually meant a mid-morning recess, but Judge Graves insisted on pushing through rather than take a break, and by the time court was finally adjourned, she was starving.

She'd lost three pounds when she was sick with the flu, but she'd gained them back fairly quickly—plus two more. Because now that her appetite had returned, she was eating regular healthy meals again—supplemented by more-than-occasional treats from Sweet Caroline's (the salted caramel brownie was her new favorite) and ice cream from Scoops (always rocky road).

As her colleagues filtered toward the exit at the back of the courtroom, Sierra found an emergency granola bar in the side pocket of her briefcase, tore off the wrapper and took a big bite.

"Sierra?"

She froze, a strange feeling—almost like dread—washing over her.

Could it be...

No, she couldn't imagine any circumstances that would have brought Eric Stikeman to Haven, Nevada.

But though she hadn't heard his voice in more than seven months and he'd only spoken a single word—her name—she knew it was him.

She chewed quickly and swallowed before glancing

over her shoulder to confirm that it was, indeed, her ex walking toward her.

He approached the prosecutor's table, a half smile on his lips. "Of all the courtrooms in all the towns," he mused.

"That's exactly what I was thinking," she said, discreetly brushing a crumb off her lapel. "What are you doing here?"

"A careless driving trial, if you can believe it."

"You came all the way from Las Vegas to argue a case in traffic court?"

"The defendant is the daughter of one of my biggest clients. I couldn't say *no*."

"I guess not," she agreed.

"What are you doing here?"

She tucked the remainder of her granola bar into her jacket pocket. "Working for the Haven district attorney."

"Do you prosecute traffic violations?"

"Not usually," she said. "Ron Harding handles most of those." She gathered up her files and stuffed them into her briefcase. "Well, good luck with your trial."

Eric took a step closer, ignoring the obvious cue that she was ready for this conversation to be over.

More than ready.

"I should have reached out to you, when I got back from—" he cleared his throat "—when I got back."

"What would have been the point?" she wondered aloud. "We'd both said everything we needed to say."

"Did I say I was sorry?"

"I think what you said was that you were sorry I didn't tell you that I'd decided to meet you in San Francisco after all."

"I know you were upset about what happened—and you have every reason to be," he hastened to assure her. "But it was a mistake—an error in judgment—and I am sorry."

"So noted." She pushed her chair back from the table and rose to her feet.

Eric sucked in a breath. "You're...pregnant?"

"Yep."

His Adam's apple bobbed a few times before he managed to speak again. "Jesus, Sierra—why didn't you tell me?"

At another time, she might have enjoyed seeing the unflappable attorney so obviously and completely flapped. But that time had passed seven months earlier when she'd caught Eric with his pants down and Aubrey on her knees.

"I didn't tell you, because it has nothing to do with you," she said coolly.

"Are you saying...the baby's not mine?"

"The baby is definitely not yours."

He exhaled an audible sigh. "Thank God."

"Don't hold back," she said dryly. "Tell me how you really feel."

He had the grace to look chagrined. "It's just that we never talked about having kids. And then, to see you now...pregnant...was a bit of a shock."

"Instead of thanking God, you should probably thank the condom manufacturer."

"Oh. Right." He attempted a smile, but it was gone before it had fully formed. "Well, if you're sure..."

"One hundred percent."

"Then I guess the only thing left to do is wish you luck."

"I don't need luck," she told him. "I'm going to be just fine."

"I have no doubt," he agreed. "And for what it's worth… I'm sorry that I screwed everything up."

She accepted his olive branch and offered one of her own. "I don't know how long your trial is expected to last, but if you have time while you're in town, you should try Jo's Pizza."

"Is it half as good as Grimaldi's?" he asked, naming what had been their favorite pizza place in Vegas.

"No," she told him. "It's better."

"Then I'm definitely going to have to check it out. Or maybe you and I could…" The question trailed off as she shook her head.

"No," she said again. "There's no way we're going to share a pizza and conversation as if you didn't screw around on me with one of my friends."

His cheeks flushed. "You have to know it didn't mean anything."

"That only makes it worse," she told him.

Turning toward the exit and discovering that Deacon was standing there, waiting for her, further compounded her humiliation.

"I thought you'd gone," she said.

He studied her carefully neutral expression for a minute before responding. "I was going to head back to the office, then I realized it was past lunchtime, so I thought I'd see if you wanted to grab a bite to eat."

"I definitely do," she agreed. "I'm starving."

"Jo's?" he suggested.

She narrowed her gaze.

"You mentioned last night that you'd been craving it," he reminded her.

He was right—she had mentioned it. Because she had been craving Jo's Pizza, and she wasn't going to let Eric's unexpected appearance in town deprive her of it.

Deacon did her the courtesy of waiting until the server had taken their order before broaching the subject she knew had to be at the forefront of his mind.

"So...that was your ex?"

She nodded.

"Obviously he's a lawyer, too."

"We both worked at Bane & Associates," she said. "I was in the criminal law division, Eric specialized in civil litigation."

Deacon smiled his thanks to the server when she delivered their drinks, then turned his attention back to Sierra, obviously waiting for her to continue.

"You really want to hear the whole sordid story?"

"I think you need to tell someone," he said. "I got the impression, during your brief exchange in the courtroom, that you'd been keeping some pretty intense emotions bottled up for a while."

"I guess I have," she admitted. "So I'll tell you—but please cut me off at any point if you get bored."

"You worked together at the same firm," he said, prompting her to pick up where she left off.

She nodded again. "Practicing law in a big-city firm can be a cutthroat business, and I didn't have a lot of close friends at Bane. Except for Aubrey. We worked a lot of cases together, which meant that we spent a lot of time together, and she was one of very few people who I confided in when I started dating Eric.

"Bane didn't have an explicit nonfraternization policy, but they discouraged professional colleagues from getting personally involved. And while my relationship with Eric wasn't a big secret, we were discreet.

"Anyway, after six months of dating, we moved in together. Actually, I gave up my apartment and moved in with him, which meant that when we broke up, I was the one who had to move out.

"But that was at the end. In the beginning, things were really good. We enjoyed spending time together—whether out with colleagues or friends or alone at home."

She paused when the server delivered their pizza to the table. Deacon transferred a slice from the tray to her plate before taking one for himself. Between bites of pizza, she continued to fill in the details for him.

"We'd been living together for almost a year when Eric was invited to present at a law conference in San Francisco. It was a huge honor, but he hesitated to accept because he didn't want to be away on our eighteen-month anniversary. He did ask me to go with him, but I already had a two-week trial on the books that conflicted with the conference dates.

"So I convinced him it was too great an opportunity to pass up, and he promised to put my name on the room registration in the hope that my trial would finish early and I could join him in San Francisco for a few days, at least.

"There were half a dozen associates from Bane who were at the conference, including Aubrey. She checked in with me every day, asking me about the trial, sharing information about the conference. And when my trial did, indeed, finish early, she encouraged me to book a flight to surprise Eric.

"'Think about how romantic it will be, to celebrate your anniversary in San Francisco,' she'd said. It did sound romantic, and I figured, after my big trial win, I deserved to steal a few days away."

She lifted her glass to her lips and swallowed a mouthful of icy water, hoping it would cool the heat of embarrassment that she could feel spreading through her body.

"I think I can guess what happened next," he said.

"I'm sure you can," she agreed. "The worst part of the whole thing is that I actually apologized. I interrupted my boyfriend in bed with my friend, and *I* said *sorry*."

It still stung to realize that not only had her supposed friend cheated with her boyfriend, but Aubrey had obviously set Sierra up to find them.

"Then I retreated to the lobby, determined to book an immediate flight back home, but I was shaking so much, I could hardly hold on to my phone. A few minutes later, Eric found me there, still shaking and crying, and tried to convince me to go back to his room so that we could talk. He actually thought I would go back to the room where I saw him…them…"

She blew out a breath. "Obviously I declined. And not very politely. Apparently I said a few words that you don't often hear in the lobby of a Fairmont hotel, and so Eric went to reception to get another room."

She managed a wry smile then. "All they had available was a deluxe balcony suite, but he handed over his credit card, and we went up to the suite to talk. Actually, he tried to convince me to understand that the scene I'd walked in on was really one of my own making, because I hadn't given him a heads-up that I was coming to San Francisco."

Deacon looked horrified. "He honestly said that?"

She nodded. "And expected me to take at least some responsibility for the situation so that we could forgive one another and move past the unfortunate indiscretion— all his words."

"Please tell me that you told him to go back to his own room and screw himself."

"Oh, I did. Several times."

Deacon wiped his fingers on a paper napkin, then folded it on top of his empty plate. "And he's really not the baby's father?"

"The San Francisco fiasco was last September. The baby is due August twenty-second. Obviously this baby isn't his."

"I guess that's good then," he said.

"It's very good," she agreed.

He handed his credit card to the server, who brought a take-out box for the leftover pizza. A few minutes later, they walked out of the restaurant together.

Sierra blinked at the bright sunshine that greeted them, her mood instantly lifted.

"I think I love northern Nevada in the spring," she said.

"There's something to appreciate about every season here," Deacon told her.

"Well, I'll still be here for the beginning of summer," she noted. "And maybe I'll come back to visit in the fall."

"Or...you could stay."

She looked at him then, her heart filled with regret. "Haven't we had this discussion already?"

"I know you think there isn't any reason to stay after your contract is up," he said, "but what if you had a reason? What if we got married?"

"There's no point in asking *what if*, because I'm not going to marry you. I sincerely appreciate the white knight routine," she said, because she did. "But I'm not a damsel in distress who needs to be rescued."

"I know you're not," he agreed. "In fact, you are one of the most amazingly capable women I've ever known.

But I grew up with a single mom, and I know the kind of struggles that she—"

"I'm not going to be a single mother, Deacon," she interjected.

"I don't understand," he admitted.

"My responsibilities with respect to the baby will be over as soon as he's born."

Deacon's brows drew together as he attempted to decipher the meaning of her words. "Are you telling me... are you giving your baby up for adoption?"

Sierra shook her head. "I'm telling you that he's not my baby."

Chapter Nineteen

"I don't understand," Deacon said again, still trying—unsuccessfully—to wrap his head around what she was saying.

"I'm not the baby's mom," Sierra told him. "I'm a gestational carrier."

Gestational carrier?

"Is that like...a surrogate?" he asked.

"Some people use the terms interchangeably," she acknowledged. "But a surrogate might allow her own egg to be fertilized while a gestational carrier does not."

"So you don't have any biological connection to the baby you're carrying?"

"Actually, this little guy—" she smiled as she laid her hands on the slight curve of her belly "—is my nephew. My brother and sister-in-law's baby."

"But...why?" he asked, equal parts baffled by the revelation and stunned by her selfless generosity.

"Because I can't imagine any couple who would be

better parents than my brother and sister-in-law. Because it totally sucks that Whitney had the option of carrying a baby taken away from her. And…"

"And?" he prompted.

"Because I owe my brother everything. Because he dropped out of college when our parents were killed to come home and take care of me. Because he put his life on hold so that I didn't end up in foster care."

"I don't know your brother," he admitted. "But I'm sure he would say that you don't owe him anything—that he did what he did because you're his sister."

"You're right," she agreed. "But he gave me so much, and I was glad to be able to do this one thing for him and his wife."

"It isn't just one thing," he pointed out. "It's nine months of your life."

"A short period of time to fulfill one of their life-long dreams."

His mind was still spinning, but one thing was clear. "You really are an incredible woman, Sierra."

"They're going to be incredible parents," she said. "Which you'd know if you ever met them."

"I hope I have the chance someday."

She smiled then. "As it turns out, they're coming to visit next weekend. Why don't you join us for a barbecue?"

"I think you might have a touch of OCD," Deacon remarked, as he watched Sierra move through the house, inspecting each room from top to bottom, straightening towels in the guest bath, wiping a fingerprint off a picture frame, fluffing the decorative pillows on the sofa, running the vacuum around *one last time* to ensure there wasn't a stray dog hair to be found. (In deference to her sister-in-law's allergies, Remy and all of his belongings had already been packed up and moved to Deacon's house for the weekend.)

"I just want everything to be perfect," she said.

"Your brother and sister-in-law are coming to see you—they're not going to care if you forgot to dust the overhead light in the dining room."

"It's called a chandelier," she told him. "And *damn*— I did forget to dust it."

He caught her hand as she started to hurry past—no doubt to retrieve her cleaning supplies. "Relax, Sierra. Nobody cares about the chandelier."

She seemed about to protest, then slowly nodded. "You're probably right."

"So why don't you tell me what's really going on?"

"I guess I'm a little bit nervous about them meeting you—and you meeting them."

"This was your idea," he reminded her. "But I can go, if you've changed your mind."

"I haven't," she insisted. "I want you to meet them. It's just that this is new territory in our relationship."

"*Our* meaning *yours and mine* or *yours and theirs*?"

"Both."

"Because you've never introduced them to a… friend…before?"

He paused to emphasize the word, as she insisted on doing whenever he hinted that their relationship might be something more. But despite her repeated reminders, and the lack of physical intimacy in their relationship, he was already more than halfway in love with her. Unfortunately, he knew she wasn't ready to hear him say it—and even less willing to acknowledge her own feelings.

So for now, he was trying to be satisfied with her

friendship. Because as much as he chafed at the restrictions imposed by the label, at least he was part of her life.

"I've introduced them to plenty of friends," she assured him.

"But maybe I'm a little bit more than a friend?" he suggested hopefully.

Before Sierra could respond to that, Nick and Whitney arrived—right on schedule.

Deacon watched from the porch as Sierra embraced her brother and sister-in-law.

Now that he knew Nick was her brother, Deacon could see a little bit of a family resemblance—mostly in the color of their eyes and the way they smiled. They were both smiling now, obviously happy to see one another for the first time in more than three months.

Whitney gave them a moment, then elbowed her husband aside to hug her sister-in-law. She was tall and slender with long reddish hair and dark brown eyes. As she made her way toward Deacon, he noticed that she had a sprinkling of freckles on her nose—and absolutely no reservations about throwing her arms around a man she was meeting for the first time.

"I'm so glad to finally meet you," she said.

"Glad to finally meet the guy Sierra told us about two days ago?" Nick said dryly, no doubt to ensure Deacon didn't get the impression he mattered enough to Sierra to have come up in earlier conversation with her family.

"Sierra has always been fiercely guarded about her private life," Whitney noted.

"But happy to introduce my family to my friends," Sierra interjected, ushering them all through the house and out to the back deck.

Now that the warmer weather had arrived, she was

apparently determined to make full use of the deck—
and the patio furniture that she'd found in the shed.
Which was why she planned to barbecue burgers and
dine alfresco (which meant that no one was even going
to be eating in the dining room under the chandelier
she'd forgotten to dust).

"Can I help you with anything?" Whitney offered,
when Sierra remarked that it was getting close to dinnertime.

"Nope. I've got everything under control," she promised. "The macaroni salad is made, potato wedges are
in the oven. I just have to get out the... Oh, no."

"What did you forget?" Deacon asked.

"Buns." She groaned in frustration. "We're having
hamburgers, and I don't have any hamburger buns."

"Is the grocery store very far?" Whitney asked.

"Nothing in Haven is very far," Sierra said, rising
from her seat.

"I can go," Deacon said.

"Thanks, but I'd rather you stayed here and started
the grill."

"Or I could do that," he agreed.

Whitney nudged her husband. "Why don't you go
with your sister?"

"Because I don't think picking up a package of buns
is a two-person job," Nick replied.

His wife gave him a look that communicated without the need for words.

Nick got to his feet. "But this is my second visit to
Haven, and I have yet to visit the grocery store," he
noted. "It might be fun."

"Only if you know a different definition for *fun*,"
Sierra said, as they walked out together.

"Are you going to grill me like I'm a burger?" Deacon asked Whitney when they were alone.

She laughed. "No, but I did want a few minutes to chat with you alone."

"I kind of got that impression," he admitted.

"I don't want to freak you out, but Sierra introducing you to her family is kind of a big deal. In fact, in the ten years that I've known her, she's never introduced us to a boyfriend. Well, except for the last one," she allowed, "but he doesn't really count, because Nick already knew Eric from when they served together on the board of a not-for-profit housing corporation. But mostly he doesn't count because he's a dick."

Deacon had to laugh at that. "That seems to be the consensus. But getting back to Sierra's introduction of me, I'm sure you noticed that she put me—firmly and definitively—in the friend zone."

"I noticed," Whitney admitted. "But the fact that she introduced you at all proves that you mean a lot to her. And I hope she means a lot to you, too."

"More than she wants to know," he confided.

"So...how did you feel when she told you that she was having her brother and sister-in-law's baby?"

"A little bit like I was in the middle of a nineties sitcom."

"*Friends*." Whitney grinned. "One of my all-time favorite shows."

"My mom was a big fan of it, too," he confided.

And then, in what seemed an abrupt conversational shift, she asked, "Do you believe in love at first sight?"

"If you'd asked me that question five months ago, I would have said no."

She smiled again. "I've always believed that we instinctively know when we meet someone who is going to play an important part in our lives. That's how it was for me and Nick. We met in law school—our first class together on our first day—and that was it for me. I was head over heels in love.

"Nick was a little bit slower to acknowledge his feelings, but he proposed at the end of our second year, and we immediately started making plans to get married after graduation. Three weeks before we were scheduled to exchange vows, I was diagnosed with cervical cancer. Nick wouldn't let me call off the wedding."

"Why did you think he would?" Deacon wondered.

"Because he hadn't signed up for that. In all our conversations about the future, we never talked about the possibility of him having to hold my hand during chemo treatments.

"But one thing we had talked about—one thing I knew Nick really wanted—was children—and my diagnosis threatened all of our plans to have a family.

"Still, Nick never wavered in his commitment to me and our future. Yes, he wanted a family, he said, but only if he could have a family with me.

"So we talked to the doctors about our options. A hysterectomy was the best choice for a positive outcome, but the result would be that I'd never be able to carry a child, so the doctors reluctantly agreed to let me postpone the surgery long enough to harvest some eggs."

She paused then to look at Deacon and ask, "Is this too much information?"

He shook his head. "No, though I am wondering why you're telling me all of this."

"Because I want you to understand what a huge deal this is—what Sierra's doing for us, against the doctors' advice."

"Why did the doctors advise against it?" he asked, immediately concerned.

"Gestational carriers are usually women who have already had at least one successful pregnancy, who have proven their ability to carry a baby to term for mothers who can't do so," Whitney explained. "This is a first for Sierra. In addition, there was some concern that the close family connection would put a lot of pressure on her. It's one of the reasons—maybe the only reason—that Nick didn't protest more vehemently when she decided to take the ADA position here."

"So why did you choose Sierra to be your gestational carrier?" he asked.

"Because I was uncomfortable with the idea of a stranger carrying our baby, even one screened and approved by the clinic for precisely that purpose. It just seemed unnatural to me to involve someone we didn't know in such an intimate part of our lives. And because Sierra understood my concerns and she offered. And because I didn't imagine—and I'm sure she didn't, either—that in the nine months she'd be carrying our baby, she would finally meet the man she was meant to be with."

Before Deacon could figure out how to respond to that, Whitney spoke again.

"Now you better get that barbecue started and get the burgers on before Sierra and Nick get back with the buns."

"Have you given any thought to what you want to do when you come back to Vegas?" Nick asked, pushing his empty plate aside.

"Actually I have," Sierra said. "I'm thinking of applying to the DA's office."

"Proof that you've officially gone over to the dark side," her brother lamented.

She rolled her eyes. "I hardly think that's the dark side."

Deacon and Whitney had been equal contributors to the earlier dinner conversation, but they both sat back now and let the siblings carry this topic.

"Well, if you change your mind, my firm is looking to hire," Nick told his sister.

"Um, no."

Nick scowled at her immediate response. "You could at least take some time to think about it."

"No," she said again. "I'm not taking a job from my brother."

"Why not?"

"Aside from the fact that it would reek of nepotism, you mean?"

"The whole law profession reeks of nepotism," he pointed out. "The directory in my building advertises Whitfield and Whitfield, Callendar and Associates—three of whom are also named Callendar—and Rowlands and Sons, and those are only the ones I remember off the top of my head."

"There's also Beringer and Beringer," Whitney chimed in.

Sierra nodded her head in acknowledgment of the point. "Nepotism aside, I need to live my own life."

"Says the sister carrying my baby," Nick noted dryly.

"For which we will be forever grateful and not interfere with the choices she makes with respect to her own life," his wife said pointedly.

"Right," Nick agreed, chastened.

"Speaking of choices," Sierra said. "We've got rocky

road, chocolate chip cookie dough and cherry chocolate chunk ice cream for dessert."

"I'd suggest you opt for the cookie dough or cherry chocolate," Deacon said.

Nick chuckled in response to the warning. "Don't worry," he said. "I learned long ago not to get between my sister and her rocky road."

Chapter Twenty

Sierra enjoyed the weekend with her brother and sister-in-law, and she'd been happy to introduce Deacon to her family. Though Nick had obviously been reserving judgment when he shook hands with her friend and canine co-parent, Deacon had soon won him over. Or maybe her brother had taken his cues from his wife, who had taken an immediate liking to "Sierra's new man," as Whitney referred to him.

In any event, they all had a good time, and when Sierra waved goodbye to them after brunch Sunday afternoon, she knew that she would be seeing them again in only seven weeks, when she went back to Las Vegas.

Which meant that she only had seven weeks left in Haven.

Seven weeks left with Deacon.

Funny how six months had seemed like so much time when she'd been moving into her temporary home, but now she suspected the last seven weeks would pass in the blink of an eye.

On her way back to the office after court Tuesday morning, she made a quick stop to grab a cranberry apple tea from The Daily Grind and spotted Deacon's sister-in-law waving to her.

"Do you have a minute?" Regan asked.

She glanced at her watch. "Sure," she decided, taking a chair on the opposite side of the table. "How can I help you?"

"I'm aware that I'm overstepping here, but I wanted to talk to you about Deacon," his sister-in-law said. "More specifically, about his feelings for you."

"Deacon and I have become good friends over the past several months," Sierra acknowledged, at the same time silently chastising herself for accepting the other woman's invitation to join her without question. "But it's not anything more than that, and he knows that I'm not looking for anything more than that."

"Does he?" Regan sounded dubious.

"He does," she confirmed. "I've also been very clear that I'm leaving Haven when my six-month contract with the DA's office is up."

"Or maybe you're just waiting for him to step up and ask you to stay."

"Step up?" Sierra echoed. Then the pieces clicked into place. "You mean because I'm pregnant?"

She was grateful that she no longer had to whisper the word. When she returned to work after recovering from the flu, she'd told her boss, and then her coworkers, about her pregnancy. It hadn't taken long for word to spread after that, and anyone who hadn't heard the gossip would be able to guess her status now that she was sporting an obvious baby bump.

Regan nodded.

"You think I'm looking for someone to be a father to my baby?" she guessed.

"I've been there," the other woman confided. "I was pregnant when Connor and I got married, so I understand that the prospect of being a single mom is daunting, and I know all the reasons that an expectant mother would want a father for her child."

"The baby I'm carrying will have a mother and a father," Sierra assured her.

Deacon's sister-in-law seemed taken aback by this response. "You're still in a relationship with the father?"

"Yes, but not in the way you're thinking."

"Can you clarify?"

"I thought Deacon would have told you," she admitted.

"Told me *what*?"

Now she did lower her voice, to tell Regan what she'd only confided to Deacon and Sky. "The baby I'm carrying isn't mine."

Regan had to close the jaw that had fallen open before she could respond. "Are you saying...you're a surrogate?"

"A gestational carrier, actually, for my brother and sister-in-law."

"I did not see *that* coming," the other woman admitted.

"It's a rather unusual situation," Sierra acknowledged.

"I can't believe Deacon didn't tell me. Actually, I can believe it," Regan quickly amended. "He's nothing if not discreet, and if you asked him not to say anything, he wouldn't. Not to anyone."

"I'm relieved to hear that," she said. "Because I'm

sure people have enough to say about my situation without adding that to the mix."

She'd heard some of the whispers and even speculation about the identity of the baby's father. Deacon's name had popped up in that conversation, notwithstanding the fact that she'd obviously been pregnant before she came to Haven. But gossips were rarely concerned about facts and, thankfully, Deacon didn't seem bothered by the rumors.

"Now I have another question," Regan said. "Since you're obviously not in a romantic relationship with anyone, why are you trying so hard to keep Deacon at arm's length?"

"Because the complication of my pregnancy aside, I'm only going to be in Haven a few more weeks."

"Because that's when your contract runs out? Or because you don't want to stay?"

"There's no reason for me to stay if I don't have a job," Sierra pointed out.

"I can understand why you might feel that way," the other woman said. "It wasn't so long ago that my career was the focus of my life. And I still love my job, but I love my family more."

"The best of both worlds," she acknowledged.

Regan smiled. "It is, indeed. Now I need to apologize for being rude, jumping to conclusions and taking up too much of your time."

"You don't have to apologize to me," Sierra said. "Not for looking out for your family."

"Deacon is family—whether he wants to accept it or not."

Sierra smiled. "He's lucky to have you."

"You really do care about him, don't you?"

"Of course I care about him. And if circumstances

were different——" She cut herself off with a shake of her head. "But there's no point in speculating, because circumstances aren't different."

The Friday before Memorial Day, Deacon rushed back to the office after court in the hope that he could finish the sentencing memo he'd been working on and escape from the office a little earlier than usual. He and Sierra hadn't made any big plans for the holiday weekend, but they did plan to spend it together.

He'd suggested packing a picnic on Saturday and taking Remy to Cutthroat Lake to hike some of the easier trails. He knew he'd likely end up carrying the dog after about twenty minutes, but he didn't mind.

Today, though, the weather was perfect for a barbecue, so he wanted to stop at The Trading Post on his way home to pick up some steaks for dinner with Sierra. And salad stuff, because she insisted on balancing her meal with healthy vegetables, and apparently a fully loaded baked potato didn't count.

He'd just clicked save on the document when there was a knock on his door. He glanced up to see his brother standing there, attired in his deputy sheriff uniform.

"Is this official business?" Deacon asked.

"No," Connor said. "It's personal."

His brother's serious expression immediately set off alarms. "Is everything okay? Regan? The girls? The babies?"

"They're all fine," his brother hastened to assure him.

"Are you okay?" he pressed, wondering if Connor had received some bad news from his doctor about his health.

"I'm fine, too."

Another thought—even more chilling. *"Sierra?"*

Deacon had seen her in court earlier that morning, but several hours had passed since then.

"As far as I know, there's no reason to worry there, either."

He exhaled a quiet sigh of relief. Now that he knew everyone he cared about was okay, he had no reason to be anxious about whatever his brother wanted to discuss. "Then what is it?"

The deputy sheriff sat on the edge of one of the visitors' chairs. "There was a fight in the parking lot behind Diggers' last night," he began. "Did you hear about it?"

"I got my coffee from The Daily Grind this morning, like I always do," Deacon told him. "Of course I heard about it."

Apparently several men from out of town had stopped in for a drink, but they were already more than halfway to being drunk—and belligerent—so Duke kicked them out of the bar. Instead of going away quietly, they started fighting amongst themselves in the back parking lot. Tempers flared, fists flew—and then one of the guys pulled out a knife.

"That about sums it up," Connor agreed, after Deacon recounted what he'd heard. "But they weren't all out-of-towners. One of them—the one who was stabbed—was Dwayne Parrish. Your father."

Deacon felt as if he'd been sucker punched and had all the air knocked out of his lungs.

Just when he was finally moving forward with his life...

"I know who Dwayne Parrish is," he said, when he'd managed to catch his breath and could speak again. "And while he might have contributed half of my DNA, he was never much of a father."

Connor nodded slowly. "I'm not going to disagree with that. I just thought you should know, and I didn't want you to hear the news from anyone else."

"I appreciate it," Deacon said.

"He's in ICU at NNRH in Elko, if you wanted to see him."

"I don't." His response was blunt and firm.

"His prognosis is pretty bleak," his brother warned. "And maybe you think I'm unfeeling, but the honest truth is, I figured he was already dead—or maybe in jail somewhere."

"Neither of those things would have surprised me, either," Connor admitted. "But he's here. And after more than twenty years, don't you want to know why he came back?"

"No," Deacon said fiercely. Because he'd stopped wondering about his so-called father years ago. Relegated him and the unhappy memories to the past. And silently cursed him now for not staying there. "I only wish he hadn't."

He sat at his desk after his brother had gone, thinking about the man he hadn't given more than a passing thought to in a very long time.

He'd meant what he'd said to his brother about wishing Dwayne had never come back. When his dad left, after that horrible fight with Connor that Deacon would never forget, he'd felt nothing but relief. Gratitude that the man was out of all their lives. That he wouldn't ever again have to hear him yelling at his mother or see him hitting his brother.

Dwayne's absence had allowed Deacon to believe that he could, if not forget about his past, at least put it behind him and move forward with his life. Recently, he'd even been foolish enough to hope that he might do so with Sierra.

But now Deacon's past had caught up with him, and he knew that did not bode well for his future.

Sierra heard the whispers around town. She usually didn't pay much attention to gossip, but when the name Dwayne Parrish caught her attention, she found herself straining to pick up the details.

Of course, there were several variations of a similar story circulating, the gist of which was that Deacon's dad had shown up in town and gotten in a fight in the parking lot behind Diggers'. According to the reports, he'd either been beaten up, stabbed or shot, and when the sheriff arrived on scene, he'd possibly skipped town, been taken to hospital or shipped to the morgue.

Back at the office, she got the official report— Dwayne Parrish had been stabbed three times and was in the hospital with serious injuries.

She wondered if Deacon had heard the same rumors and how he was handling the news. Though she felt certain that the deputy sheriff would have apprised his brother of recent events, she still felt compelled to reach out.

Heard about your dad. Just wanted to let you know that I'm here if you want to talk.

A few minutes later came a brief reply:

Not necessary, but thanks.

And that was the last she heard from him until two hours later.

I'm not going to be able to walk Remy tonight—and I have to bail on our plans for the lake tomorrow, too. Sorry.

Their planned visit to Cutthroat Lake (named for the fish that inhabited the water, he'd assured her) had been his idea. Since the warmer weather had arrived in northern Nevada, they'd been taking Remy to explore some of the local hiking trails. She'd enjoyed their outings and was looking forward to the picnic he'd promised her.

She responded:

Remy's going to be disappointed.

Because it was easier to blame the dog than admit that *she* was disappointed.

But even more than she was disappointed, she was worried about Deacon. Worried that this sudden change of plans was somehow linked to the news about his dad.

Maybe we can do it another time?

She held her breath, waiting for his reply to her suggestion. For his assurance that, of course, they would do it another time.

Or you could take Remy on your own. The trails are clearly marked.

As if she needed his permission or approval to take the dog hiking.

But she didn't want to take Remy on her own.

And she wanted to know why the man who'd been

making up all kinds of excuses to spend time with her over the past several months was suddenly bailing on her.

Why the change of plans?

It took him a while to respond to that one. So long, in fact, that she thought he might call rather than text, taking the opening she'd given him to talk.

In the five months she'd known him, he hadn't told her much about his family aside from the facts that his dad was an abusive alcoholic and his mom never should have married him. Still, she was sure he must have conflicted feelings about the man's return—and his injury—and she wanted him to trust her enough to open up to her.

Finally three little dots appeared, indicating that he was responding to her question. But his answer, when it came, wasn't anything she would have anticipated.

I ran into Madison Russell this afternoon and she invited me to a party at Spring Creek.

A party?

He was blowing her off to go to *a party*?

Maybe she shouldn't have been surprised. After all, she'd been pushing him to get out and do things with other people. She'd even specifically mentioned Madison—and he'd claimed to not be interested, that the judge's clerk was too young.

But maybe after hanging out with Sierra, who really wasn't that much older but whose activities were somewhat restricted by her pregnancy, he'd decided that he wanted to be with someone more fun and spontaneous. Someone with whom he could enjoy physical intimacy.

Because he'd been spending a lot of time with Sierra. Days out and about with Remy and quiet nights in front of the TV. And while they occasionally held hands—Deacon always took hers to help her navigate a narrow part of a trail—and cuddled on the sofa—there was no kissing (at least, not since the day she'd kissed him in her kitchen) and definitely nothing more.

And the thought of Deacon with Madison...doing *more* with Madison—

No. She couldn't go there.

Instead, she stared at his message on the screen, the letters blurred by the tears in her eyes, and wondered if he was waiting for her response.

Or maybe a reaction.

She swiped impatiently at the solitary tear that spilled onto her cheek before composing a reply.

Sounds like fun. Have a great time.

Her thumb hovered over the arrow that would send the message, a sick feeling churning in her belly.

Why should she send him off with her best wishes when he'd just ditched her and their weekend plans?

She knew it wasn't the same as saying *sorry* to Eric and Aubrey after catching them in bed together, but it felt a little bit similar. And she was *not* going to apologize for being wronged again.

Instead, she pressed the backspace key until every last letter of her reply was deleted from her screen.

Chapter Twenty-One

Saturday afternoon, Sierra took Remy to the lake.

She refused to sit at home alone and mope because Deacon had decided he'd have more fun at Spring Creek with another woman.

Even worse than moping was speculating about the kind of fun they might be having. And scrolling through Madison Russell's Instagram.

After she'd tortured herself with the pictures Madison had posted—of the five-bedroom house on the water that had been rented for the weekend (#funwithfriends), the refrigerator stocked with beer and coolers (#drinkingwithfriends), the volleyball net on the beach (#gettingphysicalwithfriends), and a photo of Madison herself in a teeny bikini top and skimpy shorts, ready to serve the ball (#tanned #toned #gigisgym)—Sierra had been desperate to get out of the house.

Because yes, she was jealous that Madison had abs.

And she was jealous that the other woman was with Deacon.

And she had no right to be jealous—because she and Deacon were *friends*.

She didn't bother to pack a picnic for her outing with Remy, but she did throw a water bottle and some snacks in her backpack, along with a collapsible water bowl she'd bought for the dog when she and Deacon had started taking him hiking.

But she wasn't going to think about those other outings today, she reminded herself firmly. She was going to focus on enjoying the weather and Remy's company.

There were a lot of trails around the lake, color coded to help hikers stay on their chosen path. Sierra opted for the purple trail—one of the shorter and easier routes. Though she prided herself on being in pretty good shape, she was carrying an extra fifteen pounds in front and didn't want to risk steep or uneven terrain on her own with Remy.

But they weren't really on their own, as Cutthroat Lake proved to be a popular destination on a sunny Saturday afternoon of a long weekend. By the halfway point, Remy was completely tuckered out, so Sierra picked him up to carry him the rest of the way. They were almost at the end of their route when she spotted Deacon's brother walking a tan-colored dog with a slightly squished face, a dark muzzle and a curled tail.

The dog barked and tugged on his leash, trying to get closer to Sierra and the Chihuahua in the crook of her arm.

"This is Baxter," the deputy sheriff said. "He's just excited because he wants to make friends, but I promise he's more pussycat than puggle."

"Puggle?"

"Part pug, part beagle."

She cautiously set Remy down so the dogs could sniff one another.

"Cutthroat Lake's a popular destination with the locals," Connor said. "But not a lot of visitors know it's here."

Though she didn't consider herself to be a visitor, she agreed that living in the town five months wasn't long enough to qualify as a local.

"Deacon told me about it," she admitted.

"I should have guessed. We used to come out here sometimes when we were kids."

"That's what he said."

"Speaking of my brother—have you seen him recently?"

"I saw him in court yesterday morning."

He frowned. "But not since then?"

She shook her head. "We exchanged a couple of text messages later in the day, though, so I know he was going to Spring Creek for the weekend."

"Oh." Connor didn't sound too pleased to hear it, and she wondered if he knew about the big house party happening on the beach. "I was hoping he would have talked to you."

"About his dad?" she guessed.

"Yeah."

"I hoped so, too," she admitted.

Remy and Baxter had apparently decided they were going to be friends and were wrestling on the ground and tangling up their leashes.

"I don't know what—if anything—he's told you about Dwayne, but I know it was a shock to him to hear that his dad came back, and that might have something to do with why he's acting like an idiot, if he is."

He definitely was, but Sierra had no intention of getting into that with the deputy sheriff.

Instead, she bent to untangle Remy's leash. "We need to be heading back to town."

"Actually, Regan and the girls are setting up a picnic over by the playground," he said. "Why don't you join us?"

"I appreciate the invitation, but Remy's more than ready for a nap."

"Are you sure? We've got three kinds of sandwiches—peanut butter, jelly and peanut butter, *and* jelly." Connor ticked off the options on his fingers.

"I'm sure," she said, and even managed to smile. "But thanks."

It turned out his brother was right.

Deacon did want to know why, after more than twenty years, his poor excuse for a father had decided to wander back into town. And since he was already in Spring Creek, Northeastern Nevada Regional Hospital wasn't much of a detour on his way home.

By the time he arrived Saturday afternoon, Dwayne's condition had been upgraded from "critical" to "serious" and he was sitting up in bed. Deacon paused in the doorway, a jolt of shock reverberating through him at the realization that the old man in the bed was his father.

Of course, more than two decades had passed since he'd last seen the man, and Deacon had only been a child then. A child afraid of the big man with the booming voice and quick fists.

But he was no longer a child, and the figure in the bed bore little resemblance to the one he remembered. His dark hair had gone gray and his formerly broad shoulders were noticeably less broad.

Everything about him just seemed…a little less.

And so, Deacon realized with no small sense of relief, was his power over his son.

"Did too many years of hard drinking catch up to you and you came back to Haven because you need a liver?" he asked, from his post inside the door.

The old man in the bed cackled as he turned his head to look at his visitor. "I wouldn't be surprised," he finally responded. "But no, that's not why I came back."

"So why did you?" Deacon asked the question he'd promised himself he wouldn't.

"Come in, boy, and let me take a look at you."

"I'm not a boy," he said, even as he stepped forward.

"I can see that," Dwayne acknowledged.

"Why are you here?" Deacon asked again.

"I heard your mom passed."

"Yeah. More than ten years ago," he said bluntly.

His father didn't look the least bit chastened by the pointed response but followed up by asking, "She leave you any money?"

"Are you kidding?" Deacon was stunned. And furious. "Is *that* why you came back? Because you thought there might be a few bucks for you?"

"She was still my wife," Dwayne said gruffly. "Anythin' she had when she died should've come to me."

"You mean like the pile of medical bills, courtesy of the cancer that killed her?"

"There must've been somethin' left," Dwayne insisted. "How else did you pay for that fancy law school diploma?"

"She had no money," Deacon said, needing to make it perfectly clear. "I had scholarships that paid for college and law school."

"No shit?"

"No shit," Deacon echoed dryly.

Dwayne scratched the stubble on his jaw. "I didn't think you were that smart."

"I was eight when you left home. And before that, the only time you thought about me at all was when you told me to bring you another beer."

The old man almost looked regretful for a minute— or maybe it was only wishful thinking on Deacon's part.

"I did my best," Dwayne said.

"Yeah, well, your best was pretty damn lousy."

"Some men just don't have what it takes to be a dad."

"Isn't that the truth?" Deacon agreed, and walked out the door.

Sky was sitting up in bed, holding her newborn swaddled in a pink blanket with a matching cap on her head, when Sierra walked into her hospital room in Battle Mountain on the first Friday in June.

"Jake was right," Sierra said. "Your baby girl is every bit as beautiful as her mama."

"When did you see Jake?"

"Two minutes ago—in the lobby downstairs."

"He's on his way home to feed Molly and take her for a run. The poor animal's been horribly neglected for the past couple of days."

Sierra set the vase of flowers she'd brought on the windowsill alongside several other arrangements, one of which she noticed bore a card signed by Paige and MG.

"The gerberas are gorgeous, thank you," her friend said. "But honestly—there are so many flowers in here, it's starting to look like the window display of Blossom's Flower Shop."

"Probably because everyone got their flowers at Blossom's," she noted.

"And I'm grateful to everyone," Sky said. "I just wish someone had thought to bring me cherry chocolate chunk ice cream."

Sierra pulled a container with the Scoops logo out of her purse.

The new mom's eyes went wide.

"Don't tease me," she warned.

"I'm not teasing you," Sierra promised, setting the ice cream and a plastic-wrapped spoon on the table beside her friend's bed. "But if you want the ice cream, you're going to have to put down the baby—or give her to me."

"I think that might have been your plan all along," Sky mused.

Sierra just grinned as she took the sleeping baby from her friend's arms.

Sky reached for the ice cream. "And now your status as my friend has been restored," she said, prying the lid off the container to dig into the contents.

"I didn't realize it had been revoked."

"It was in jeopardy," Sky told her. "Because Maya was born a full nineteen hours ago and you're only showing up here now."

"Not because I wasn't eager to get a look at your gorgeous baby, but because I knew your room would be overflowing with family and friends, and I didn't want to get in the way."

"You're one of my friends, too," Sky reminded her, as she dipped her spoon into the container. "My best friend again now," she added, with her mouth full of ice cream.

"I still think I got the sweetest part of the deal," Sierra said, cuddling the baby.

"She is pretty great—but trust me when I say that I now understand why they call it labor."

"I don't want to hear any details." Carrying her brother and sister-in-law's baby was one thing, bringing him into the world was another—and she was admittedly a little apprehensive about that part of the process. But right now, holding her friend's newborn in her arms, she was filled with awe and wonder.

"I promise not to share the details," Sky said, "except to say that every minute of the sixteen hours was worth it."

"Well, that's obvious," Sierra said, smiling at the sleeping baby.

"And while I'm thrilled that you're finally here, I'm a little surprised that Deacon didn't come with you."

"He was out with Remy when I left."

"Did something happen between you two?"

"Nothing except that he's suddenly decided that we've been spending too much time together."

Her friend frowned. "That doesn't sound like the man who's been chasing you for months."

"There was no chasing," Sierra denied.

"Well, whatever's going on with him, I'm sure he'll come around."

"Maybe it's better if he doesn't."

"Why would you say that?" Sky demanded.

"Because I'm only going to be in town another three weeks."

"No," her friend said. "If we're not talking about my childbirth experience, we're not talking about that, either."

"I'm going to miss you, too," Sierra told her.

"Not talking about it," Sky said again.

And for the next half hour, they talked about everything except the fact that the clock was ticking down on Sierra's time in Haven.

Chapter Twenty-Two

Early the following Saturday morning, Sierra dragged herself out of bed because someone was pounding on her door. Not knocking, pounding. Remy wasn't happy about the early morning interruption, either. His hackles were up and he was growling deep in his throat as she carried him down the stairs.

Scowling with annoyance, she peered through the sidelight to see Deacon standing there before unlocking the door and yanking it open.

"Do you know what time it is?" she demanded.

"Eight thirty... Almost."

"It's eight twenty-two on a Saturday morning."

"You were still in bed," he realized.

"What do you want, Deacon?"

He held up the tray of drinks and bakery box from Sweet Caroline's.

"Not even a salted caramel brownie can make up

for you showing up at my door before nine o'clock on a Saturday morning."

"How about a salted caramel brownie and a heart-felt apology?"

"Maybe," she allowed, after a moment of hesitation.

"Can I come in? Or are you going to make me grovel on your porch?"

She looked at the dog in her arms. "What do you think?"

Remy let out a sigh and rested his chin on her arm.

"I guess you can come in." She opened the door wider. "Actually, I'm a little surprised you didn't let yourself in. Did you lose your key?"

"I didn't think it was an appropriate time to use it."

"But you thought it was an appropriate time to bang on my door?"

"Only when you didn't respond to my knock."

She put the dog on the floor, and he immediately headed to the kitchen for his breakfast.

Deacon set the drinks and pastries on the counter while Sierra filled Remy's bowl.

Then she took a seat at the island and removed the lid from the to-go cup Deacon handed to her.

"Let's try this again," she suggested. "Why are you here?"

"Because I can't pretend anymore that I don't want to be with you."

Her heart bumped against her ribs. "Were you pretending?"

"I was pretending. I was an ass."

"Actually, I'd argue that you really were an ass."

His lips curved a little, but his expression remained contrite. "And I'm sorry."

She opened the bakery box to peer inside, waiting for him to continue.

He cradled his cup in two hands. "You asked me once about my mom, and I gave you a flippant response," he said.

"I remember."

"I don't like to talk about my childhood—or even think about it most of the time. It's easier to believe that I've moved on and left my past in the past. But I want to tell you some of that history now, so that maybe you'll understand why I acted like an ass."

"Okay," she said.

"My mom, by her own admission, was a little wild in her younger days. She was barely seventeen when she got pregnant the first time, and when she told the baby's father he was going to be a father, he drifted out of town again as aimlessly as he'd drifted into it, leaving her on her own.

"Despite her age and lack of a high school diploma, she insisted on keeping her baby. But she struggled to make ends meet as a single mom and occasionally found herself in...unhealthy relationships, because she was desperate for help to pay her bills and looking for a father figure for her son.

"Connor was five when she met Dwayne Parrish, six when she got pregnant again and seven when they got married—a few months before I was born. Of course, plenty of people had things to say about the fact that she'd been six months pregnant when they exchanged vows, but the consensus was that at least this one did the right thing and put a ring on her finger, because Connor's dad never did.

"Of course, it's easy for people to pass judgment based on what they can see from the outside, without ever knowing—and probably not caring about—the rest of the picture. Because marrying Dwayne wasn't the right thing for my mom, who didn't know he was an abusive alcoholic until it was too late. And it wasn't the right thing for my brother, who was frequently knocked around by Dwayne when our mom was out.

"And she was out a lot, because Dwayne was injured on a construction site job shortly after they were married and wasn't able to work after that. So my mom got a job—sometimes she had two or three jobs—to pay the rent and utilities and put food on the table and—far more important to Dwayne—beer in his belly."

Sierra's heart ached for the boy he'd been, living a life that no child should have to live. And it ached for the man he'd become, still living with the scars of his childhood.

She wanted to reach out to him now, to offer him comfort—or at least support—but she knew it couldn't be easy for him to talk about any of this, and she was reluctant to interrupt. So she held on to her cup with both hands and didn't let them tremble.

"That was my life. My family," he continued. "So you can maybe understand why I didn't grow up thinking that I'd ever want a wife and kids. The atmosphere in the rented, rundown bungalow on Second Street wasn't anything I'd ever aspire to emulate. All I ever wanted was to get out of that house, that neighborhood, the whole damn town.

"I was determined to make something of myself. To prove that I was better than who and where I came from. Going to college was the first step. Being accepted into law school was the second. When I got that letter from Columbia... I was blown away.

"Not that I actually had any plans to attend. I'd applied just to see if I was good enough, and I figured I'd hold on to the letter for the rest of my life, because it proved that I was. But there was no way I could afford to go to an Ivy League school.

"Connor was beyond proud—he was insistent that the opportunity was too big to pass up. I pointed out that I had other options—the William S. Boyd School of Law at UNLV, the University of Idaho College of Law or S.J. Quinney College of Law in Utah."

None of which was ranked number four of all law schools in the country, as she knew Columbia was.

"So I decided to go to New York—and tried not to freak out about what it would cost and how I would pay for it.

"Connor came through for me again, taking out a second mortgage on his house to pay for my tuition. Then I got a scholarship from Blake Mining, which coincidentally came through around the same time that Connor and Regan got married, so I suspect my sister-in-law had a hand in that."

"I didn't realize Regan was a Blake," she said, her surprise momentarily eclipsing her determination to stay mum.

"A Channing, actually," he clarified. "But her mom was a Blake."

"The Blakes and Gilmores really do have connections to everyone in this town, don't they?"

"It certainly seems that way," he agreed.

"So you went to law school in New York," she said, prompting him to pick up the thread of his story again.

He nodded. "And when I left, I was certain that I'd never want to come back. But the time away gave me perspective—and made me realize how much I'd miss

Connor and Regan—and later Piper and Poppy, too—if I decided to live and work anywhere else.

"When I came home that first summer, I thought I'd have to get a job bagging groceries or cutting grass—both jobs that I'd done in the past. Because despite the fact that I already had one college degree and a year of law school under my belt, I knew no one in town would be eager to hire Dwayne Parrish's kid. Because even though he'd been gone a long time by then, the shadow of his reputation remained.

"But the sheriff told my brother that I should send my résumé to Katelyn, and I did, not really expecting anything to come of it. I was thrilled to score an interview, but my cautious hope was trampled when I learned that she'd also interviewed Isabelle Graves."

"Judge Graves's daughter?"

He nodded.

"I was certain Katelyn would give the job to the candidate with the pedigree. Instead, she hired me. And now people who once looked down on me because of where I came from seek my counsel and representation. Because Katelyn gave me a chance when I didn't think anyone would."

"Which proves that she's a very smart woman."

"Anyway, the point of all of that was to show you that Mr. Columbia Law, as you like to call me, is really just a poor kid from the wrong side of the tracks, albeit grown up now and wearing a suit—and occasionally 'designer original' Cole Haan loafers."

She smiled at that, then her expression turned serious again. "Or maybe that poor kid was always a Columbia-educated lawyer just waiting to prove to the world what he was capable of."

"That's an interesting spin," he said. "But the fact

remains, the earliest years of my childhood aren't something I like to revisit, and my fear of turning out like my...like Dwayne...made me reluctant to even consider getting married and having a family. Until I met you.

"And just when I was starting to think that I could have everything I never knew I wanted, Dwayne showed up in town again.

"That's why, when I saw Madison later that day, after hearing about his return, I jumped at her invitation to go to Spring Creek for the weekend. Because she didn't tempt me to want anything more than what I already had, whereas every time I'm with you, I find myself wanting to believe that I can be the man you deserve."

It was an effort to hold back the tears that burned the backs of her eyes. "You're making it really hard for me to stay mad at you."

"I'm...sorry?"

She managed a chuckle. "I'm grateful to you for telling me all of that, but none of it changes what I already knew—that you're a good man, Deacon Parrish. One of the best I know."

"Does that mean I'm forgiven?" he asked.

"You're forgiven," she said, and gave him a quick hug.

"There's one more thing I want you to know."

"What's that?"

"I didn't spend the entire weekend at Spring Creek."

A fact of which she was already aware, as she'd spotted his truck in his driveway when she returned from her trip to the lake with Remy on the Saturday afternoon. And because she'd later overheard one of the court admins whispering to another that Madison was annoyed "Dekes" hadn't stuck around.

"Also, I didn't sleep with Madison," he told her now.

"Your personal life isn't any of my business," she said, dropping her gaze to stare into the bottom of her now empty cup.

"The reason I didn't sleep with Madison," he said, continuing as if she hadn't spoken, "is that the whole time I was with her, I couldn't stop thinking about you. Because I don't want to be with anyone but you."

The sincerity in his tone tugged at her heart—a heart that she suspected might already be his.

But she was almost seven months pregnant and couldn't be sure if her feelings were real or a by-product of all the baby hormones in her system, so she kept them buried deep inside.

Or at least tried to.

But his words had touched her deeply, and the single tear that slid down her cheek felt as if it had been squeezed out of her heart.

Twenty-three weeks down, one to go, Sierra noted, as she walked into the DA's office early on the last Monday of June.

She anticipated a busy week, tying up lots of loose ends. But aside from writing case summaries for Jade on current cases, a few hours in First Appearance Court and a couple of bail hearings, Brett kept her close to the office. And anything new that came in went to one of the other ADAs, since Sierra wouldn't be there to see the charges through to trial.

It was understandable, and yet the restrictions on her duties were yet another reminder that her time in Haven was rapidly counting down.

Tuesday night, she started to pack. An hour later, she texted Deacon and asked him to come over to get Remy. He was there in five minutes.

"What's going on?" he asked, lowering himself onto the floor near where she sat, cuddling the little dog.

Judging by the sympathy in his tone, he could tell that she'd been crying.

"I'm trying to pack and he keeps climbing in to whatever box or suitcase I'm trying to fill."

"Obviously he wants to go with you."

"I can't take him," she said. "And we all knew that from the beginning."

"I'm not sure that he did," Deacon countered gently. "Aside from sit and stay, I'd guess the rest of our words are gibberish to him."

"He also knows t-r-e-a-t, w-a-l-k and s-h-e-l-t-e-r," Sierra noted, opting to spell the words that were likely to get an excited reaction from the dog.

"Do you want me to take him for a w-a-l-k now, while you finish up in here?"

"It would have to be a really long w-a-l-k. I've still got a fair amount of packing to do."

"Should I take him home with me tonight?"

Her eyes filled again as she nodded. "That's probably for the best."

"C'mon, Remy," he said, lifting the dog from her lap. "Let's give Mommy some space."

"I'm not his mommy," she protested. "I'm not anybody's mommy."

And, inexplicably, she began to cry.

Or maybe her roller coaster emotions weren't so inexplicable. After all, she was seven months pregnant with all kinds of baby hormones running rampant through a body that didn't seem to understand the baby she carried wasn't her own. And while her mind understood that basic truth, the knowledge did little to help control her emotions.

She wouldn't have blamed Deacon if he'd taken the dog and ran. Instead, he placed Remy in her lap again and put his arms around her, holding her while she cried.

His wordless support and understanding only made her cry harder as she realized how much this man had come to mean to her in such a short time—and how much she was starting to wish that she could hold on to him forever. But right now, she wasn't feeling strong enough or brave enough to risk her heart on a future filled with so many uncertainties.

"I'm sorry for the meltdown," she said, when she'd finally pulled herself together enough to be able to speak.

"You don't have to apologize to me," he assured her.

She brushed her hands over her tear-stained cheeks. "I'm such a mess."

"You're beautiful," he said.

She managed a laugh. "You really do need to get out and spend time with other people."

"I tried that," he reminded her. "It didn't go so well, because I only want to be with you."

"I'm leaving, Deacon."

He held her gaze for a long minute before he replied, "I know."

She wished he would ask her to stay, even though she knew that she couldn't and that his asking wouldn't change that fact.

And apparently he knew it, too, because, in an abrupt change of topic, he asked, "Do you have any plans for Friday night?"

"Just hanging with Remy, like I do most Friday nights. And almost every other night." Except this Friday would be her last Friday night with the little dog that had stolen her heart.

Her last night in this town.

The realization made her throat tighten again, but this time she managed—barely—to keep the tears at bay.

"Do you think Remy would mind if I took you out to dinner Friday night?"

They'd shared several meals together but, aside from that long ago Valentine's Day invitation, this was the first time Deacon had formally asked her to go out with him, which almost made it seem like a date...

"Not a date," he hastened to assure her, as if privy to her innermost thoughts. "Just an informal meal at Diggers'."

"I don't think he'd mind," Sierra said. "And I'd like that very much."

Chapter Twenty-Three

The job was supposed to be something to tide her over—and provide much needed medical insurance—until Sierra had the baby and could get serious about looking for a more permanent position. And when she first came to Haven, she never would have imagined that she might someday envision a future here.

But the six months that she'd spent in the northern Nevada town had both challenged and fulfilled her in ways she hadn't anticipated. She'd enjoyed her work and made friends. She'd become part of the community. And she knew that she was going to miss this place and its people when she was gone.

She could promise to keep in touch with friends and plan to come back to visit, but she wasn't sure it was realistic that she'd be able to do so if she went back to working sixty-plus hours a week in Las Vegas. Because that was what was expected of an associate who wanted to make partner in the big firms—and didn't every attorney want to someday be a partner in a big firm?

Certainly it had been her goal when she first started at Bane & Associates. But now... Now she knew she was going to miss working in the Haven DA's office—and especially all the people she'd met through her job there.

When Deacon picked her up Friday night, she was feeling a little out of sorts that everyone at the office had gone about their business as usual, with only the occasional mention of the fact that it was her last day. And then, when they walked into Diggers', she paused in the doorway, an odd sense of déjà vu stealing over her as she took in the colorful streamers and balloons. But instead of a generic *Happy Birthday* banner there was one that read *Farewell Sierra*.

"This time it's your party," Deacon said with a smile.

"You said an informal meal at Diggers'," Sierra reminded him.

He shrugged. "I had to get you here somehow."

"I didn't expect anything like this." She wasn't just surprised, she was overwhelmed—and very much afraid that she was going to melt down in front of him again.

"Good, because if you'd expected it, it wouldn't have been much of a surprise," he pointed out.

Then, as if sensing that she needed to be rescued from her own emotions, he nudged her farther into the room. And suddenly she was surrounded by friends and colleagues. Even her boss was there, and her prenatal yoga instructor and Harvey—the courthouse security guard that she'd been certain didn't like her because he only ever responded to her good morning wishes with a grunt.

"I guess everyone likes a party," she mused. "Or at least cake."

"Cake?" Deacon's eyes went wide. "Was I supposed to get cake?"

It was a good time—with a lot of laughter and more than a few tears—and over the course of the evening, it seemed as if everyone she'd ever met in Haven had stopped by for at least a minute or two. Including Sky with Jake and their now three-week-old baby. They didn't stay long, and Sky refused to say goodbye, but Sierra was okay with that, because she didn't think she would be able to say the word to her friend, either. Deacon's brother and sister-in-law showed up, too. And Regan hugged Sierra and told her that she sincerely hoped she'd find her way back to Haven someday.

When there was nothing but crumbs remaining of the cake—because of course Deacon had arranged for a cake (delicious red velvet, layered with chocolate mousse and cherry *pâté de fruit* jelly)—he took her home. After he walked her to the door, he kissed her—a kiss so achingly sweet, it made her want to cry all over again.

When he eased his lips from hers, he lifted his hands to cradle her face and said, "I love you, Sierra."

They were the words she'd both longed for and dreaded. Words that simultaneously filled her heart and made it ache.

"Did you really think that now, only hours before I'm leaving town, was a good time to tell me?" she asked, her voice wavering more than a little.

"I'll admit the timing isn't ideal, but I didn't think you were ready to hear it before." He held her gaze as his thumbs gently brushed away the tears that spilled onto her cheeks. "I'm not entirely sure you're ready to accept the truth of my feelings now, but I couldn't let you leave without telling you.

"I understand why you have to go," he said. "But I hope, after the baby's born, you'll consider coming back."

She'd thought about it, of course. In recent weeks, she'd found herself thinking about it a lot. But her emotions were a tangled mess, and she didn't know how much of that was a result of her growing feelings for Deacon and how much was pregnancy hormones or even how much of her feelings for him could be attributed to those same hormones.

"I can't make a decision about this right now," she said.

"I'm not asking you to make a decision right now," he told her. "I'm asking you to think about it."

"I can do that," she agreed.

The drive to Vegas seemed to take a lot longer than any other time that Sierra had made the journey.

Maybe it was because she had to stop four times to use a restroom, as the baby had recently taken up position on her bladder.

Or maybe it was that she wasn't as eager to return to Sin City as she'd been on previous trips, because she knew this might be the last time she'd ever travel this route.

Because whatever else might have drawn her and Deacon to one another, proximity had undoubtedly been a significant factor. And now that proximity would no longer factor into the equation, he might soon forget about her.

Out of sight, out of mind.

Besides, Vegas was her home. It had been her home

her entire life. It was also where her brother and sister-in-law lived. Where her soon-to-be-born nephew would live with his parents.

She'd never imagined living anywhere else. Had never—except for a few days immediately following her trip to San Francisco and her breakup with Eric—wanted to live anywhere else.

Had Eric broken her heart?

She'd thought so, at the time.

He'd certainly wounded her pride and made her question her judgment.

She'd been duped—not just by the man she'd loved but also by a woman she'd considered a friend.

Still, she hadn't actually planned to leave Las Vegas. But when the job posting for a six-month position with the Haven District Attorney's Office appeared the same day she'd given her notice at Bane & Associates, she'd decided it was fortuitous timing. (Deacon probably would have said it was destiny.)

In any event, when she'd packed up her car and headed to Haven, she'd vowed to never succumb to the yearnings of her heart again.

And then she'd met Deacon Parrish.

Was it foolish to let herself believe that her feelings for him could be real?

She didn't know, and the pregnancy hormones running rampant through her system, messing with her brain and her heart, gave her reason to be cautious.

Which was why she couldn't make any decisions about her future right now. Why she needed some time and distance to think about her life and future more clearly. Because when she was with Deacon, she didn't want anything else.

Time and distance would give them both some necessary perspective, she decided.

If, after she had the baby, she still had feelings for
him, maybe she'd reach out.

But she probably wouldn't.

Two months was a long time, and by then, he was
certain to have moved on without her.

It was the third week of August—seven weeks after
he'd said goodbye to Sierra, and Deacon had missed
her every single day. Despite his best efforts to keep
himself busy, she was always his first thought in the
morning and his last thought at night.

He'd planned—and canceled—several visits to Sin
City, because as much as he wanted to see her, he knew
that he had to respect her request for space. She was
reluctant to believe that her feelings for him were real,
concerned that her emotions were amplified by her
pregnancy. And he knew that any effort to insert himself back into her life while she was still pregnant would
not serve any purpose.

But *damn*, he missed her.

"Deacon?"

He dragged his attention back to his sister-in-law.
"Did you say something?"

"Your mind is a million miles away today, isn't it?
Or would four hundred and fifty be a more accurate
number?"

"Does it matter?" he said. "The babies' room is getting painted, isn't it?"

"It is," she agreed. "And I'm happy to say I love that
color even more on the wall than on the paint chip."

He stood back to examine his handiwork. "It does

look good," he agreed. "But are you sure it's blue? It almost looks purple to me."

"It's periwinkle."

"Sounds like a girl color."

"I don't believe in boy colors and girl colors," she said.

"So why is Double Trouble's room the color of Double Bubble?"

"Don't call them that," his sister-in-law admonished.

"They don't mind it," he pointed out.

"Well, I do. And don't think I don't see what you're doing."

"I'm painting your walls."

"You're sidetracking the conversation because you don't want to talk about Sierra."

"There's nothing to talk about."

"You miss her," Regan guessed.

"Yeah," he said, because there was no point in denying it.

He'd missed her every minute of every day since he'd watched her drive away. He'd thought he would get used to her absence over time, but he still looked for her car in the driveway when he drove down Larkspur Lane and Remy still wanted to run up to the door when their walk took them past her former house.

"You do realize that missing her is silly, don't you?"

"Gee, why wouldn't I want to talk to you about my feelings when you're so quick to dismiss them?" he said dryly.

"I'm not dismissing your feelings," she denied. "I'm saying that it's silly to be moping around here because you miss her when you could be in Vegas with her."

"Then who would be painting your walls?"

"The walls could wait another week or two."

He continued to paint.

Regan sighed. "Have you talked to her since she went back?"

"Almost every day." He also texted her when they didn't talk—and even sometimes when they did. "She's applied for a few jobs and even had an interview last week."

"How did it go?" she asked cautiously.

"She said they sounded really excited about her qualifications when they called to set up the interview—and a lot less enthused after she showed up for the interview."

"Because she's pregnant?" Regan guessed.

"Probably," he agreed. "Not that they were foolish enough to say anything that might open them up to a discrimination suit, but even after Sierra explained her unique situation, the interview ended pretty quickly."

"You keeping your ear to the ground so you can let her know if any jobs open up here?"

"I am," he confirmed. "I've also been looking at potential employment opportunities in Las Vegas— for me."

Sierra couldn't sleep.

It was hard to get comfortable when her belly was approximately the size of a beach ball.

She didn't know if it was the bed in her brother and sister-in-law's guest room that was responsible for her backache—or the fact that she was hauling an extra twenty-five pounds around with every step every day.

Not that she'd been hauling it too far.

She still walked every morning, but since her return to Vegas, she hadn't had to do much of anything else. She did have a doctor's appointment scheduled the following day, and Nick and Whitney were both planning to go with her. It would be her thirty-nine-week checkup—due date *finally* just around the corner!—and while Sierra absolutely understood that she was carrying their baby, she was also starting to realize that moving in with her brother and sister-in-law for the last two months of her pregnancy had not been the best idea.

Maybe it was because she'd had so much space in Haven—not just an apartment of her own but an actual house—and now she was essentially living in a bedroom. A spacious and beautifully decorated bedroom, but still only a single room.

Of course Nick and Whitney encouraged her to make herself at home, but it was their home—she was only a guest. The room she slept in wasn't her own, just like her body wasn't her own right now.

It wasn't just that the baby had stretched her out of shape and was making her get up to pee three times in the night and giving her heartburn when she ate anything spicy. It was that she rarely had five minutes to herself without her brother and sister-in-law hovering over her, which was another reason that she got up early to walk every morning.

She enjoyed the fresh air and the exercise, but she missed walking with Remy. And while the heat of a Las Vegas summer was more familiar to her than the cold of a Haven winter, she found herself missing the cooler temperatures of northern Nevada—among other things.

On her way back to Nick and Whitney's, she passed the same little convenience store that she passed every day. Today she stopped in to pick up a snack.

Whitney was in the kitchen, refilling her coffee mug when Sierra walked in. Her sister-in-law had greeted her with a smile that quickly slipped when she saw the bag of salt and vinegar potato chips in Sierra's hand.

It was only a snack-sized bag—just enough to satisfy her craving.

"There's a fruit plate in the fridge," Whitney told her.

"Thanks," Sierra said. "I'll have some later."

Whitney's gaze dropped to the bag of chips again, and she opened her mouth as if to say something, then snapped it shut.

Sierra tossed the chips into the trash can and retreated to her room, where she cried for no particular reason, as she seemed to be doing a lot in recent days.

She knuckled away a tear as a phone chimed with a text message.

Bail court with Judge Longo this morning.

The message was followed by a face screaming in fear emoji, making her smile.

Hope your client has a comfy cell.

She spent the rest of the morning thinking about Deacon. She wanted to blame his text message, but the truth was, he was never far from her thoughts.

Earlier, when she'd caught Whitney's disapproving look toward the bag of chips, she couldn't help but remember how Deacon had gone out of his way to get some for her, just because she'd had a craving.

Because that was the kind of man he was—and she missed him so much more than she could ever have imagined.

Whitney came home with a bag of chips.

A family-sized bag that she set on the end table beside the sofa, where Sierra was sitting reading a book.

"A peace offering," she said.

"Not necessary," Sierra told her.

"I think it is," her sister-in-law insisted. "And so is an apology. The closer we get to the baby's due date, the more I realize how ill-equipped I am to be a mom, and I think I've been trying to micromanage you because it gives me something to focus on rather than admitting my own fears."

She closed her book and set it aside to give Whitney her full attention, silently chastising herself for not considering that the baby's mom was dealing with a plethora of emotions, too.

"You better not be saying that you changed your mind," she said lightly. "Because this baby is yours, for better or for worse."

Her sister-in-law managed a watery chuckle. "I haven't changed my mind. I'm just scared that I'm not going to have a clue about what I'm doing."

"I'd bet that most first-time parents don't have a clue about what they're doing."

"Maybe not," Whitney agreed. "But sometimes I wonder..."

Sierra waited.

"I wonder if maybe God took my womb because I wasn't meant to be a mom."

Religion had always been boggy ground for Sierra. Though she'd been baptized in the Catholic Church, her parents had encouraged kindness and generosity over attendance at weekly mass. Her sister-in-law, on the other hand, had been born into a devout family, and Sierra knew that she needed to respect her beliefs as much as reassure her.

"God didn't take your womb," Sierra said gently. "The doctors did. And not because you did anything wrong but because cancer is a horrible, insidious and indiscriminate disease.

"But if you want to look for God's hand in some part of this process, perhaps you could trust that he gave the doctors the skills they needed to not only save your life but allow your eggs to be harvested so that the children you deserve to have could be born someday."

"Do you really think so?" Whitney asked hopefully.

"I really do," she said sincerely.

"You're giving us the greatest gift, and I know there's no possible way we'll ever be able to repay you."

"I was glad to do it and would happily do it again for you and Nick. In fact, I *want* to do it again," Sierra told her. "So that this little guy can have a brother or sister to grow up with."

"Really? Even after all my hovering and nagging, you'd be willing to do it again?"

"Well, maybe I shouldn't make any promises before I've been through the experience of childbirth, but I figure you'll be so busy with this little guy, you won't be able to hover or nag half as much."

Whitney brushed away the tears that spilled onto her cheeks. "The day I met Nick was the best day of my life—not only because I met the man I love more than I ever thought possible but also because I gained a sister that I couldn't love any more if she was my own."

"It was a good day for all of us," Sierra said. "But I think today's going to be a good day, too."

And it was, because just before midnight, Jameson Nicholas Hart was born.

Chapter Twenty-Four

Sierra scrolled through job posting after job posting, inexplicably irritated to discover that most of the positions weren't anywhere nearby. Because what was the point of setting the parameters of her search to the Las Vegas area if Carson City was still going to pop up?

And if she was willing to go that far, she might as well go back to Haven.

It was a far-too-tempting idea—and apparently a feasible option. Because after only six weeks back in the DA's office, Jade Scott had decided to take a job as a victim services advocate.

Deacon had texted Sierra as soon as the first whispers started circulating around the courthouse, and even Sky—preoccupied as she was with her new baby—reached out when the news made its way to her. Sierra didn't reveal to either of them that she'd already been contacted by her former boss, who'd assured her that the DA's office would be thrilled to have her back, if she was interested.

At that time, she'd still been two weeks away from her due date and told Brett she wasn't ready to make any decisions about her future. He'd assured her that he understood and promised not to post the position until he heard back from her.

Now, though, Sierra was tempted to leap at the opportunity to return to her former job. Haven was admittedly farther away from Nick and Whitney and three-week-old Jameson than she wanted to be, but she needed to move on with her life. And maybe doing so with a little distance from the baby she'd carried would be better for all of them.

Another factor in favor of accepting Brett's offer was that she'd made friends in Haven. Skylar, of course, but also Julie and Brenna and Lucy and Erin.

But the biggest factor was Deacon.

Because even after two and a half months apart and with four hundred and fifty miles between them, he still texted her every morning, just to say good morning, and again every night.

Those brief communications were always the highlight of her day. And their less frequent FaceTime calls put a smile on her face that lasted for days afterward.

But was this love?

After weeks—maybe months—of pondering that exact question, she was finally starting to believe that it was.

A seven-hour drive was a lot of time to have second thoughts, and Sierra had plenty of them as she drove the now-familiar route from Las Vegas to Haven.

She should have called to tell Deacon that she was

coming, but she'd wanted to surprise him. And that impulse was the cause of most of those second thoughts, because the last time she'd traveled out of town to surprise someone, she'd caught him with his pants down. Literally.

Of course, Deacon wasn't anything like Eric.

He would never break a promise he'd made.

But he'd never made her any promises, and she wouldn't have let him if he'd tried.

And now she was both incredibly nervous and ridiculously excited about the prospect of seeing him again. So much so that she could hardly sit still in one of the two Adirondack chairs that flanked his front door as she waited for him to return home from work.

Finally, his vehicle pulled into the driveway. Her hands gripped the arms of the chair more tightly.

He got out of his truck, a grin spreading across his face as he made his way toward her.

She rose to her feet as he approached, a kaleidoscope of butterflies taking flight in her tummy.

"Well, this is the very best kind of surprise," he said.

"I should have called—"

"No," he interjected, cutting off her apology before dipping his head to brush his lips over hers.

The casual kiss quickly became something more, and when they finally drew apart, they were both breathless.

"You haven't even asked why I'm here," she noted.

"Because I don't care why," he told her. "I only care that you are. Although I am curious to know why you're sitting outside. Don't you still have the key that I gave you?"

"I do," she confirmed. "But I learned the hard way that you can't know what you might be interrupting when you walk into a room unannounced."

"The only thing you'd be interrupting here is Remy's all-day nap."

She smiled at that. "Life is exhausting when you're a four-pound dog carrying forty pounds of anxiety."

"He's got some baggage," Deacon acknowledged. "Which you, apparently, do not."

"My suitcase is in the car."

"Well, let's go get it," he said. "Then we can go inside so you can fuss over Remy while I figure out something for dinner."

"Actually, I didn't want to presume that you'd want to cook, so I brought Jo's pizza."

"Even better," he said, walking beside her to her vehicle to help with her things.

"I picked it up about an hour ago, so it will probably need to be reheated, but I figured we could do that... after."

His brows winged up. "After?"

She smiled.

He unlocked the door and ushered her inside.

Remy danced around her feet in excited circles, and while Deacon took the pizza into the kitchen, Sierra set her small suitcase on the floor to scoop up the little dog. The happy Chihuahua proceeded to lick her face all over, making her laugh—which resulted in a tongue in her mouth.

"I appreciate your enthusiasm, but you really need to work on your technique," she told the Chihuahua, as she set him on the floor again.

"And right now, you need to get lost," Deacon said, returning to offer the dog a treat that he knew would occupy him for quite some time.

Once Remy had wandered off, he took both of Sierra's hands in his. "Are you sure about this?"

She nodded.

"It's not too soon? After the baby, I mean."

Now she shook her head. "My doctor gave me the go-ahead. Though I feel I should warn you that it's been a while for me."

"I'm guessing at least nine months, since you were adamantly opposed to having sex while you were carrying your brother and sister-in-law's baby."

"And Eric and I broke up a few months before that, so it's actually been more than a year."

"It hasn't been quite as long for me," he confided. "But there's been nobody else since the first time I saw you."

"Really?" she asked, sounding equal parts surprised and dubious.

"Really," he confirmed. "I haven't wanted anyone but you since I saw you standing beside the last box of Frosted Flakes in the grocery store."

"Of course, that was before you knew I was pregnant—and before I got fat."

"You were never fat," he chided. "And you're even more gorgeous now than you were then."

"It's my breasts," she said. "They're up a whole cup size, but they should go back to normal when my milk supply dries up, so don't get too attached to them."

"I'm sorry," he said. "I didn't hear anything you said after *breasts*."

She laughed softly. "You're such a guy."

"Thank you for noticing."

"Believe me, I've noticed."

He kissed her again.

She parted her lips, allowing him to deepen the kiss. The sensual flick of his tongue against hers sent flames of heat licking through her veins, making every part of her burn.

She wanted him with a desperation that was both scary and unfamiliar. Had wanted him from the first moment she saw him. She'd tried to blame the instantaneous and intense attraction on pregnancy hormones, except that he wasn't the only man to have crossed her path, but he was the only one to have elicited such a reaction.

That first moment had been a long time ago. They'd waited so long for this moment now, and she didn't want to wait any longer.

She eased her lips from his to say, "Take me to bed, Deacon."

He lifted her into his arms and carried her upstairs to his bedroom.

She only had a brief moment to register her surroundings—pale gray walls, dark furniture, a wide bed covered with a sage green comforter—before he stripped away her T-shirt and jeans and deposited her on top of that cover. His shirt and tie and pants joined the pile of clothes on the floor, then he stretched out beside her.

"I've dreamed of you here, just like this, more times than I could count," he confided.

"If this is a dream, don't wake me up."

"It's not a dream." His fingertip traced the lacy edge of her bra, skimming over the swell of her breast, the slow sensual touch making her shiver. "It's a dream come true."

He opened the front fastening of her bra and peeled back the cups, exposing her breasts to his gaze. Her nipples immediately tightened, and his eyes darkened with desire before he lowered his head to swirl his tongue around one turgid peak. Sensations ricocheted through her system, like sparks dancing along a live wire, intensifying the ache between her thighs.

"You might not want to spend too much time up there," she warned, when he shifted to give the same attention to her other breast. "There's a very real possibility that I might start leaking."

"I don't care," he said. "After waiting so long to have you in my bed, dreaming of touching and tasting every inch of your body, I'm not willing to skip any parts."

"There are other parts—a little further south—that wouldn't mind some attention."

"I'll get there," he promised.

"Soon?" she asked hopefully.

He chuckled at that.

"It's been more than a year," she reminded him. "At least thirteen months since I've had a man-made orgasm."

"But not more than thirteen months since you've had an orgasm," he mused thoughtfully.

She felt her cheeks burn. "I'm going to shut up now."

"Don't." He brushed his lips over hers again. "In fact, I'd like to hear more about the ways you pleasure yourself. There's nothing sexier than a woman who goes after what she wants."

"That's why I'm here," she reminded him. "Because you're what I want."

"You're changing the subject," he protested.

"On the contrary," she said, reaching between their bodies to slip a hand into his briefs and wrap her fingers around him, making him groan. "I'm going after what I want."

"I know what else you want," he said.

He hooked his fingers in the sides of her panties and

tugged them over her hips, dragged them down her legs and tossed them aside.

When she was finally, completely naked, he took a moment to strip away his boxer briefs before returning to the bed.

She sighed when his body came down on hers, relishing the feel of his skin against hers, the weight of his hard body pressing her into the mattress.

She lifted her hands to explore the taut muscles of his shoulders...arms...chest. She paused with her hand splayed over his heart, smiled to discover that it was pounding as fast and hard as her own.

At the same time, he was engaged in his own exploration. His hands were strong and sure as they moved over her, seeming to know just where and how to touch her. Apparently he was every bit as confident in the bedroom as he was in the courtroom, and she felt grateful to be the recipient of his careful and thorough attention as sparks flew through her body, igniting new wants, new desires.

She pressed her thighs together, as if that action might ease the desperate ache between them, but she already knew that relief—and satisfaction—would only be found when he was inside her.

His hands skimmed down her torso, touching, testing. His mouth followed, tasting, teasing. He nudged her legs farther apart and settled between them. His thumbs parted the slick folds of skin at the apex of her thighs, exposing her most sensitive core first to his avid gaze...then the gentle brush of his thumb...and the stroke of his tongue.

Her head fell back against the pillow and her hands fisted in the comforter as he continued to do wicked and wonderful things to her with his mouth. She bit down on her lip to hold back her cries of pleasure as he drove her ever closer to the edge of oblivion...and finally...over.

Delicious shudders continued to wrack her body as he made his way up her body again, dropping leisurely kisses along the way—on her abdomen, her navel, the valley between her breasts. He kissed her throat, then the underside of her jaw, then her lips. Lingering there for a long, breathless moment.

"I'm happy to reciprocate," she said. "Just as soon as I get feeling back in my body."

"No reciprocation required," he assured her, reaching into the drawer of his bedside table for a condom.

Required or not, she wanted to do for him what he'd done for her. To make him feel as good as he'd made her feel.

After he'd taken care of protection, he shifted so that his body was poised over hers, his weight braced on his forearms.

Later, she promised herself, as his erection nudged at the soft, swollen flesh between her thighs, and she drew her knees up, digging her heels into the mattress and tilting her pelvis to facilitate his entry.

In one deep stroke, he pushed inside her. Not just filling but fulfilling her.

She moaned her pleasure as he began to move, the glorious friction causing a whole new avalanche of sensations to crash over her, leaving her battered and breathless, flailing to hold on to something...someone.

He caught her hands and linked their fingers together, then let the storm take them both.

Deacon brushed a strand of hair off her cheek, tucked it behind her ear. "Can I tell you now?"

Sierra tipped her head back as she snuggled closer. "Tell me what?"

"That I love you."

He was obviously referring to the first time he'd spoken those words to her—and her subsequent admonishment about the timing. And though she was more amenable to believing him now, she felt compelled to protest again.

"No," she said. "Postcoital declarations of affection are inherently untrustworthy, more likely a response to dopamine lingering in one's system than an expression of genuine emotion."

"Sometimes you sound just like a lawyer," he mused.

"Imagine that."

"And if we were arguing this case in a court of law, I would suggest that declarations of affection, at any time, increase feelings of intimacy and provide an opportunity to communicate hopes and dreams of a future together."

"And I would have to object," she told him.

"On what grounds?" he asked, sounding more amused than offended.

"That counsel needs a recess—and food."

"Objection overruled."

"You can't be both advocate and adjudicator," she protested.

"Sure I can." He grinned. "It's my bed."

Her stomach growled.

Loudly.

"Perhaps court can adjourn for a brief recess," he allowed, rolling to the edge of the mattress. "I'll go put the oven on."

He scooped up his pants from the floor and stepped into them but didn't bother with anything else.

Sierra didn't mind watching him walk around half-naked. In fact, she wouldn't have minded watching him walk around completely naked. Unfortunately, she didn't get to watch him for long, as he exited the bedroom to deal with her dinner.

So she found his abandoned shirt and slipped her arms into the sleeves. Fastening only two of the middle buttons, she made her way downstairs.

He glanced over when he heard her enter the kitchen, then did a double take.

"That's my shirt you're wearing."

"Is it?"

"You know it is."

"Do you want it back?" She reached for one of the two buttons that held it closed, slid it through the opening.

He swallowed. "Maybe you should keep it until after we eat."

She glanced at the timer on the stove as she took a step closer. "We've got almost twelve minutes."

"I don't know whether to be flattered or insulted that you think…" His words trailed off when she unfastened the second button.

"You were saying?" she prompted.

"I have no idea," he admitted.

Her lips curved as she reached now for the button at the top of his pants.

"Tell me, Deacon, in all of those dreams you had of the two of us together, did any of them take place in the kitchen?"

"My fantasies of you encompassed every room of the house—and several other places," he confided. "But I never thought those fantasies might someday become a reality, or I would have prepared."

She pulled a condom out of the pocket of his shirt.

"You are full of surprises today, aren't you?" he mused.

And they forgot about the pizza and everything else for more than twelve minutes.

"Even slightly overcooked, this really is the best pizza," Sierra remarked, licking a smear of sauce from her thumb.

Deacon's lips twitched as he lifted the piece he was holding to peer at the very dark crust on the bottom. "I think this is a little more than *slightly* overcooked."

"Should I apologize for distracting you?"

"No. In fact, feel free to distract me like that any time you want."

She smiled as she rose from the table, then nudged his chair back so that she could straddle his lap and draw his mouth to hers for a kiss.

"I love you, Deacon."

He drew back to look at her.

"Did you just break your own rule against postcoital declarations of affection?"

"It seems that I did," she admitted. "Throughout the whole drive from Las Vegas, I've been thinking about how and when to tell you, and I didn't want to wait a minute longer."

He gently brushed her hair from her face and smiled. "I love you, too, Sierra."

"I know we've still got some logistics to figure out, but I'd really like to see if we could make this work."

"Me, too," he told her. "In fact, I've been looking at job postings in Las Vegas. I wanted to talk to Katelyn before I actually sent any applications, but I think she'd give me a favorable reference."

"It means a lot to me that you'd be willing to uproot your life and your career here—"

"I would do anything for you."

"—but I don't think that's going to be necessary."

"Why not?"

"Because I sent my application to Brett yesterday, and he said the job is mine."

"And you waited until now to tell me?"

She shrugged, a smile tugging at the corners of her mouth. "It didn't seem quite as important as the other things we were doing earlier."

"I can't disagree with that," he said, lifting her with him as he rose and carried her back to bed.

Epilogue

Fifteen months later

"This one's a girl," Sierra announced when she and Deacon returned to the house on Sherwood Park Drive after her three-month appointment with Dr. Amaro.

Nick and Whitney, who'd brought their now fifteen-month-old son, Jameson, to Haven for a weekend visit, beamed happily in response to the news.

"Did you hear that?" Nick asked his son. "You're going to have a little sister."

"Cah!" Jameson said.

His mom laughed. "No, you can't trade your sister for a car."

"Cah!" he said again.

"Everything's good?" Whitney asked Sierra.

She nodded. "The doctor said there's no reason to believe that this pregnancy won't be every bit as uneventful as the last one."

"She also said there's no need to restrict your physical activities," Deacon said, with a wink.

"What does that mean?" Nick asked his sister. "You're not planning on taking up rock climbing or something like that, are you?"

Whitney looked at her husband with amusement. "It means that they can have sex."

"Please." Nick put his hands over his ears. "I don't want to hear that kind of stuff about my little sister." Then he removed his hands from his own ears to cover his son's. "And Jameson definitely doesn't need to hear it about his aunt."

"I doubt that you guys are abstaining because you're expecting another baby," Sierra pointed out.

"No. We're abstaining because we have a toddler who ends up in our bed almost every night," Nick grumbled.

"And since that's more information than I need to know, I'm going to go start the grill," Deacon decided.

Nick grabbed a couple of bottles of beer out of the fridge and followed him onto the back deck.

"Thanks," Deacon said, accepting the proffered beverage.

"Actually, I wanted to thank you," Nick said. "Whitney and I really appreciate you supporting Sierra's decision to be our gestational carrier again."

"It was always her choice," Deacon said.

"She'd certainly argue that point, but the first time she offered to do this for us, there wasn't anyone else to factor into her decision. This time, she obviously talked to you about it, and we're grateful that you didn't have any objections."

"No objections," he confirmed. "But I will confess to hoping that the next baby she carries will be ours."

"Are you going to put a ring on her finger before then?" Nick wanted to know.

Deacon grinned at his hopefully future brother-in-law. "That's the plan."

And six months after that...

Six weeks after Everleigh Sierra Hart was born, Deacon's plan was proving a little more difficult to implement than he'd anticipated, forcing him to improvise.

"What happened to the raisin bran?" Sierra asked, staring into the almost empty cereal cupboard Friday morning.

"It must be all gone."

"But I just opened the box on Tuesday."

He shrugged, playing it casual. "I guess I ate a lot of raisin bran this week."

She turned to look at him, a slight frown marring her brow. "You don't even like raisin bran."

"Just have something else today," he suggested, a hint of impatience leaking into his voice.

"Apparently all we've got is Frosted Flakes." But she took the box out of the cupboard, opened the flaps and tipped it over her bowl.

He sipped his coffee, pretending that his heart wasn't pounding wildly in his chest.

"What the—" Her breath caught, and she reached into the bowl to fish out the diamond solitaire engagement ring.

She stared at it for a long moment—an *endlessly* long moment from where he was standing—before she shifted her attention to him and said, "When I was a kid, I felt lucky to get a plastic ring in a box of cereal."

"How are you feeling now?" he asked cautiously.

The smile that curved her lips was reflected in her gaze. "Very lucky."

The vise that had tightened around his chest loosened, allowing him to release the white-knuckled grip on his mug.

"Are you going to try it on?" he prompted.

"Are you going to ask me the question?" she countered.

"Should I get down on one knee?"

She shook her head. "No. I don't want you on your knee but beside me, every day for the rest of our lives."

"You're kind of infringing on my territory now," he cautioned.

"Sorry," she said, but the sparkle in her eyes told him she wasn't sorry at all.

He set his coffee down and took her hands. "I love you, Sierra. The day that I met you was the best day of my life—until the next day and the day after that, because with each passing day I fell more in love with you. And though I can't imagine loving you any more than I do right now, I look forward to being proven wrong every day of the rest of our lives together and hope you will do me the honor of being my wife."

She was sniffling just a little as she offered her hand to him.

"I'm going to need a verbal answer to my question," he said, holding the ring poised by her third finger.

"Yes," she said. "I will marry you and prove you wrong every day of the rest of our lives together."

"I guess that's what I get for falling in love with a lawyer," he said, chuckling as he slid the ring into place.

"I can empathize with that," she said, drawing his mouth down to hers for a kiss. "Happily and forever."

* * * * *

*Look for Michael "MG" Gilmore's story,
the next installment in Brenda Harlen's
Match Made in Haven miniseries,
on sale October 2023, wherever
Harlequin Special Edition books
and ebooks are sold.*

#2995 A MAVERICK REBORN
Montana Mavericks: Lassoing Love • by Melissa Senate

Handsome loner cowboy Bobby Stone has his issues—from faking his own death three years ago to discovering a twin brother he never knew. But headstrong rodeo queen Tori Hawkins is just the woman to break through his tough facade. First with a rambunctious fling...and later with the healing love Bobby's always needed...

#2996 RANCHER TO THE RESCUE
Men of the West • by Stella Bagwell

Mack Barlow may have broken Dr. Grace Hollister's heart in high school, but sparks still fly when the now-single father walks into her medical clinic. His young daughter is adorable. And he's...too dang sexy by far! Can a very busy divorced mom take a second chance on loving the man who once left her behind?

#2997 OLD DOGS, NEW TRUTHS
Sierra's Web • by Tara Taylor Quinn

When heiress Lindsay Warren-Smythe assumes a false identity to meet her biological father, she's not expecting to develop a connection with her new coworker, Cole Bennet, and his lovable dog. Cole has learned the hard way not to trust beautiful liars with his heart, so when he lets his guard down with Lindsay, will her lies tear them apart?

#2998 MATCHMAKER ON THE RANCH
Forever, Texas • by Marie Ferrarella

Rancher Chris Parnell has known Rosemary Robinson all his life. But working side by side with the beautiful vet to diagnose the sickness affecting his cattle kicks him completely out of his friend zone! Roe can't deny the attraction sizzling between them. But will her friend with benefits stick around once the cattle mystery is solved?

#2999 HER YOUNGER MAN
Sutton's Place • by Shannon Stacey

Widow Laura Thompson falling for a younger man? Not on your life! Except Riley Thompson is so dang charming. And handsome. And everything Laura's missing in her life. The town seems to be against their romance. Including Riley's boss...who's Laura's son! Are Riley and Laura strong enough to take a stand for love?

#3000 IN TOO DEEP
Love at Hideaway Wharf • by Laurel Greer

Chef Kellan Murphy is determined to fulfill his sister's dying wish. But placing an ocean-fearing man in a scuba diving class is ridiculous! Instructor Sam Walker can't resist helping the handsome wannabe diver overcome his fears. And their unexpected connection is the perfect remedy for Sam's own hidden pain...

Get 3 FREE REWARDS!

We'll send you 2 FREE Books plus a FREE Mystery Gift.

FREE
Value Over
$20

Both the **Harlequin® Special Edition** and **Harlequin® Heartwarming™** series feature compelling novels filled with stories of love and strength where the bonds of friendship, family and community unite.

YES! Please send me 2 FREE novels from the Harlequin Special Edition or Harlequin Heartwarming series and my FREE Gift (gift is worth about $10 retail). After receiving them, if I don't wish to receive any more books, I can return the shipping statement marked "cancel." If I don't cancel, I will receive 6 brand-new Harlequin Special Edition books every month and be billed just $5.49 each in the U.S. or $6.24 each in Canada, a savings of at least 12% off the cover price, or 4 brand-new Harlequin Heartwarming Larger-Print books every month and be billed just $6.24 each in the U.S. or $6.74 each in Canada, a savings of at least 19% off the cover price. It's quite a bargain! Shipping and handling is just 50¢ per book in the U.S. and $1.25 per book in Canada.* I understand that accepting the 2 free books and gift places me under no obligation to buy anything. I can always return a shipment and cancel at any time by calling the number below. The free books and gift are mine to keep no matter what I decide.

Choose one: ☐ **Harlequin Special Edition** (235/335 BPA GRMK) ☐ **Harlequin Heartwarming Larger-Print** (161/361 BPA GRMK) ☐ **Or Try Both!** (235/335 & 161/361 BPA GRPZ)

Name (please print)

Address _____ Apt. #

City _____ State/Province _____ Zip/Postal Code

Email: Please check this box ☐ if you would like to receive newsletters and promotional emails from Harlequin Enterprises ULC and its affiliates. You can unsubscribe anytime.

Mail to the **Harlequin Reader Service:**

IN U.S.A.: P.O. Box 1341, Buffalo, NY 14240-8531
IN CANADA: P.O. Box 603, Fort Erie, Ontario L2A 5X3

Want to try 2 free books from another series! Call 1-800-873-8635 or visit www.ReaderService.com.

---

*Terms and prices subject to change without notice. Prices do not include sales taxes, which will be charged (if applicable) based on your state or country of residence. Canadian residents will be charged applicable taxes. Offer not valid in Quebec. This offer is limited to one order per household. Books received may not be as shown. Not valid for current subscribers to the Harlequin Special Edition or Harlequin Heartwarming series. All orders subject to approval. Credit or debit balances in a customer's account(s) may be offset by any other outstanding balance owed by or to the customer. Please allow 4 to 6 weeks for delivery. Offer available while quantities last.

Your Privacy—Your information is being collected by Harlequin Enterprises ULC, operating as Harlequin Reader Service. For a complete summary of the information we collect, how we use this information and to whom it is disclosed, please visit our privacy notice located at corporate.harlequin.com/privacy-notice. From time to time we may also exchange your personal information with reputable third parties. If you wish to opt out of this sharing of your personal information, please visit readerservice.com/consumerschoice or call 1-800-873-8635. **Notice to California Residents**—Under California law, you have specific rights to control and access your data. For more information on these rights and how to exercise them, visit corporate.harlequin.com/california-privacy.

HSEHW23

HARLEQUIN
PLUS

Try the best multimedia
subscription service for romance
readers like you!

Read, Watch and Play.

Experience the easiest way to get
the romance content you crave.

Start your **FREE TRIAL** at
<u>www.harlequinplus.com/freetrial</u>.